SAPPHIRE 1 BRIDES

# A Treasure Concealed

# TRACIE PETERSON

BETHANYHOUSE
a division of Baker Publishing Group
Minneapolis, Minnesota

© 2016 by Peterson Ink, Inc.

Published by Bethany House Publishers
11400 Hampshire Avenue South
Bloomington, Minnesota 55438
www.bethanyhouse.com

Bethany House Publishers is a division of
Baker Publishing Group, Grand Rapids, Michigan

Printed in the United States of America

Library of Congress Cataloging-in-Publication Data
Names: Peterson, Tracie, author.
Title: A treasure concealed / Tracie Peterson.
Description: Minneapolis, Minnesota : Bethany House, a division of Baker
    Publishing Group, [2016] | Series: Sapphire brides ; book 1
Identifiers: LCCN 2015037999| ISBN 9780764213342 (hardcover : acid-free paper) |
    ISBN 9780764213243 (softcover) | ISBN 9780764213359 (large print : softcover)
Subjects: | GSAFD: Love stories.
Classification: LCC PS3566.E7717 T73 2016 | DDC 813/.54—dc23 LC record
    available at http://lccn.loc.gov/2015037999

Scripture quotations are from the King James Version of the Bible.

This is a work of historical reconstruction; the appearances of certain historical figures are therefore inevitable. All other characters, however, are products of the author's imagination, and any resemblance to actual persons, living or dead, is coincidental.

Cover design by LOOK Design  Studio
Cover photography by Stephanie Rau

16  17  18  19  20  21  22        7  6  5  4  3  2  1

Dedicated to Katie and Randy Gneiting
at Montana Gems in Columbus, Montana,
with much gratitude for their help in understanding
the reason Yogo sapphires are so special.

I appreciate the information you gave me regarding books to read and places to visit. Katie, thank you for answering my ten thousand questions with such patience, and thank you, Randy, for allowing me to watch you work with the stones. You are both amazing!

# 1

"*M*ama?" Emily Carver whispered the word as she opened the door to her parents' bedroom.

Her mother looked peaceful. Her ragged breathing punctuated the otherwise silent house, giving Emily confidence that her mother was only sleeping and hadn't passed on. Closing the door with great care, Emily sighed.

She knew her mother's illness was terminal. The doctor had told her father it was probably only a matter of weeks before she would die, but he couldn't tell him why. Emily felt a tight clenching in her throat. Tears formed, but she blinked them back. She would have a good cry later—when her work was done and she could slip off to be alone. All of her life she'd had to be strong, and now was no different. Her unconventional upbringing amid the mining towns of the West had taught her to be tough and fearless. Well, almost fearless. She feared her mother's death.

*I don't know what I'll do without her.*

How would she ever manage without her mother? How could

she keep her spirits up without Mama to talk to? Throughout the years of her father's dragging them from one gold strike to another, Mama had always been there. And even though the last few years had proven to be too much physically for her mother to bear, Emily cherished her wisdom and comfort. It was impossible to imagine enduring this life without her.

*But Mama never really wanted me to continue with this kind of life.*

The thought did nothing to comfort Emily. Many had been the time when her mother had encouraged her to break away from the family. She had high hopes of Emily marrying and having a home, and God knew Emily longed for such things. She wanted a permanent home and family of her own more than she could express. The idea of living in one place she could call home was even more tantalizing than the idea of marriage.

Pulling on an old hat with one hand, Emily carefully tucked her long single braid up under it with the other. She tugged the broad brim down low, then felt to make certain every strand of her brown hair was concealed. Next, she checked the pocket of her overly large coat to find her pistol ready for whatever need she might have. She'd killed many a varmint with it and prided herself at being a good shot.

She looked once again at the door to her parents' room. Her mother slept more and more these days, and Emily knew she'd probably be back from town before Mama even noticed she was gone. Still, Emily hated to leave her. With Pa panning down at the river's edge, Emily knew he'd never hear if her mother called out for help.

"I need to be two people," she muttered and headed outside.

The sun bore down, making the cumbersome coat even more uncomfortable, but Emily didn't consider leaving it behind. She had learned quickly and at an early age that it was best she conceal any hint of her gender and shapely figure. Most of the folks in Yogo City, Montana, knew she was a young woman, but they understood her need to be protected. From a distance the filthy coat disguised her age and gave a rather nondescript impression. This generally kept most of the men from bothering her. Most, but not all. A great many men didn't care what a woman looked like so long as she was . . . a woman. Mining towns were lonely places, and women were scarce.

Emily glanced down at her appearance. Her coat was only one of many ill-fitting pieces of clothing. Her skirt, under which she wore canvas duck pants rather than petticoats, was ragged and patched many times over. It had belonged to her mother long ago, but now it was one of only two Emily owned. Instead of a blouse, she wore an old flannel shirt of her father's, which hung long, nearly to mid-thigh. Wearing it in this fashion gave her a shapeless, odd look that suited her purpose. The only feminine articles she wore were a fine lawn chemise and a loosely tied corset. Of course, neither of those were visible. She hadn't wanted the addition of the corset, but after a time, she found that the bracing actually kept her back from aching so much at the end of the day.

She glanced up at the clear sky wishing there might be a sign of clouds to offer shade. There wasn't a single one set against the seemingly endless blue. The rolling hills and distant mountains stood out in stark contrast, but even those would offer little shelter from the heat.

Turning her attention back to the dirt trail, Emily tried to bolster her spirits. She thought of a poem by Theodore Tilton that was in one of her poetry books.

> Once in Persia reigned a King,
> Who upon his signet ring

Graved a maxim true and wise,
Which, if held before his eyes,
Gave him counsel, at a glance,
Fit for every change or chance:
Solemn words, and these are they:
"Even this shall pass away!"

But would it? Would this gypsy life—this endless road—would it truly ever pass away?

The walk to town, if Yogo City could be called a town, would take no time at all. Emily could walk a fast pace, and her endurance did her proud. She could even walk the eighteen miles to Utica, the only real town near to this collection of miners and reprobates, in less than half a day. Once she'd had to do just that when her father had been away and her mother's pain medication had run out. It wasn't a trip she wanted to make again, however. There was no telling when a bear or some two-legged creature might try to complicate the journey.

Sweat trickled down her face. They'd lived in one part of Montana or another for the last few years, and generally the summers had been mild. This year was a blazer, as her father put it, and there was no end in sight. Emily pulled out a dark blue handkerchief and wiped her face and neck. It would be winter soon enough, and then everyone would complain about the cold.

She tucked the handkerchief away and gave a wave to one of the locals who sat whittling under the shade of a pine tree. The man claimed to be Scottish and called himself Rob Roy after some famous ancestor. Emily knew there was a book by Sir Walter Scott that told of that man, but as of yet she'd never come by a copy.

"Hot enough for you?" the man asked without pausing in his work.

10

"Reckon so." She kept her voice low, almost gravelly. The man said nothing more but gave a nod. The heat left neither of them wanting to talk. The effort was just too great.

The friends they'd made here in Yogo City were good ones, and Emily knew they looked out for her and her mother. These few men were good to bring them extra game or offer up warnings about bear in the area. And Emily felt confident that when her father had to leave for several days, those same men were watching over them. No one had said a word about it, but the effort was there all the same. Of course, the area was hardly thick with people. Most of the population that had flooded the claims just a year earlier had moved on to more promising ground when the mother lode failed to be found.

*But Pa won't leave. He's sure there's gold here somewhere.*

Just as he was always sure that God was about to help him strike it rich. Emily sighed once again and tried to put it from her mind. She wasn't even sure that God knew where Yogo City, Montana, was, much less who lived there.

The landscape around her was dotted with pines and aspen, as well as tall wild grass and a wide variety of vegetation, which Emily gleaned for herbs that she could use in cooking and healing. However, in the dry heat of the late summer, most everything was brown or wilted. The river and creeks that flowed quite full in the spring were now low, making everyone's life more challenging.

A mule and cart approached with one of the local miners at the helm. One-eyed Tom tipped his hat ever so slightly as his wagon kicked up a thick cloud of dirt. Emily nodded even as she tasted the dust upon her lips and felt it sting her eyes. She blinked several times, but it did little good. She muttered disgust at the heat and dust, then chided herself and decided she would do her best to endure such annoyances without complaint. Mama always said that complaining was the easiest of goals for a person to accomplish. Refraining from such despair was far more difficult but would, in time, prove the merit of the man. Or woman, in her case.

Emily arrived at Millie Ringgold's place and stepped inside. The small building was a combination of saloon, grocery store, restaurant, and boardinghouse, and Millie was well known by one and all. Yogo City was, for all intents and purposes, Millie's town, and no one knew it as well as the former slave woman.

Emily blinked a few times, letting her eyes adjust to the darker room. An old black woman looked up from where she sat at a table and smiled, revealing the double row of front teeth for which Millie Ringgold was famous. "Goodness, chil', you look dressed for winter and covered in dust. You gwanna faint dead away wearin' all dat. Why don't you shed some of dem clothes?"

"I doubt that would be to my benefit. The heat is one thing, but having to fight off hooligans and their ideas for me would be even more difficult." She pulled the felt hat from her head and fanned herself with it. "There are too many lovestruck old men looking for a woman to ease their miseries."

Millie laughed. "Sho nuff, you's right on dat account. I gets offers to come tend 'em too. Seems dey ain't all dat particular." The old woman laughed and motioned for Emily to join her. "I gots some nice root beer here if you'd be wantin' a glass. Ain't cold, mind ya, but it's wet."

"No thanks, Millie. I just came to see if the laudanum arrived. Mama used all of hers, and if I have to walk to Utica to get more, I will." She ignored the perspiration that trickled down her neck.

"No sense doin' dat, chil'. I gots it this mornin'." Millie pushed up from the table and made her way behind the makeshift bar, where she sold watered-down whiskey and warm beer to the miners. "I put it back here to save for ya." She produced the bottle and handed it to Emily.

"Thank goodness. I had no desire to make that walk in this heat." A grin cut across Emily's face. "I'm afraid I might have had to shed an article of clothing every few miles and pick them up on the way back."

Millie laughed and slapped her stout belly. "Now, wouldn't dat have been a sight."

Emily nodded. "Too much of one." She turned for the door and stopped. "Did I pay you enough when I ordered this?"

"We're square, chil'. In fact, take dis." She came around the counter and went to the far side of the room, where shelves were lined with canned goods and other articles for sale. Millie returned with a can in her hand. "Dis be peaches. I know Mr. Henry likes 'em. Oh, and Jake says to tell yo he'll be comin' by with meat one of dese days. He was in here last night to say he means to shoot him another grizzly bear. He gots the record for the most, and aims to keep it dat way."

Emily couldn't help but laugh. "And Jake Hoover makes sure we all know it. Nevertheless, if he gets another one and wants to share a portion with us, that'll be fine. Tell him I'll be happy to use the fat to make us all some candles, even if bear fat does make the worst-smelling ones around."

"Dat a fact," Millie said, nodding. "Still ain't gwanna be sensible to let it go to waste, no sir. 'Course Jake'll sell it to grease wagon axles if nuttin' else."

Emily tucked the laudanum into her pocket and did likewise with the can of peaches. Her father would be pleased with the surprise. She secured her braid and hat before opening the door. "I'll be bringing you eggs as soon as I can, Millie. The heat has the hens kind of slow in laying, but I expect things will pick up soon seeing how it's almost September."

"I'll be here," Millie said, flashing another toothy smile. "Ain't goin' nowhere."

*None of us are.*

Emily bit back a comment and pulled the door open. The harsh Montana sun momentarily blinded her, but she knew the way well enough, and by the time she returned to the cabin, Emily found that her mother had awakened. The laudanum had come none too soon.

"I'll get you a glass of water, Mama," Emily said, pouring the medication into a wooden spoon. Her mother took the foul-tasting stuff without even a pretense of refusal. It used to be she wouldn't take the medicine, hating the sleepy, drugged state it put her in. The fact that she took it almost eagerly now proved to Emily that the pain had grown far too great for her mother to try to be brave.

She fetched the water and helped the sick woman hold it while she took several sips. "I wish it could be cold for you, Mama." Emily straightened with the glass. "I'm afraid, however, there's nothing even remotely cool about these days."

"It has been horribly hot, but at least the nights cool down," her mother replied, falling back against the pillow. "If a person wanted to avoid hell for no other reason than the heat, I would understand it."

Emily smiled. "I'm going to wet down this sheet for you." She lifted the cloth from her mother's body. The woman looked so tiny in her cotton nightgown. It was as if she were disappearing a little each day. Emily bit her lip to keep from letting her emotions take charge. Of late it seemed to take very little to bring on tears. "Oh, Millie sent a can of peaches. Would you like some?"

Her mother shook her head. "I'm not hungry, Em. I'll just lie here and let the medicine take the pain." She closed her eyes. "I'm sure your father will be happy for the treat."

"That's what I figure. He's no doubt already wondering where his noon meal is." Emily headed for the main part of the house, leaving the bedroom door open. She took the sheet to the washtub, where water awaited. It took very little effort to dampen the material, and when she returned to the bedroom to place it on her mother's weary body, Emily was rewarded with a smile.

"Ah, that feels so nice, Em. Thank you. You are a good girl."

Mama never opened her eyes, so she couldn't see the tears that sprang unbidden to Emily's eyes. Emily dug her nails into her palms and hurried from the room. "I'll let you know when I take Pa his lunch."

Mama said nothing, but that wasn't at all surprising. Talking seemed to drain the older woman of what little strength she had. By the time Emily had fried up some bacon and soaked a few hard biscuits in the leftover grease, her mother was sound asleep.

The afternoon sun bore down on Emily as she made her way to the river, where her father had set up his sluicing frame. He was faithfully panning in the water, humming a favorite hymn, while their old mule, Nellie, grazed on dry grass a few yards away, mindless of the cart she remained harnessed to.

Emily had to smile at the sight. Pa had rolled up the legs of his pants and stood barefoot in the shallow but rapidly moving river. "That looks like a good way to bear up under the heat."

"Emmy, I'm mighty glad to see you." Her father straightened and held out his pan. "I found some color. Look here."

For a moment Emily allowed herself the tiniest spark of hope. "Truly?"

She came to where he stood and peered into the iron pan. There at the bottom were a few flecks of gold mingled with blue pebbles. It wasn't nearly enough to get excited about. She sighed.

"Now, don't go gettin' all sad," her father said. He came out of the water to take a seat on the bank of the river. Once seated, he placed the pan between them. "I'll add it to what I already have, and at this rate I'll be able to head into town tomorrow or the next day and get a few supplies. Just remember, any color is proof that there's a whole lot more somewhere upstream."

"Oh, Pa. We've talked about all of this before. There was a gold strike here last year, so of course there's gold, but you know as well as I do what everyone said about it."

"I do know. I just don't happen to agree."

Emily handed him his lunch and sat down beside him. "It's played out around here, and what's left will take too much energy and money to retrieve. We don't have a whole lot of either commodity."

He laughed and pulled apart one of the biscuits. Bending a piece of the thick bacon in two, he sandwiched it between the biscuit halves. "I got plenty of energy left, and I'll show 'em all. I ain't giving up."

Emily had heard this speech on many occasions. He'd never quit looking for that next strike—that big find. Henry Carver was absolutely convinced that God himself had ordained it. And God knew better than anyone that her father had looked for just such a treasure in every nook and cranny in the western United States.

"Oh, I just about forgot." Emily withdrew the can of peaches. "Millie sent this as a gift."

Her father took the can and smiled. "Good ol' Millie. I'll get this open right now and we can share it." He unsheathed a knife he kept on his belt. "Yes, sirree, nothin' quite as good as peaches."

In no time at all he had the can open and offered Emily a small peach half at the end of his knife. She took the slimy piece and popped it into her mouth. The sweetness made her smile.

Her father had always had a sweet tooth, and this would no doubt offer some satisfaction. Of course, it didn't take much to give Henry Carver satisfaction. Emily had never known her father to be all that unhappy.

*Now, Ma on the other hand . . .*

As if her father could read her thoughts, he asked, "How's your mama doin'?"

"She's fine now. I picked up her laudanum at Millie's."

"Oh, that's good. She'll rest better now." Her father wiped peach juice from his graying beard. "She's quite a woman, your ma. Never complains. Ain't seen any woman who could come close to bein' as patient in adversity."

Their peaceful lunch was disrupted by the sound of rustling in the trees beyond the riverbank. Emily put her hand in her pocket to reassure herself that the pistol was still there, but her father stood and took up his rifle. Scouring the area for any sign of life, he waited. More than once they'd been surprised by a bear, so there was no need in taking any chances.

"I ain't a grizzly," a man's voice called out in amusement. A big man, bigger than any of the regulars in Yogo City, came out from behind a clump of pines.

Emily watched him, careful to keep her hat low so he couldn't see her face very well. In spite of the heat, she was grateful for her heavy coat. Her father lowered the rifle. "That's a good way for a man to get shot," he answered.

The man crossed the distance between them in what Emily thought was no more than ten steps. His long legs made strides that would have taken at least two and possibly three for most folks. She looked up, shielding her eyes by bending the brim of her hat down a little lower. The stranger had to be at least six and a half feet tall. Her own father stood at six feet, and this man was another head taller.

"Name's Kirk Davies."

The man looked down momentarily at Emily. She quickly lowered her head. There was something about him she didn't trust—something that suggested trouble. Davies was certainly no more scruffy and dirty than the other men who lived in the area, but he had an air about him that almost frightened her.

"I'm Henry Carver. What can I do for you?"

"Well, the fact is, I'm here to do something for you. I understand you own the claim just up the hill and back of these trees."

Emily glanced back up to find that Davies' attention was completely fixed on her father. The scowl on Pa's face told her he didn't like the intrusion and arrogance of this man any more than she did.

"I reckon I do, but I hardly see how that's any of your business."

Davies' jaw clenched and Emily could see his eyes narrow. He had beady eyes that reminded her of a rattlesnake. "I'm here to offer to buy you out. I'm employed by a man who wants to buy up as many of these claims as possible."

"Well, you're wastin' your time with me. I ain't lookin' to sell."

"Now, just a minute," Davies countered. "You haven't even heard what I'm set to offer."

"Don't much care what you're offerin'. I don't have any intention of sellin'."

"Well, if you ain't an ingrate." Davies reached out faster than Emily or her father could react. He took hold of Henry's upper arms, making it impossible for him to raise the rifle in defense.

Emily forgot about hiding her face and jumped to her feet to confront Davies. "Leave him alone."

Davies looked at her a moment. Then his face seemed to light up in amusement. "Now, ain't you a sight. You got eyes darker than stout ale. In fact, you're kind of pretty. Be even better in the right clothes. Or out of them."

Emily stiffened, but it was her father who made the next move. He punched Davies square in the belly, loosing the big man's grip.

Davies fell back a few steps, and his eyes narrowed. "You ought not to have done that, mister. I can't abide a man who hits me."

"And I can't abide a man who lays hands on me and treats my daughter like a common strumpet," Carver replied, once again bringing up the rifle. "Now, get outta here before I forget I'm a good Christian."

Davies' scowl deepened. "You're gonna need more than God to protect you. I'll go for now, but I'll be back in a week for your answer."

"You already have my answer," Emily's father declared. "I said no. I'm not lookin' to sell."

Davies' expression changed to a cold, calculated smile. "You will be—only then my offer ain't gonna be half as generous."

He turned and headed back the way he'd come, leaving Emily and her father to watch. Despite the heat, Emily shivered. She could only hope he would forget about them, but unfortunately, she knew that wasn't likely.

# 2

*Caeden* Thibault stepped from the stage in Utica and glanced around. He saw a hotel, several saloons, a post office and bank, stables, and a mercantile, just like any other small frontier town. A person could blink and miss it if they weren't headed here as their final destination.

Over one building the sign read *Silver Dollar Saloon*. It looked like a popular place with plenty of men standing in the shade of the structure. Another sign caught his attention, however. *Feed Stable*. He hoped he could rent himself a reliable horse there. He'd already received permission to leave his things at the blacksmith's, which doubled as the stage office. The man there assured him his things would be safe there.

Caeden studied the main street again. He was tired and thirsty. Mostly thirsty. He needed something to wash down all the dust he'd eaten on the stage ride from Great Falls. Not given to hard drink, Caeden had little desire to head to one of the saloons. Maybe the mercantile would have a soda fountain. It was at least worth a look.

He dusted off his traveling clothes as best he could, then made his way to the store. The place wasn't nearly as well supplied as he'd hoped. He looked around, disappointed to realize there was no sign of anything to quench his thirst.

"Howdy, stranger," a clerk said to him from behind a counter. "What can I do for you?"

Caeden fixed the man with a look. "Just came in off the stage and hoped you might have some soda water."

The man shook his head. "Ain't got any. You can get powdered lemonade made to drink at the hotel restaurant down the way. Sometimes they got root beer. 'Course, there's beer and whiskey to be had at the saloons."

Caeden nodded and was turning to leave when an older man approached him. "Why don't you come with me, and I'll get you fixed up with a drink. Name's Henry Carver."

The bearded older man smiled and waited for Caeden to say something. He seemed friendly, but Caeden hadn't really come to Montana to make friends. "I, uh, don't drink."

"What's that?" Carver asked. "Sounded to me like you were thirsty."

"I am, but I don't drink alcohol."

The old man began to chuckle. "Me neither. Never did develop a taste for it. No, I was suggestin' you join me for a bite down at the hotel. I was headed that way, and frankly, I'd enjoy the company."

Caeden was surprised by the old man's openness. It had been his experience that a great many Montana men were more inclined to keep their own company, which generally suited him just fine. However, he was hungry and even more so needed something to drink—even water at this point.

"I suppose I might as well," Caeden finally answered.

"Good," Mr. Carver declared. He looked back over his shoulder. "Sam, I'll be back to load up that stuff after I get a bite to eat."

"Sure thing, Henry. I'll have it ready."

The older man left the store without another word. Caeden glanced after him and finally followed. Henry Carver seemed to have little doubt he would and kept walking toward the northern end of town.

Caeden had no trouble catching up and keeping stride with the older gentleman. He let the awkward silence stand between them until they reached the door, where Carver bounded in like he owned the place and motioned Caeden to a table and chairs by the back wall.

"Bring us two, Sarah," Carver called out to no one in particular.

Caeden looked around at the numerous people gathered there to eat, but he saw no one who fit the name Sarah. The place was full of older men and cowboys, not a single woman that he could see.

"It's cooler back here," the old man explained, pulling out a chair. "That big old window up front makes it feel like an oven when the sun comes bearin' down. Back here's much better."

Caeden did likewise, still not entirely sure why he'd joined Carver.

"So what brings you to Utica, young man?" Carver pulled off his kerchief and wiped his face.

"Name's Thibault. Caeden Thibault."

"Tee-bow. Now what kind of name is that?" He resecured the kerchief.

"French, I believe. At least that's what my mother used to tell me." Caeden put his hat upside down on the chair beside him just as an older woman came to the table with two large mugs of dark liquid.

"Thanks for the root beer, Sarah," Carver declared, taking

23

the mugs from her hands. He handed one to Caeden. "Best in the West."

Caeden didn't bother to answer. Instead he put the glass to his mouth and drank nearly half of the cool liquid. It went down easy and eliminated the burning dryness in his throat.

"You'd better bring him another, Sarah. Looks like Mr. Thibault ain't had a chance to clear the stage dirt from his gullet."

The older woman smiled. "I will. Now, how about something to eat?"

Carver looked to Caeden. "They got the best ham and beans to be had."

Caeden gave a nod. "That's fine with me."

Sarah smiled. "Coming right up."

Henry Carver eased back in the chair and smiled at Caeden. "So I'm sorry for repeating myself, but what brings you up this way? You don't talk like nobody I've ever heard. Where you from?"

"I was born and raised in New York. I'm out here doing some work for the government."

"What's the government got to do with Montana? Ain't been a state long enough to cause any real trouble."

Caeden couldn't help but smile. "No trouble. Actually it has more to do with the mining resources. I'm a geologist, and I'm cataloguing some of the mining sites in the state. There's actually a team of us out here, and this area of the state is my responsibility."

"A geologist?" Henry shook his head. "What exactly is that?"

"To put it simply, I study rocks—dirt—and the things that can be found in either one."

"And somebody in the government pays you to do that?" the

older man asked, shaking his head. "Seems hard to believe, but I always did figure the government wasted more money than anyone."

It was clear that the old man lacked education and understanding of what his government would find of value in such an investigation. Caeden took another long draw from the mug and emptied it just as Sarah brought another and hurried away with the empty glass.

Caeden picked up the new mug and gave Henry a nod. "There's a lot of good that can come out of such studies." He took another long drink, finally feeling that his thirst was being sated.

He put the mug down and continued. "By figuring out what resources a state has to offer, the government can get an idea of what the worth of the area is and how they can best utilize it to serve the nation, rather than just a few individuals."

"Figures they'd find a way to stick their noses into our business," Henry said, sounding none too happy.

Just then Sarah returned with two oversized bowls of beans. "I'll have some bread out to you shortly, unless you'd just as soon have crackers."

Henry looked to Caeden. "Makes me no nevermind, but I'm gonna need some vinegar."

Sarah looked at Caeden and put her hands on her hips. "Well, how about you?"

"Crackers are fine." Caeden picked up the spoon that had been placed in the bowl. The aroma of the beans reminded him he'd not eaten since breakfast. "Smells good." He smiled up at the older woman. "Thank you."

Sarah relaxed her stance and smiled in return. "You're welcome, stranger." She turned and headed back to the kitchen without another word.

"I'll offer a blessing." Henry bowed his head and jumped right in. "Lord, we thank you for this meal and for your providence. Amen."

Caeden had barely closed his eyes before the old man's prayer was through. Sarah brought the crackers and a jug of vinegar, and Henry went right to work, first adding a healthy portion of vinegar to the beans and then crushing crackers into the soup. Caeden merely sampled the fare. It was simple but tasty. Carver was shoveling in his food as if it were some sort of eating contest. They passed the time in silence for a few minutes, and Caeden didn't complain when Sarah appeared after a time and offered to refill his own bowl. It would seem Henry Carver's enthusiasm for eating was contagious.

Now, however, with his own urgency to eat and drink satisfied, Caeden slowed down to enjoy the flavors of the second bowl of ham and beans. Crumbling a handful of crackers into the bowl, he posed a question to Carver. "I wonder, can you give me directions to a place called Yogo City?"

Carver's face split into a broad smile. "I can do one better than that. I can lead you there. I have a claim down that way. I need to load up my mule and cart with goods first, but then I'll be headin' back down."

It seemed most fortuitous that Caeden had run across the older man. He nodded, realizing that this unexpected new acquaintance might make his duties a great deal easier. Folks didn't take well to strangers asking permission to inspect their properties.

"That would be most helpful. I need to rent a horse and get a few supplies myself."

"No problem at all," the old man said, pushing his bowl away. "I can wait. Where you staying down in Yogo?"

"Wherever I can pitch my tent."

"That's easy enough. You can pitch it by my cabin. You can take your meals with us when you're around."

"Us?"

"I have a wife and daughter, but they won't mind. They'll be glad for the company. You play chess?"

Caeden nodded, memories washing over him. "I do. I used to be pretty good at it. Played quite a bit with my uncle."

"Then we can spend some time playin' this evenin'. I think you'll like Emmy's cookin'."

Caeden finally finished off the second bowl of beans. "Is Emmy your wife?"

"No, she's my daughter. Her given name is Emily, but we call her Em or Emmy most of the time. My wife's name is Nyola." For the first time Henry Carver's expression took on a look of sorrow. "She's not been well."

"I'm sorry to hear that." Uncertain what else he could say, Caeden looked at his pocket watch. "I suppose we should get to it before we lose too much more time. I'd like to be set up before dark."

"Well, won't be dark for hours around here. That's the joy of a Montana summer." Nevertheless, Carver got to his feet. "I'll pay Sarah and then we can head out to get your horse."

"No, this is on me." Caeden reached into his pocket. "The government has provided funds for my meals."

Carver grinned. "Well, that's right kind of ya. I don't suppose I can argue with lettin' the government pay."

Caeden settled the bill and found Henry waiting for him just outside the front door. They headed back down the street to the stable.

"I'll go load up my cart and meet you in front of the mercantile," the older man told him.

Caeden pushed his hat back just a bit. "Once I secure a

mount, I have some things to pick up at the stage stop, but that won't take much time."

With a nod, Henry took off for the store, while Caeden turned his attention to renting a solid-looking black gelding. The rental prices for the horse and saddle were steep, but he'd expected no less. When there's only one show in town, folks will pay whatever they're asked and be grateful, albeit poorer.

It took less than half an hour to gather his things and visit the mercantile for necessities. Since Henry Carver spoke of his taking meals with the family, Caeden thought it only proper that he supply some of the food. He purchased a variety of canned goods, oatmeal, flour, sugar, salt, and beans, hoping Carver's daughter would be able to make use of it. Last of all, he pointed to a large ham and told the proprietor he'd take that as well.

"Ready?" Carver asked as Caeden came out the door carrying a large wooden box heaped with goods.

"Do you have room for this in your cart?" Caeden looked at the small conveyance and old mule with doubts. "I figured I'd bring something to add to our meals."

"Old Nellie can pull most anything. She might look old and feeble, but there's a lot of gumption left in her. Just throw it in back with the rest of the stuff."

Caeden deposited the load, then went for his horse. Once he'd mounted, he urged the horse to step up alongside the cart and mule. "Ready?"

Carver nodded and gave the reins a slap. "Get on with ya, Nellie." The mule pulled forward without hesitation.

The old man waited until they were out of Utica before resuming their conversation. "So can I ask you a question?"

Caeden couldn't very well refuse him. "Of course." He gave a hint of a smile. "But I might not have an answer."

"I'm bettin' you will," Henry replied. "Just don't know if you'll be wantin' to share it."

"Go ahead."

"I was just wonderin' about you not drinkin'. Most of the men I know drink and do so frequently. Liquor keeps 'em company on a lonely night. Now, I know it's a personal matter, but since I'm an abstainer too, I reckon I just found it interestin'."

Caeden felt himself go rigid at the thought of answering. He had long abstained from alcohol, but seldom did anyone question him as to why. "It *is* a personal matter, but I suppose I don't mind telling you. My father drank heavily, and it ruined our family. That's the simple truth. My mother had great faith that he would change, but he didn't."

Henry nodded. "Usually takes somethin' like that to keep a fellow off the bottle. Liquor has a powerful pull, and it's been known to ruin many a good man."

"What about you? Is there a reason you refuse to drink?" Caeden kept his gaze on the road ahead. He hadn't wanted this conversation, but now that he'd made his reply, it didn't seem right to go silent.

"My Nyola prefers it that way. She's a strong woman of God, and she took me to a church meetin' once where the preacher spoke out against the evils of liquor. I tell you that man very nearly made me feel the fires of hell lightin' up my backside, even though I weren't much of a drinker." Carver chuckled. "Well, I figured if Nyola could say yes to marryin' a man like me, I could say yes to abstainin'."

Caeden nodded but said nothing more. He hoped they might pass the remaining miles in silence, but it wasn't to be. Carver continued with his comments and questions.

"So you mentioned your ma's faith. Is she a woman of God?"

"She was." Caeden's hands tightened on the reins. "She's dead now."

"Gone to glory," Carver murmured. "Bless her soul. And how is it with your own soul, Mr. Thibault?"

The question took him by surprise, but he kept his expression as emotionless as possible. "Call me Caeden. My soul is . . . well, I'm not sure how to answer that question. My mother taught me to have faith in God, but . . ." He fell silent. Caeden wanted no part of a conversation that exposed his anger toward God.

"But?" Henry prodded.

"But she's gone now."

"And so's your faith? Is that it?"

Caeden turned to face the older man. For some reason he found himself wanting to discuss the matter with this stranger. It was almost as if a spring had been unplugged and water was gushing out without restraint.

"Something like that. It's hard to have faith in God when He clearly allowed my father to inflict such misery on the family. The hard truth is, my father was an abusive and hateful man, and drink only made him worse. My mother encouraged me to have faith that God would deliver us, but He never did. My mother died heartbroken. My father followed her two years later—last year, in fact. Given Mother's faith and my father's lack thereof, I feel rather confident she will not have to face him in eternity."

"She must have loved him a good bit to keep hopin' he'd change," Henry said. "You can't beat havin' a woman who believes in you."

"Well, her beliefs in my father and in God did her little good. The way I see it, she was disappointed by both. It was an utter waste of her time and life."

Henry surprised him by laughing. "With women you can

never tell for sure what they're thinkin', but I'm bettin' *she* didn't think it was a waste of time or of her life."

Not knowing how to respond, Caeden fell silent. To his surprise, Carver said nothing more either. They rode in silence, and Caeden began to relax. He studied the scenery around him, noting the rolling hills and occasional open valleys. A small river twisted back and forth alongside the road for most of the way. Occasionally they saw another person. It seemed a wonderful country to lose himself in.

They stopped a couple times to water the animals and stretch, then resumed their travel with Henry sometimes whistling, sometimes humming. Caeden thought him a strange fellow, but amiable enough. From time to time Henry pointed out a cabin or some other place of interest, but otherwise they didn't talk, and that was just fine by Caeden.

After some time, Henry spoke. "My place is just over the hill this side and to the west of Yogo City. Ain't much of a city since the gold seemed to play out. But I'm of a mind that there's still plenty to be had, and I figure as soon as I hit the mother lode, folks will flock back to find their fortunes as well."

"You're that sure there's a big strike to be made?"

Caeden's question seemed to give the older man pause. Finally Carver spoke up. "I've always figured that a big strike is comin' my way. I feel it in my bones. I know the Good Lord has a fortune for me out there—somewhere. Just don't know for certain where it might be. But when I do find it, I'm gonna use the money to give Nyola a proper home and the doctorin' help she needs."

"You mentioned she wasn't feeling well. Is it serious?"

Carver nodded. "The doctor says she's dyin'. He don't give her long."

"What's wrong, if you don't mind my asking?"

The old man shook his head. "In all the places we've been, doctors can't rightly say or agree. Some think it's a weakness in her heart. Some think it's a cancer. She has pain and faints a lot and grows weaker by the day." His voice had taken on a sorrowful tone, and Caeden regretted having posed such personal questions.

"Perhaps one of the bigger cities might have doctors with a deeper understanding of her condition. Have you thought to take her back east?"

"Thought about it. Truth is, I think Nyola's given up." He shook his head, and the look of sadness in his eyes, a deep defeated sorrow, reminded Caeden of his mother.

"I am sorry. I know that can't be easy for you or your daughter."

Henry gave a sigh, then straightened. "Em is tough as nails—stronger than anybody else I know. She keeps me goin'. She and the Good Lord."

Caeden didn't understand how the man could call the Lord good after all he'd just explained.

"Well, we're here. You can pitch your tent wherever you like. If the weather's bad, you can stay in the cabin. We ain't got but one bedroom, but if it's stormin', you and I can bed down in the front room, and Emmy and her ma can sleep in the bedroom."

"I'm sure the tent will suffice." Caeden could see the cabin just ahead of them. Smoke trickled out of a small flue on the roof. From the size of the cabin, Caeden surmised he might have more room in his tent. "I've slept out in some fearful storms, and the tent has served me well. You needn't worry." He continued to study the cabin. At least it had a couple of windows and looked to be fairly solid in its log construction.

"Well, the offer stands just the same. Wouldn't feel right otherwise."

Caeden nodded and followed Carver to the far side of the

cabin. He had no idea of what awaited them, but he found the old man had returned to his happy-go-lucky countenance. Henry was even humming a tune as he jumped down from the wagon.

"Em's fixing venison stew tonight, and with any luck at all she'll have made us some bread puddin'. It's my favorite. Yes, sir, I think you're in for a real treat," Carver added. "Why don't you deposit your things, and I'll go stake out your horse to graze. You can just go on up to the cabin and let Em know who you are and why you've come. She won't mind at all."

3

Because of the heat of the day and the dirt caking her face and clothes, Emily decided to treat herself to a tepid bath. Her father was going to be in Utica until late, and her mother was once again sleeping. The evening belonged to her.

The small tub they used for bathing was barely large enough to submerge herself, but Emily had learned how to make the most of it. By drawing her knees to just under her chin, she could soak her entire body. At least the lower half.

Leaning her head back, Emily relished the way the water cooled her. This was a luxury she didn't indulge in very often, given the amount of work it took to haul in enough water. Of course, that didn't mean they were filthy people. During the summer Emily made sure to daily wash her mother's weak body. A bed bath always made Mama feel better, even if just for a few minutes. And while her father had never been one to keep all that clean, he was occasionally known to take time out during his hunt for gold to enjoy a dip in the river.

*I wish I could just shed my clothes and frolic in the river like the men around here.* Emily smiled at the thought. Many had been the time that she'd had to avert her eyes to keep from seeing far more than she'd bargained for. Up and down the Judith River, a person could see most any kind of spectacle imaginable.

With a small bowl Emily scooped water and poured it over her head. She had taken down her long brown hair with the intention of washing it and letting it dry throughout the evening. She repeatedly poured water over herself until her hair was thoroughly saturated, then took up her one and only bar of rose-scented soap and began to lather her hair and body. How wonderful to smell of something other than animals and sweat.

The scent made her favorite daydream come to life as she pictured a home with a fine picket fence and rosebushes. Emily could see herself, dressed in a simple but feminine fashion, tending to her roses. She thought of how neighbors would stop on their walks to bid her good morning and ask about her husband and children.

*Why, they are all doing just fine,* Emily imagined herself saying. *My littlest one just turned two, and the doctor tells me I'm expecting again.* She would smile as the neighbor gave congratulations and commented that having six children would make for a nice-sized family. Emily always thought of having six children. Perhaps even more. She often fancied a family of three boys and three girls, with the oldest two boys and the youngest two girls. The other two would be one of each—perhaps even twins.

And their house would be large and airy with a huge yard and a place to garden. There would be plenty of rooms—at least four bedrooms, so there would be no need to put more than two children in a room. Of course, that wouldn't figure right with three of each gender. She shrugged. As long as she was dreaming, perhaps she should have eight children and make it an even number of each. It didn't cost any more to dream up eight than six. Dreams were after all . . . free.

Reluctantly she opened her eyes and let the beautiful dreams fade away. The small cabin seemed to close in on her. The air was warm and stale, and the room was far from beautiful. It was, as her father called it, "mostly adequate." Realizing time had gotten away from her, Emily knew she needed to put an end to her bath. When her father did finally arrive home, he'd be starved.

She stood and picked up the nearby pitcher to pour clean rinse water over her hair and body, then stepped from the tub. A rough towel served for drying off. With laundry to wash, Emily dressed only in her clean chemise, hoping to remain as cool as possible for as long as possible. Her wet hair trailed down her back, dampening the thin material to her skin. She gathered her dirty clothes, picked up a bar of lye soap, and deposited both in the water.

The tub water would serve to wash her dirty chemise and a few other things that she'd saved for such an occasion. Laundry was another thing that didn't get done as often as Emily would have liked. Other chores over the last few weeks had taken over most of her free time. Between seeing to her mother, tending the garden, cow, and chickens, as well as cooking, cleaning, and occasionally helping her father pan for gold, Emily found laundry to be an extravagance.

She let the clothes soak and the lye soap soften while she went to get supper started. She stoked up the fire in the stove, regretting the added warmth it would give the house. If not for the laundry she needed to tend to, she might have gone outside to set up a cook fire. But time was getting away from her. Emily checked the venison stew she planned for supper. Giving it a big whiff, she was relieved to find it hadn't yet gone bad. She put it on the stove and gave it a quick stir before turning to mix up a quick pan of corn bread. After slipping the corn bread into the oven, Emily went back to the washtub. Thankfully she'd washed her father's extra shirt the day before. She had only her few things—chemise, stockings, and skirt.

She began scrubbing her things with the strong lye soap. No sweet scent of roses for her clothes, for even while there remained a scent of that precious soap in the water, the lye would soon erase any trace.

"When I have a home of my own, I shall have one of those wringer washing machines," she announced while doing her best to squeeze the water from her newly washed clothes. She draped the wet things across a small line that her father had secured for her in the corner of the cabin. Given the warm Montana air, she knew they'd be dry in no time at all. Meanwhile she would wear her other skirt and one of Mother's old blouses. She had just gathered the pieces from her trunk when the cabin door opened without warning.

Clutching the skirt and blouse to her, Emily looked up to meet the gaze of the most beautiful eyes she'd ever seen. The serious but handsome face they belonged to remained fixed on her face. Emily all but forgot her state of undress. She found it impossible to speak. The stranger continued to stare as if transfixed. Who was he? Why had he come?

All at once he turned away. "Excuse me." He called over his shoulder. "You must be Emily. Your father told me to just come on in. I'm sorry if I frightened you."

"I am . . . Emily." Her voice sounded strange in her ears. "And you are?"

"Caeden Thibault."

He remained with his back toward her, and only then did Emily remember her situation. "Oh my!" She hurried into the bedroom and pulled the door closed behind her. Her breath caught in her throat at the thought of what Mr. Thibault must think of her. Not only that, but to appear before a complete stranger in nothing but one's undergarments was more than a bit unnerving. Emily wasn't at all certain she could even face him again.

With shaking hands she secured her corset. Since Mama had fallen ill and Emily's workload had been so heavy, she never pulled the lacings all that tight, but in her state of mind, she seemed to have uncanny strength and flexibility. The corset cinched tight, further accentuating her small waist. Emily tied off the laces and drew in a breath. There wasn't time to even give her attire much thought. She pulled on her blouse and did up the back buttons as best she could. Next she stepped into her skirt and could barely make her fingers work to secure the hooks and eyes. Mama remained asleep; otherwise, she might have seen how disturbed Emily was by this strange turn of events. She had done such a good job of keeping herself hidden from the eyes of men, but now one very handsome man had seen almost all of her there was to see.

"Em? Where'd you get to?" her father called from the front room.

She felt her face grow hot. "I'll be right out, Pa." Emily swallowed the lump in her throat. There was little she could do about her embarrassment. She took up her mother's hairbrush and hurried to put her wet hair in some semblance of order. Braiding it into a single plait, Emily tried to think of how she would face the stranger.

"Caeden Thibault," she murmured. Who was he, and why was he here?

Her hands once again shook so hard it was difficult to secure her braid with a short piece of red ribbon. "This is silly," she chided herself. "It was a simple mistake, and with the dim light and the clothes I held, I'm sure it wasn't all that immodest."

But she wasn't convinced. With her hair complete, Emily glanced at the heavy coat and canvas pants she'd deposited near the end of her parents' bed. She had hoped to give both a good brushing off before donning them again, and she hadn't had any intention of wearing them that evening. Of course, she hadn't figured they'd have company, nor that there would be any reason for her to hide her appearance. If anyone had ventured to come over that evening, she would have hidden herself away with Mama or else taken refuge in the bedroom to redress at that time. Now, however, she was about to face Mr. Thibault again.

"Well, there's no fooling him now."

Without concern for stockings or shoes, Emily squared her shoulders and decided the time had come to face the music. She reminded herself that she'd done nothing wrong, but it was hard to shake the feeling that she had.

She opened the door to find her father had already set up the chessboard and was telling Mr. Thibault about his exploits when they'd lived in Bozeman.

"Oh, there you are, Emmy." He looked at her a moment as if seeing her for the first time. "I haven't seen you dressed so . . . nice in a long while."

She felt herself flush again and turned her back to her father. "Would you mind doing up the rest of my buttons?"

"Not at all." He made quick work of it, then turned her to face him and planted a kiss on her cheek. Motioning to their guest, he said, "This is Mr. Caeden Thibault. He's a government geologist. They pay him to study rocks and such. Can you even imagine it?"

Emily forced herself to turn from her father to face Mr.

Thibault. He wore the same serious expression, but there seemed to be just a hint of amusement in those lovely brown eyes.

"Mr. Thibault." She gave a nod and hoped that might be the end of the introductions, but the man got to his feet and gave her a slight bow.

"Miss Carver, it is a pleasure to meet you." His lips curled just a bit in a smile.

"We don't stand on formalities around here," Emily's father declared. "No, sirree. Why, Emmy, I see that you're not even wearing shoes and stockings."

*I was wearing a whole lot less a few minutes ago.* "It's too hot."

Her father totally surprised her by turning back to Thibault. "Em usually wears a lot of heavy clothes to disguise her appearance. It's useful for keeping the young men in line. Most folks around here don't know Emmy's young, much less pretty. Some don't even know she's a girl."

"I wouldn't think that any amount of clothes could hide that." His gaze traveled the length of her before he looked again into her eyes.

Emily found it hard to draw a breath and wished she hadn't laced the corset so tight. She finally found her voice. "I've started supper. Should be ready in another half hour."

"That's fine, Em. You'll find a stack of supplies in the corner. Mr. Thibault figures to be around for a while doing his studies, and seeing as how he plans to eat with us, he's donated to our stores." He didn't wait for her response. "We're gonna play us a game of chess while you see to supper. Mr. Thibault here reckons himself to be pretty good at it." Her father paused after making his first move. "Em doesn't do too bad herself. She's got a quick mind and can move fast when she sees her position being threatened."

Thibault coughed but gave a nod. Emily could only imagine what he was thinking. She hadn't moved all that fast earlier. At least not until her senses returned and she realized her situation. Goodness, but how embarrassing to have to deal with that memory day in and day out for however long Mr. Thibault decided to stay.

She hurried to the stove and checked the corn bread. Next she gave the stew a stir, then replaced the lid. Uncertain what else she could do to busy herself, Emily decided to put away the store goods. She was pleased to find sugar, flour, vanilla, and cornmeal, just as she'd requested from her father. Along with this, however, were a great many canned goods, a sack of beans, a smaller sack of oatmeal, flour, sugar, and salt, and a ham. No doubt these were Mr. Thibault's contributions. Well, at least they wouldn't starve anytime soon.

Her father had nailed several wooden crates to the kitchen wall, and these acted as cupboard space for food and dishes. With her mother sick, Emily had arranged the kitchen to suit herself. She liked things orderly. Baking supplies went together in one crate and canned goods in another. Once these items were tucked away, Emily went to work making a bread pudding. She needed to use up what little milk she'd gotten from Bonnie-Belle, their one and only real money-making possession.

Bonnie-Belle was good for breeding, and Emily's father always arranged for a calf out of her each year. Emily was never quite sure how he managed this, for breeding cost good money, but once a year her father would take her off into the "tall and uncut" as he called it, and roughly nine months later Bonnie-Belle was a mother again. Once the baby was weaned, Emily's father would take the calf to market and bring back much-needed supplies. It had kept them going the last six years. That and Emily's ability to garden. The chickens were a fairly new idea of Emily's. She'd been offered four sitting hens in trade when they lived in Bozeman. After a man's wife died, Emily had watched his children until his mother could travel to be with them. In return, he'd given her the chickens, plus three worn-out quilts from which Emily made rag rugs. She hadn't been sorry for the trade.

Taking up some dried bread she'd been saving, Emily continued to wonder about Mr. Thibault. Her father said he was a geologist. The thought intrigued Emily. In her youth she'd attended school, albeit not on any regular basis given her father's propensity for moving them around the country. However, Emily enjoyed learning, and she determined early on to read everything she could get her hands on. She always prayed that one day they would live where there was a library, and when they did, she intended to spend her every free moment there. Books were a way to experience things she might never otherwise know, and for Emily that list was quite long. Perhaps Mr. Thibault had brought some books with him and she might be allowed to borrow them. The thought excited her.

Mixing eggs, milk, and seasonings in with the bread, Emily tried not to think too much on books or Mr. Thibault. She knew that longing for dreams that were completely out of reach could bring heartache and bitterness. She added sugar and butter and again gave the mixture a thorough stirring before plopping it into a bread pan. The corn bread was ready to leave the oven, so she exchanged one baking pan for another.

"Well, Emmy, Mr. Thibault wasn't lyin'. He's mighty good at this," her father called.

"I'm not surprised." At least not about the chess match. Mr. Thibault had an attitude about him that spoke of cunning, intelligence, and confidence.

"I would much prefer you both call me Caeden."

Emily tested the corn bread and found it perfectly baked. She wiped her hands on her apron as she made her way to the bedroom to check on her mother. She found Mama awake but drowsy. Laudanum wreaked havoc with her mind, but Mama seemed alert enough to ask about the male voice she'd just heard.

"Who have you got out there?"

"Pa brought home a man who's working for the government. He's a geologist. His name is Caeden Thibault."

The older woman seemed to come more awake at this. "What's he like?"

Emily shrugged and helped to raise her mother to a sitting position. "I can't really say." She tried not to think of her embarrassment at their first meeting. "He's tall and has brown hair and dark brown eyes." *Beautiful brown eyes that look as if they can see through to your soul.*

"Is he young?"

She nodded, then reached for her mother's pillows to plump. "Probably late twenties, early thirties."

"And is he handsome?"

Emily chuckled. "Ma, you're a married woman."

"But you aren't," her mother replied without pause.

"Well, Mr. Thibault isn't for the likes of me. He's educated and refined. He no doubt has a young lady waiting for him somewhere. Men like that don't go long without a woman securing him for their own."

Mama surprised her by making a request. "I wonder if you would turn around for me."

Emily frowned in confusion. "Turn around?"

"I want to see you. Turn in a circle."

Emily gave a turn and met her mother's smile. "Emmy, you look mighty pretty today. I don't think I've seen you lookin' like this for quite a while."

"Well, it was warm, and I decided to take a bath. One thing led to another, and I just couldn't bring myself to put on all the other clothes. I didn't realize we'd have company. But then Pa came home with Mr. Thibault, and I needed to put supper together." She smoothed out the sheet and tried to keep her nerves from showing. With the bed put to order, Emily helped her mother to lie back.

"Speaking of supper, do you think you might take a little something? Mr. Thibault added to our stores, since he intends to be surveying the area for a while. Pa told him he could stay here on our property and eat with us, so he felt obligated to share food."

"That was very kind of him." Emily saw her mother grimace and knew the pain was back. "I'd like . . . very much to meet him. Perhaps after supper you might bring him to me."

Emily thought it odd but said nothing. Mama was rarely interested in other people these days. "I will, but you need to eat something first. I have some corn bread. I could put some milk and sugar on it. That would be easy to eat and keep down."

"I will try, Emmy. For you I will try."

Emily returned to the stove. "Supper's nearly ready," she told the men. She set the table with plates, cups, spoons, forks, and knives before returning to check the bread pudding. She'd all but forgotten that with the new supplies she could whip up a nice little sauce to go over the dessert.

Emily busied herself with putting the food on the table and found herself hoping it would meet with Caeden's approval. But why? Why did it matter if this stranger enjoyed their meager fare? Her mind began to whir with thoughts.

*He came in here without warning and embarrassed us both. And even if Pa did tell him to just walk in, he might have knocked. I doubt Pa would approve if he knew what happened.*

Still, it was all innocent. Emily put a wooden spoon in the venison stew and placed the kettle on the table. "Food's on. Be careful of the pot; it's still quite hot." Emily didn't wait to see if they would give up their game and come to the table. There were only three chairs in the house, and they would need to bring the two they sat on if they wanted to sit at the dinner table. She figured when they were ready, they would do just that.

So instead of worrying about it, Emily set out to create a sauce for the bread pudding. She needed to keep her mind busy. Perhaps later she could explain the importance of keeping her youth and feminine appearance a secret. Pa had mentioned it, but maybe if she stressed the dangers, then Mr. Thibault would honor her request and not tell anyone else. Caeden Thibault certainly seemed honorable. He hadn't taken advantage of their encounter, nor leered at or ogled her afterward. If it had been Kirk Davies instead, there was no telling what he might have done. She shuddered. No, Mr. Thibault seemed to be a perfect gentleman. She only hoped he would consider her a perfect lady despite her earlier display. Emily felt her cheeks grow hot but told herself it was from the heat of the stove rather than the memory of Caeden seeing her in that thin, damp chemise. She tried to reassure herself once again.

*I was holding my clothes. He couldn't have seen all that much.*

Why couldn't she just forget about the incident? If she kept worrying about it, her father was sure to sense that something was amiss, and then she'd be obligated to explain. That would only make matters worse.

Emily left the sauce and began fixing her mother some corn bread. She mixed it with a little milk and sugar until it turned to mush. Seeing that the men were still finishing up their game, Emily took the bowl to her parents' room.

"I think you'll like this, Mama." Emily put the corn-bread pudding on the nightstand and then helped her mother to sit. "Just let me get these pillows plumped up behind you." Emily pushed and pulled at the pillows until they seemed fuller. She stacked them, then stuffed a rolled-up blanket back there as well. She eased her mother against the pillows. "How's that?"

Mama gave a weak smile. "You do a good job, Emmy." She closed her eyes and seemed to just concentrate on breathing.

Emily sat beside her on the bed. "I'll help you with this. It's a bit soupy. I probably shouldn't have added so much milk."

"It'll be fine," her mother murmured, then opened her eyes. "What about that young man?"

"Mr. Thibault? He and Pa are still playing chess. I figure they'll be committed to finishing their game before either will have any interest in supper. Now, here. Please try a spoonful." Emily put the spoon to her mother's lips.

The older woman took a tiny taste and nodded. "It's real good, Emmy."

Emily knew her mother wouldn't eat much, but she had to try to get some sustenance into her waning body. She coaxed her mother to take a few more bites by entertaining her with news about the area.

"Millie said that more men are giving up on their claims and selling out. She figures pretty soon there won't be anybody here but her and Jake. I don't think she ever means to leave." Her mother gave a little nod to acknowledge the conversation. "Oh, and apparently there's a fella who wants to buy up all the land around here. I don't know what he plans to do with it." Emily put the spoon aside, seeing that her mother wouldn't take any more. "He offered to buy Pa out, but I suppose Pa already told you about that."

Her mother nodded. "Yes, Henry said he was figuring to come back this week to ask again."

Davies' actions and threats made Emily shudder. She and her father both agreed to say nothing about Davies' heavy-handed actions. "He probably thinks Pa will soften to the idea." She laughed and got up from the bed. "Would you like to lie flat again?"

"No. I think this is just fine. Don't forget, I mean to meet this Mr. Thibault. Bring him in after supper."

Emily knew she meant business. Despite her weakness, her mother had a way of finding just enough energy to see her plans through. And for some reason, she seemed bound and determined to meet this young man. It was that kind of stubborn resolve that had kept her alive this long.

"I'll see to it that he visits you, Mama." She placed a kiss on her mother's forehead.

⌒⧢⧢⌒

Caeden didn't know when he'd enjoyed supper quite so much. The food was simple, certainly nothing like the grand meals he'd grown up with, but far better than what he usually scrounged up for himself when out in the wilds. He'd even joined Henry Carver in eating two helpings of the delicious bread pudding before announcing he couldn't eat another bite.

Now while Emily went about cleaning up and putting the leftover food away, Caeden couldn't help watching her. She exuded a quiet grace that he'd known only in his mother. Although clearly a beauty, Emily Carver was unconcerned with her looks. She dressed simply and without fuss, something he couldn't imagine his own sisters doing, much less Catherine Arnold. Catherine was the daughter of his father's former business associate, and she and her father clearly had designs on Caeden. Caeden, however, wanted no part of such an arrangement. Catherine only served to remind him of his painful past.

Henry Carver stood and stretched. "Em, I'm gonna go work a bit at the sluice. It's not that late, and there's still another hour of good light."

"Please be careful, and don't forget to take your rifle in case . . ." She gave a quick glance at the bedroom door and lowered her voice. "In case that Davies returns."

"I'll be careful. Why don't you take Caeden outside and show him where he can set up his tent and where the river is."

Emily flushed and nodded, not even looking up as she continued clearing the dishes from the table. Caeden wondered if she resented the task or was simply still embarrassed at their earlier encounter.

Once Emily's father had gone, Caeden waited for her to say something or direct him where to set up camp, but instead she continued to see to the dishes. He knew it would have been polite to offer his help, but he couldn't seem to stop watching her. She was a shapely young woman, curvy in all the right places, and just the right height—he figured her to be about five feet four. But her best features were her dark brown eyes. His own eyes were a deep, dark brown, and oftentimes people had mistaken them for black. Emily's eyes, however, were a rich cocoa color, framed by thick black lashes.

All at once Caeden realized he was staring, and Emily had stopped in her work to stare back. He coughed lightly and lowered his gaze. "I apologize. It's rude to stare."

"We might as well clear the air," she replied.

He looked up again. "Clear the air?"

"From our earlier encounter. I can say without a doubt that your untimely arrival was the most embarrassing moment I've ever endured. I go out of my way to keep my . . . form from being the focus of men, and now all I can do is ask that you keep my secret."

"You have my word."

"Thank you." She lowered her gaze. "Now, if you'll excuse me, I need to dress to go outside. It'll only take a minute. First, however, I promised my mother I would bring you to meet her."

He had wondered about Mrs. Carver all through dinner. It seemed strange to have her there in the other room but unable to join them. Emily opened the door and called to her mother.

"Mama, I've brought Mr. Thibault to meet you."

Caeden followed her into the dimly lit room. The air was stale, and a bed and nightstand along with a large trunk were the only things in the tiny room.

"Mr. Thibault, I'm glad to meet you" came the weak voice of the older woman.

Caeden went to her bedside and extended his hand. He took hold of her hand and held it very gently. "Please call me Caeden."

"Caeden. Such a beautiful name. Gaelic, I think."

"Yes, but in my case it's a variant on the French name Cade. I was named after my grandfather."

"How nice." Mrs. Carver closed her eyes. "I would very much like to visit with you again, but for now I'm afraid I'm quite tired."

"I will come again when you are more rested." Caeden let go of her hand. He looked to Emily, not quite certain what he should do.

"I need to change my clothes. If you'll wait in the front room, I'll only be a minute," she said, directing him toward the door.

Caeden paced the small cabin while he waited. Mrs. Carver stirred images and memories of his own dying mother. How she had suffered. All of her life she had tried her best to please her husband—to be the wife he needed. But to him she was never enough, and sadly, she knew this better than anyone else.

His fists clenched. His father had never done anything to reassure Caeden's mother that she was a good wife and mother. Instead he had been harsh and critical. Always demanding more and more. A low growl escaped him as Caeden fought to put aside his anger. It would serve no purpose now.

Caeden's geological work had helped him reorganize his thoughts and plans for the future. After the death of his father little more than a year ago, Caeden knew that his sisters and their husbands, as well as his uncle Jasper Carrington, expected things to change. Caeden had left home to attend college and had seldom ventured back for any reason. Everyone knew it was because of his father. After his mother had died, Caeden hadn't bothered to return at all, but he'd sent an occasional letter to his sisters to let them know he was alive and well. He hadn't been there when his father passed, nor had he cared to be. Uncle Jasper had caught up with him in Washington, DC, to give him the news and urge him to return to Albany. It seemed that despite their hatred of each other, Caeden's father had left almost everything to him, and everyone expected him to come home and run the family's various business ventures.

But to him that wasn't home. It was merely the place he'd grown up. A house of painful memories and broken promises. He had no desire to ever return to the Thibault estate. In fact, he'd immediately tried to sell the place, but Uncle Jasper had encouraged him to wait at least a year. Now that year was up, and Caeden felt no different about his childhood home.

"Sorry to keep you waiting."

He turned to see a raggedy and stocky woman where earlier had been youth and beauty. Emily smiled from beneath the wide brim of an old hat.

"I know your father said you tried to disguise your . . . beauty, but I didn't see how that was possible." Caeden continued to take in the sight.

"But now you can," Emily replied. "It's hard to wear all of this in the heat of summer, but I have little choice. I've lived in mining camps all of my life, and women are always scarce. If you have any looks at all, you're in for constant attention." She laughed. "Fact is, even if you don't have looks, you tend to get plenty of attention if you're a woman."

"So why wear the disguise? If you're only going to get attention anyway, you might as well be comfortable."

"I have thought that a few times myself. Still, it seems that taking care to hide my figure and face has at least lessened those who come to pester me. Here in Yogo City it's not so bad. Pa's made good friends with what few men have remained. They seem to be a decent lot, but there's always the chance that someone will arrive who isn't so decent." She moved to the door. "Even so, I'm content to endure. If you're ready, I'll show you around."

Caeden followed Emily outside. The heat of the day had passed, and in its place had come a pleasant evening with an occasional cool breeze. He knew as well as anyone that once the sun set, the night would actually grow cold.

"This might serve you well," Emily said, pointing to an area behind the lean-to where Bonnie-Belle quietly munched on dried grass. "You could use the back of the lean-to to cut the wind in case of storms. The river's just down that path about two hundred yards. The water is way down, but it's still crystal clear and cold. Tastes good too."

A couple of hens clucked and pecked at the ground, while not so far away, another two sat atop their nests on a small raised platform. Emily paused to shoo them inside the small fenced area. "I pen them up at night and let them out during the day. Usually they aren't bothered, but occasionally a fox has been known to come visiting."

Caeden smiled. "You have quite the arrangement here."

"I do. On the other side of the house is my garden. It helps to have your own vegetables when the pan doesn't give you much color." There was a hint of something negative in her tone.

"I suppose it's a hard life," he murmured.

She looked at him as if he'd grown horns. Her frown lasted only a moment, however. "It can be, but that's just the way it is. I don't suppose we have it as bad as some, and we definitely have it worse than others. A person doesn't always get to have a say over how things will be." She barely paused for breath. "Do you need help assembling your tent?"

"No. I can handle it. I'm sorry if I offended you."

Emily shook her head. "You didn't."

"You sounded upset. Yet not that as much as . . ." He struggled to find the right word.

"Cynical?" she asked.

He met her gaze. Those cocoa brown eyes fixed on him, and her mouth tightened into a straight line.

"Perhaps cynical is the right word."

She shrugged. "I'm tired and I suppose the worst comes out of me in such a state. Now, if you'll excuse me, I need to tend to the garden before I retire for the night."

He gave her a nod but couldn't help wishing she would stay. There was something about Emily Carver that held his attention as nothing else had in a long, long time.

# 4

*W*ell, if it isn't Jake Hoover. Millie told me you'd be making your way here." Emily stepped back from the door to admit the smiling man.

"Millie said you'd be up to makin' candles, so I brought you some of the fat from this old bear I kilt." Jake held up a gunnysack.

Emily wriggled her nose. "I can smell it from here."

Jake chuckled as he stepped into the house. He hoisted the sack onto the kitchen table and straightened himself while smoothing the sides of his thick mustache. "So what do you have to trade today?"

"I baked you three loaves of bread and two dozen oatmeal cookies. Will that do?" She saw the look of pure joy on his face. Jake loved her oatmeal cookies.

"I'll say it will. I was just telling Hobson—you know he's my friend and partner who runs the Fergus County Bank over in Lewistown—well, I was tellin' him that you make about the best cookies I've ever had the privilege of eatin'. He told me next time I got some, I should bring him a batch, but I told

him they'd never make it all the way from Yogo to Lewistown."
He laughed and slapped his canvas-clad thighs. "Fact is, they
seldom make it back to my ranch."

Emily couldn't help smiling. She was dressed in her heavy
clothes but without her hat, and she knew that the forty-five-
year-old Jake could have been one of those seeking her favors
had it not been for the friendship he bore her father.

"Well, maybe next time you can get Mr. Hobson to come
here. After all, since he's a partner in your gold venture, I would
think he'd want to check things out." She went to fetch the
bread and cookies. "I put your goods in one of my old flour
sacks, but I'd like to have it back if you don't mind. That way
I can refill it for you."

"That's good incentive for me." He took the bag from her.

"Why don't you sit a bit, and I'll get you a cup of coffee. And
maybe I'll throw in a couple of extra cookies." Emily went to
the stove and picked up the pot. "It's still warm."

That was all the encouragement Jake needed. He pulled out
one of the chairs and plopped down, placing the sack of bread
and cookies directly in front of him. "So I met that geologist
fella who pitched his tent by your lean-to."

"Caeden Thibault." Emily nodded as she placed a mug of
coffee in front of Jake. "He's studying the area's minerals."

"That's what I heard. He came to look over our ditch and
flume system. He thought it looked mighty well done."

"Pa has always admired it. It was impressive to see how you
could divert water from the upper creek to the lower area where
you were working."

"Cost a pretty penny. Much more money than I'd ever have.
If it hadn't been for Hobson and our other partner, we'd never
have gotten it done. Now I'm not so sure it was worth it. I mean,
there is gold to be had, but not in the abundance I'd hoped for.

Seems I'm always a day late to the big finds, or if I find 'em, I sell out before the big strike."

"Just like my father." Emily placed a dish with three oatmeal cookies on the table. She moved the sack of bear meat and fat to the pan she used for washing dishes. "Pa is convinced, however, that there is gold and he will find it."

"I think there's a good fortune to be had as well." Jake sampled a cookie before continuing. "Mighty good, Miss Emily. Mighty good." He ate the rest of the cookie and chased it down with hot coffee before settling back in the chair.

"Frankly, my efforts have turned to disaster. I do better selling meat to the trading post in Fort Benton and the folks along the way."

"Then why bother looking for gold?" Emily joined him at the table and took a seat.

"For the thrill of it, I guess. And the fact that oftentimes it turns to good. I've made my share of money here and there. I seem to have a knack for finding bits and pieces but never the mother lode, but one of these days . . ." He gobbled down another cookie and again followed it with coffee.

Emily had for so long heard the same stories of glory from her father. The entire idea left her frustrated and more than a little cynical. And try as she might to hide her feelings, even Caeden had picked up on them. "Well, for your sake and ours, I hope you're right. I would love to see Pa sluice out something other than those pretty blue pebbles."

"To be honest, I've been setting aside some of those blue pebbles that seem so plentiful. I have a feeling they're worth something." Jake rubbed his whiskered chin. "I'm of a mind that they're sapphires. Not like those ugly green-and-white ones they found up on the Missouri River, but real quality ones."

Emily perked up at this. "You really think so?"

Jake shrugged. "I figure it's worth checkin' into. You suppose that geologist fella would know about 'em?"

"I suppose he would. Seems if he's studying minerals, he'd know about gemstones."

Emily tried not to get excited. She'd heard tales of men uncovering everything from diamonds to rubies to gold, and it always seemed the stories were more exaggeration than substance. Even so, she had a tin of the little blue stones sitting in the corner of the cabin. She'd been collecting them since last year, when her father first brought the family to Yogo City.

"What makes you think they're sapphires?" She hadn't meant to ask the question aloud.

"Well, they're harder than just about anything save diamonds," Jake replied. "One fella in Great Falls told me they weren't nothin' but blue bottle glass, but I know the difference. If your geologist comes around, ask him to take a look at the ones you've found and let me know. I'm not sure but what Hobson will end up sending some to a friend of his for inspection. But if you can get this fella to let us know sooner, that would be helpful. Then maybe we could put our efforts on finding the stones instead of gold and make us a fortune that way."

Emily shook her head. "Wouldn't that be something, now, if those cursed blue pebbles turned out to be valuable." She couldn't imagine what her father would think if those rocks that troubled him so much turned out to be his salvation.

"When you've finished your coffee, I'll walk you down to see Pa. He won't be happy if you leave and don't take time to catch him up on all that's happening."

"Your pa's a good man. I wouldn't think of missing out on talkin' to him." He drank the last of the coffee, then put the mug down with one hand and picked up the remaining cookie with the other. "I'm ready whenever you are."

Emily got to her feet. "Let me check on Mama."

Jake's expression sobered. "How is your ma?"

"About the same. Doctor says she probably won't make it through the winter." Emily tried to sound matter-of-fact.

She went to the closed bedroom door and opened it just a crack. Her mother was sleeping soundly thanks to the laudanum. Emily closed the door again and crossed to the crock where she'd stored the cookies. "I'd best take a few of these to Pa. He won't care a bit about having more coffee, but he'll feel mighty abused if I fail to deliver him a sweet treat."

Jake laughed and pushed back from the table. "He's a man after my own heart."

Emily pulled on her broad-brimmed hat and grabbed a handful of cookies for her father, while Jake took up the sack she'd given him and cradled it like a baby. She would have laughed out loud at the sight had she not held a genuine fondness for the man. She wouldn't want to embarrass him for all the world.

They made their way down to the sluice, admiring the day as they went. Emily was glad the temperature had cooled a bit.

"I think we're in for an early fall," Jake said. "I've been watchin' the critters. The signs say that fall will come early and winter will come hard."

"I hope you're wrong."

"I seldom am," he said in a boisterous tone. "I know this land like the back of my hand. That's why I'm sure there's a treasure here to be had."

Emily paused. "Jake, would you do me a favor?"

"You know I will if I can." His smile assured her of his sincerity.

"Please don't say anything to Pa about the sapphires. I don't want him getting his hopes up. I'll ask him to save me all the pebbles—he usually does anyway. That way if they do turn out

59

to be valuable, we'll have them set aside. But if you get his hopes up and they aren't worth anything . . . well . . ."

"Little gal, I understand. Your pa may hear rumors about them, but it won't come from me. Once I know for sure, I'll let you know. Either way."

She smiled and began to head down the path. "Thank you, Jake. I'll have to make you an extra batch of cookies."

The older man chuckled. "Miss Emily, if I were of a mind to take a wife, I'd come courtin' you."

She laughed. "Only for my bread and oatmeal cookies." Emily spied her father and called out to him. "Pa, look who's come to visit."

Her father glanced up and pulled off his hat long enough to wipe the sweat from his forehead. "Jake, good to see you. I wondered when you might show up."

Pa put aside his tools and motioned Jake and Emily to join him on the ground. The trio sat in a casual manner, and Emily handed her father most of the cookies, saving one back for Jake. He grinned like a schoolboy and snatched it from her hand as if he feared she might change her mind.

"So what's the word, Jake?"

"I was just tellin' Miss Emily here that I think we're in for an early fall. Weather's changin' and the signs tell me it's comin'. Early winter too—probably heavy."

Her father frowned. "Can't say that's good news."

"No, I don't suppose it is." Jake shook his head and gazed out past the sluice. "You finding any gold?"

"Bits, but nothing much. I figure if I work it day and night, I might lay by enough to get us through the winter."

"So you mean to stay?"

"We did last year," Emily's father said with a shrug. "I still think this claim is worth workin'. I'm not ready to give up yet.

I kind of like it around here. Not only that, but Em put in a good garden and canned some and dried some. We should be well enough."

"You might be better to get you some ranchland like I did." Jake stretched out his legs. "I don't know that it'll amount to anything, but at least it's something to fall back on. I got me a few steers I can sell if things get bad."

Emily wasn't sure her father could ever find contentment on a ranch. Staying in one place just wasn't in his blood—not only that, but the lure of gold was too strong. Every time a new strike was announced, her father was ready and raring to head out in search of his fortune.

"I think I'd best get back to the house and check on Mama." Emily got to her feet. "I'll probably have those candles made in a couple of weeks at the latest, Jake. Feel free to check in with me sooner, though, if you're around."

"I'll do that, Miss Emily. But I'm thinkin' I might make me a trip over to Great Falls. I can lay in some supplies and see the Kid."

"How's he doing?" Emily's father asked.

"Not too bad. He's givin' his full attention to his art. I figure the name Charlie Russell is gonna be famous one day. Sure a far sight from that scrawny kid I found half starved on the trail. I'm right proud to call him friend."

Emily smiled. She'd heard Jake's tales of Charlie, or the Kid, as he usually referred to him. She'd even seen one of the sketches he'd done for Jake. He was quite talented, but it was hard to imagine anyone making a living at drawing and painting. Humming to herself, Emily made her way back up the path to the cabin she called home. It wasn't much, and it wasn't pretty, but it was all she had.

*Help me to be content, Lord.* It was a prayer she prayed

more and more often. Why did it have to be so hard to find contentment? It didn't help that her mother urged her to find a good, godly man and settle down to have a family. Did Mama honestly think such a man would just appear in the middle of this isolated state?

Caeden had just appeared. She shook her head. He wasn't going to stick around. He had business to do and then he'd be gone. There was no sense in building an interest only to have her heart broken. Emily had been much too cautious over the years to give her heart so easily to this handsome stranger now.

She checked on Bonnie-Belle and the chickens before deciding to take a turn through the garden. A few tomatoes were ripening nicely, and she found herself very impatient to pick them. What a tasty treat they would make! Even Pa would be glad for them. Finding them still not quite ready, Emily decided to give them another day. She looked over the beans, carrots, and potatoes, then dusted off her hands and trudged back to the house. Jake had provided a pleasant diversion, but she couldn't forsake her duties forever. If he was right that fall was about to settle over the land, there was plenty to do.

Reaching the front door, Emily pulled off her hat and entered the cabin. She put her hat up on the peg and shed her coat and the long flannel shirt she'd pulled on over her blouse. She hadn't bothered to put on her duck-cloth pants that morning and felt amazingly free without the encumbrance. Someday she would wear silk petticoats and dainty drawers made from the softest cotton. She'd never again wear anything that even remotely resembled a man's costume. Someday.

Emily went to the kitchen, then felt an uneasiness come over her. She listened, wondering if her mother had called out, but there was only silence. She turned back to the still-open front door. What if Kirk Davies had returned? He was due back anytime now to make good on his threats to buy them out. She hurried to close the door, but still the feeling lingered.

Unable to ignore the sensation, Emily decided to check on her mother. Fear washed over her. What if she found Mama dead? She drew a deep breath. Sooner or later that would be the case. If it turned out to be today, then she would face it as best she knew how.

Emily put her hand on the door and paused for courage. It didn't come. Her hand trembled as she pushed the door open. She gasped at the sight of her mother on the floor, her legs tangled in the sheet. Apparently she had wanted to get up and had decided to try it on her own.

Yet she was so incredibly still that Emily feared her first suspicions had been right. Closer inspection proved her wrong, however. Her mother was breathing, albeit in a most shallow manner. Emily carefully unwound the sheet from Mama's feet and set it aside. She hadn't realized that tears had trickled down her cheeks until she brushed back a few errant strands of hair. Feeling the dampness only served to stir her emotions.

*I can't give in to tears. I have to remain strong.*

"Mama? Mama, can you hear me?" Her mother moaned slightly, but she didn't wake up.

Emily bolstered her courage and forced herself to remain stoic. She struggled to lift her invalid mother but found it impossible. Getting to her feet, Emily reassessed the situation and tried again. It was a lot different lifting someone from a chair and maneuvering them to bed than picking them up off the floor.

Panic began to course through her. She would have to go get her father. If Jake was still there, she knew the two men would have no trouble getting her mother back to bed. Still, she didn't want to leave. What if her Mama only had minutes left to live? Emily didn't want her to die alone. Her eyes welled again with tears.

She glanced heavenward. At times she wasn't convinced that God was still listening, but her mother was certain He did. "God, I need help."

⌒∾⧵⧵∾⌒

Caeden heard Emily's moaned prayer just as he entered the cabin. Not seeing her in the front room, he made his way to her parents' bedroom. "Emily?" he called out.

"Caeden!" Her voice was very close to a scream. "Hurry."

He rushed into the room and immediately saw the problem. "What happened?" He pushed Emily aside and easily lifted Mrs. Carver into his arms.

"I came back from seeing Pa and found her on the floor. Please put her in the bed. I'll go for Pa. He'll want to make sure she's . . . all right." Emily hurried from the room, leaving Caeden to put her mother to bed.

Caeden frowned at the poor woman's bony structure. She was all but wasted away. He immediately thought of his own mother. She too had wasted away. Wasted away from heartbreak. Caeden swallowed hard. Instead of Nyola Carver, he saw his mother lying there and, without thinking, reached out to touch her cheek.

The moment made him wish he could go back in time. Not because he wanted to endure the pain all over again, but rather to say all the things he'd left unspoken. So many thoughts and feelings coursed through him. He had kept so much to himself. He hadn't wanted to add to his mother's troubles by telling her how hurt he was—how much he hated the way his father treated her—treated all of them. Of course, she knew it anyway.

"Nyola?" Henry Carver called as he entered the house.

Caeden stepped back. "She's . . . alive, but unconscious."

Henry came closer and sat on the bed. "Oh, Nyola." He took hold of her hand and held it tight.

Caeden felt he was intruding and decided to go check on Emily. She was no doubt quite shaken. He stepped into the front room, but she wasn't there. He frowned. Had she decided to take herself off for a good cry? Surely a young woman in her position couldn't stay strong all the time.

He walked out of the cabin, noting as he passed by the door that her big hat and flannel shirt and canvas coat were still hanging on the pegs. She must have been seriously upset to leave the house without them.

*Of course she's upset finding her dying mother in that condition!*

He looked around the landscape, hoping to spy some sign of her. A thought came to mind that perhaps she was at the sluice site. Caeden went back to the cabin and retrieved her hat and coat and headed down to the sluice. He was nearly there when he heard the unmistakable sound of crying.

He found her sitting in a tight ball. She'd pulled up her knees and buried her face in the voluminous folds of her well-worn skirt. Her arms were wrapped tightly around her legs as if she were holding on to a lifeline. For a few minutes Caeden stood stock-still and waited to see if she would sense his presence. If she did, she made no indication of it.

Caeden eased down onto the ground beside her, and only then did she look up with a start. He smiled. "I didn't mean to frighten you."

"Oh . . . oh, please just go away." She hid her face again.

"I thought you might need your hat and coat. I knew you wouldn't want anyone to see you without them."

For a minute he wasn't sure she'd heard him, but finally she looked up and gave a nod. "Thank . . . thank you." She quickly pulled on the coat and hat. Then a sob broke from her, and once again Emily buried her face.

Caeden had comforted his mother and sisters on more than one occasion when his father had been particularly ugly. He knew very well how to offer gentle support and reassuring words. But Emily wasn't a family member. She was a beautiful young woman. She might misinterpret his actions for taking liberties.

"Emily." He spoke her name soft and low. "I want to help."

She shook her head without looking up. "You can't." Her words were muffled against her skirt.

"It's not good to bear this alone. Maybe you'd feel better if you talked about it."

For some reason this set her off. Without warning she jumped to her feet and looked down at him as if he were crazy. "Nothing will make me feel better. My mother is dying a little each day, and I cannot stop it. My father insists that he'll find a fortune each day, and he never does. Talking to you won't make this madness stop."

Caeden got to his feet. "I didn't mean to suggest it would. I only thought you might need a shoulder . . . or rather a sympathetic ear."

She shook her head. Her eyes were red and swollen, but they stared out at him with all the emotions a heart could contain. Caeden found that he very much wanted to hold her and assure her that everything would be all right. But, of course, he knew firsthand that often things were never made right. He wouldn't further her pain by lying.

"I have sympathy enough to last a lifetime," she said.

He could barely hear her words. She stared at him a moment longer, then sank once more to the ground.

"Sympathy has never done me a lick of good. Pity is even worse. So I don't want either from you."

Caeden made a bold move, moving in and sitting down right beside her again. When she didn't move away, he decided to share a bit of his heart.

"My mother wasted away much like yours. My father was a heavy drinker, and his business dealings were far more important than his family. My mother used to say that he was really married to liquor and kept his business as a mistress. It broke her heart. She knew he didn't love her or care that she was dying. She knew he would never give her a second thought once she was gone. But she kept hoping anyway."

Emily turned her face to his. "How terrible! At least Mama knows that she's loved and that she'll be missed."

Caeden nodded. "And that is worth more than all the gold in the world. Love is something you cannot buy or discover hidden in the ground. You can't find it in liquor or business dealings either." He tried to keep the bitterness from his tone, but he couldn't hide it when it came to memories of his father's abuse.

For several minutes neither said another word. Emily looked away to stare out at the river, while Caeden found it impossible to watch anything but her. Why was it she so captivated him? Was it because of their first encounter? Or because he had come to see how hard she worked to hide her identity and her heart, all while laboring to ease her mother's final days?

"All I've ever wanted was a home." Emily sighed and shook her head. "A home where we could stay and not have to leave for the next gold strike or mining camp. A home where I could plant flowers and a real garden and have a nice little fence around it all."

She surprised him by giving a small laugh. "I suppose that sounds childish, but I've never had it. Whenever Mama and

I walked to town, I used to pretend we were actually going home—that one of the houses in town belonged to us. I imagined the details of the house right down to the rugs on the floor and the curtains in the bedrooms. I would let that dream carry me past the mud and muck, the gloom and filth of the hole where we made camp. I held it tight until there was no other choice but to face the reality of my life once more.

"Sometimes I got to go to school, and when I did I was always so impressed by the children who came from real houses and homes, where their mothers dressed in beautiful clothes and their fathers worked regular jobs that provided a living. I got invited once to a birthday party for one of the children, but Mama didn't let me go. We had nothing I could give as a gift, and she said it would have been rude to show up empty-handed. That was one of the biggest disappointments of my life. I wanted so much to see the magic—the life I would never have."

"A house doesn't make a home. I ought to know that better than anyone." Caeden looked down at the ground. "It's the people that make it home. Or in my case . . . a nightmare. Don't let yourself get trapped in a lie, Emily. A house and little fence will not be what make you happy. Don't be deceived and throw away the good things you have in search for something that doesn't exist."

# 5

*K*irk Davies sat in the saloon and sipped a beer while his employer, Septimus Singleton, explained his next move. Davies was bored with the man and his plans, but he paid well and served Davies' purpose all at the same time, so it was worth the trouble to hear him out.

"I want you to close the deal on the rest of these claims," Singleton said. "We need to get all that we can and clear out those who had the mines originally. Once we have them gone, I can bring in new buyers. We certainly don't want anyone hanging around who can tell the prospective buyers that the claims are basically worthless."

Davies nodded. He'd heard all of this before. Singleton had no idea, however, that there were people who still believed in those claims. Folks like Millie Ringgold and Henry Carver would stay until they exhausted all possibilities.

"I've already been advertising. We need to have this all sewn up by the end of September and hopefully before the weather turns bad."

"Some of those folks aren't inclined to sell. Millie Ringgold, for example. She's a tough old woman—former slave, as I hear it. She owns a bunch of claims and has no desire to sell. She told me Yogo was her home and she intended to stay right there until she died. Jake Hoover has two other partners and quite a few claims, and they are unwilling to sell or even consider your offer. However, that could be to your benefit. I heard that their consortium put in over thirty-eight thousand to fix up those claims and make a way for the water to reach where they needed it. That's a good investment that might show other buyers that gold has to be there or else they wouldn't have spent that kind of money." Davies could see he had Singleton's interest with the mention of such hefty sums.

"Then there's that Carver fellow. He lowered his rifle on me and told me he wouldn't sell. He could be trouble for sure. He hasn't struck it rich, nor does he have much to show for his time. Some folks might be dissuaded if he started telling tales."

Singleton shook his head. "It won't work to have folks lingering around who can speak to my potential customers and discourage them with stories about the lack of gold. We need to get rid of the men who are still there. Hire some men to help you get rid of Carver. Burn them out if you have to. Just like other vermin, once their nests are destroyed and their welfare threatened, they'll move on. Offer the slave woman more money. We can always shortchange her. I still have some of that counterfeit money we could use. If she refuses to go . . . well, I can't see that she'd do too much harm. After all, no one's going to listen to a black woman speak out against a white man."

Kirk leaned his chair back on two legs against the wall. "You really don't know much about those folks, Mr. Singleton. I'm telling you it won't be that simple."

The stocky man narrowed his eyes and hit the table with

his fist. "And I'm telling you that some folks just need a little incentive. I'm sure you have a few rowdies who can help you accomplish the job. I want those claims, and I want them right away. I need time to salt the mines with gold and make the setup look promising to those men who are gullible enough to buy in. We have several things in our favor. First, that area experienced a resurgence of mining just last year. Second, folks who are looking to get rich quick never pay as much attention to the negative things folks say as to the positive. Then too we're heading into winter, and most of the miners will be hard-pressed to make much progress until spring. By then, we'll be long gone. I've made money all over the West this way."

Davies picked up his beer. "I've got someone in mind who might help. It'll cost you, though. He doesn't come cheap. Sure not as cheap as I do."

Of course, he hadn't worried about the money. He wasn't in this just for a job. He had other ventures to see to, and Singleton was just a means to an end.

Singleton pushed a bag of coins toward Davies. "The money isn't a problem. Take this and get some help. I want this resolved. Do you understand?"

Davies looked at the stocky man in his ill-fitted suit. More than anything, he would have liked to punch the man in the face. Nobody talked to him in such a condescending tone and got away with it. "I understand, but you'd do well to treat me with some respect. I may be workin' for you, but I could just as easily work against you."

The other man's face darkened, and he got to his feet. "There's no reason to take that attitude, Davies. I'll double what I'm paying you—just get the job done."

Davies pushed off the wall and reached out for the bag of

money. He liked the feel of it. It was good and heavy, suggesting gold pieces. "Is this all real? You didn't throw any of that counterfeit in here, did you?"

The man looked at Davies as though surprised by the challenge. "I wouldn't cheat you. You're working to my benefit."

He could see the man was telling the truth. Singleton knew better than to double-cross him. "I'll get the job done."

"Good. Then meet me back here in two weeks. I'm heading to Great Falls to meet up with investors who want to buy these claims. I'll send you a wire if I can't make it for some reason, but otherwise plan to see me here."

"I'll do that," Davies said. He watched Singleton leave the saloon, then settled his attention back on the warm beer.

Utica wasn't exactly his idea of a great place to hang around, but it had served his purposes while he was waiting to revisit the miners in Yogo City. One man in particular.

Davies hadn't known the man by sight, but he had held a grudge against him since learning of his responsibility for taking the life of Kirk's younger brother Lenny. It had taken nearly six years to hunt down that man. Kirk's patience had won out, however. He now knew exactly where to find Henry Carver, and how to make him pay.

He smiled. Revenge was something he relished. There was nothing quite like it to get a man's blood up. Not only that, but he was good at killing. He'd had a lot of practice.

He looked at the bag of gold in his hand and tossed it up and down. For now, he had to put his own plans on hold. He needed to get the rest of those claims for Singleton. First, however, he'd need to ride to Lewistown. He knew of some less-than-desirable sorts there who might want to earn a little money.

Davies tucked the bag of coins into his pocket and got to his feet. He glanced down at the unfinished beer and decided to leave it. It wasn't that good anyway. He could always get drunk in Lewistown.

⁂

Caeden found the Carver cabin surprisingly quiet when he returned after visiting several of the area mining claims. He'd figured to at least find Emily there, but she appeared to have gone to town. All of her heavy clothes were missing from the pegs by the door.

Hanging his coat on one of the free pegs, Caeden wondered if Mrs. Carver was awake. He'd heard from Emily earlier that day that her mother had regained consciousness and had seemed no worse for her fall. He had to admit he was happy to see at least a hint of Emily's lighthearted nature return.

The door to the bedroom was open, so Caeden decided to see if Mrs. Carver was awake. It would be only courteous to let her know he was there in the cabin. He wanted to work at the table and organize some of his notes from his work journal.

"Mrs. Carver?"

"Mr. Thibault, please come in."

He was surprised to find her quite alert. "I didn't want to disturb you, but I had some work to do at the table and didn't want to alarm you in case you heard someone moving about the cabin."

She smiled. "I'd like it if you'd come sit with me a spell."

He couldn't imagine why she'd want his company, but he nodded and went to fetch one of the chairs. Returning to her room, he positioned the chair beside the bed. "What can I do for you?"

Nyola Carver reached out her hand. Caeden took hold and smiled, waiting for her to speak. There was a glimmer in her brown eyes that reminded him very much of Emily.

"Mr. Thibault—"

"Call me Caeden, please."

"Caeden." She nodded. "I do like that name." She drew a breath and closed her eyes for just a moment. Caeden wondered if she was in pain, but when she opened her eyes again, she seemed to have the same peaceful look on her face.

"I want your promise that you'll hear me out."

"Mrs. Carver, I don't know what it is you want to tell me, but I promise to hear you out." He squeezed her hand in a gentle fashion. "So please go on."

"I've been praying for Emily. Praying that God would send her a good Christian man to love her . . . and I believe that man is you. I think God has put you here to marry my Emily."

Caeden looked at the woman in complete silence for several long moments. Shocked by her frank confession, he struggled to know how to respond. What could he do, he decided, but speak in just as frank and forthright a manner as she had?

"Mrs. Carver, I'm pretty sure *God* hasn't sent me here for any reason, but especially not for that purpose. First of all, I'm not a good Christian. You wouldn't say that if you knew more about me. Second, I have no intention of ever marrying. My parents were a miserable example of marriage, and I've no desire to repeat their mistakes."

She didn't so much as blink. "You aren't here by mistake or chance, Caeden. I've been praying in earnest to meet the man who would marry my Emily. I've asked God to let me meet him and know him before I die, and I haven't much time."

"But you can't think that it's me." He wanted more than anything to convince her she was wrong. He found Emily quite charming and beautiful, but he wasn't the right man for her. She wanted a home and a place to plant flowers. She wanted a fence, for pity's sake. He couldn't bear the idea of returning to

74

such a life. At least not in Albany, New York, where everyone expected him to return and settle down.

"Caeden, I know you've endured a great deal in your life. I can see that in your eyes." She patted his hand. "We all have burdens we bear and pain that has left us fearful of living life. But God has a plan for you. He brought you here for a reason, and I believe that reason is Emily. Why don't you try talking to Him and see if you don't find that to be true?"

He didn't want to tell her that such an idea terrified him right down to his boots. He swallowed, but his throat was dry and gave him no relief. "I doubt God would listen to me. He hasn't exactly stayed close." It was all he could bring himself to admit.

"God never is the one who walks away, Caeden. Only we can do that. Jesus promised to never leave or forsake us. Unfortunately, we can leave and forsake Him. I think if you take a good hard look at the situation, you'll find it's an easy walk back. He's waiting there for you, and I know He'll give you the answers you need."

Caeden heard the cabin door open and Henry Carver's whistling. "Sounds like your husband has come back." Caeden got to his feet and let go of his hold on Mrs. Carver's hand.

"You promised to hear me out, and I appreciate you keeping your word. Could you please promise me one more thing?" she asked.

He didn't want to promise her anything, but at this point he didn't know what else to do. "I'll try."

"Just give God a chance. If you take yourself back to Him and talk it out, I know He'll show you the way. He has a lot of mercy and tenderness for His children."

"He didn't seem to have much for my mother." Caeden's bitter tone echoed in the tiny room. "She lived in a loveless marriage to a violent man, always hoping for that mercy and tenderness. Apparently God didn't have any such thing to give her."

Nyola Carver smiled. "He took her home, didn't He? She's not here to continue in her burden of pain and sorrow. That suggests mercy and tenderness to me. And as a mother I can assure you that our children are often oblivious to the comfort we find even in the face of adversity—especially when that comfort is found in God."

"Nyola, you're awake," Henry Carver said, strolling into the room. He gave Caeden a nod. "Where's Em?"

Caeden shook his head. "I haven't seen her. I just got back and had some journal work to do. If you'll excuse me."

He heard Nyola tell her husband that Emily had gone to trade some eggs and would be back shortly. Thoughts of Emily's whereabouts were not enough to take his mind off of the disturbing conversation with Mrs. Carver. He took a seat at the table and crossed his arms. Nyola's words had taken root, and no matter how hard he tried to push them aside, Caeden couldn't forget what she'd said. Like a stubborn child refusing to eat his vegetables, Caeden shook his head.

*I am not the man she thinks I am, and God is definitely not the compassionate deity she believes Him to be.*

෴

Henry Carver closed the bedroom door, then took a seat in the chair Caeden had just vacated. "It's good to see you awake and smilin', Nyola. I know I haven't given you much to smile about all these years."

She shook her head. "You are the joy of my life. You and Emmy. I'm the one who's sorry. Sorry for quitting on you like this."

Henry took hold of her hand. It was cold and thin. Much too bony. Her skin was like translucent paper. "Those doctors could be wrong, Nyola. Maybe this is just a bad spell. Could be you'll snap out of it and feel a whole sight better in a few months."

"Now, Henry." She made a *tsk*ing sound, chiding him. "You and I both know that isn't the way it is. I am ready to go when my time comes. Of course, I do worry about you and especially about Emily."

"I don't know what I'll do without you." Henry looked at her. His breath caught in the back of his throat. Facing her death was harder than anything he'd ever done.

"You'll get by, Henry. But you need to promise me that you'll let Emily go her own way. She's stayed with us all these years because she knew I needed her. She knows you're strong enough to go off on your own, but she may need convincing that you want her to do just that for herself."

"But I don't know that I do." He looked toward her hand, unable to meet her gaze. "Fact is, Nyola, I don't know that I could bear to be alone."

"Then find another wife, but don't force that child to give up her dreams of a home and family of her own just to ease your loneliness. We've taken far too much from her already."

For several silent moments Henry thought on her words. "I hate that I've let you down. I'm sorry as I can be that I didn't turn out to be the husband you needed me to be." He looked up to find her smiling.

"You are the man I love, Henry Carver. I married you for better or worse, in sickness and health. I don't regret it. Not even now."

"I hope you'll forgive me. You deserved so much more." Henry's eyes welled with tears. "I promise you, if you can just hang on a little longer, I'll find that gold, and then I'll be able to take you back east to a proper hospital and better doctors."

"They wouldn't be able to help me any more than the others have, Henry." She squeezed his hand. "There's nothing for me to forgive. I want you to remember that. My only regret is that I would have liked to have lived long enough to see Emily married with a babe of her own. I think I would have liked being a grandmother." She winced and closed her eyes.

"You would have made a good grandmother, Nyola." He wiped at the tears with the back of his sleeve. "I can see that you're hurtin'. Would you like me to fetch the laudanum?"

"No. Not just yet," she replied, still not opening her eyes. "I want to talk to Emily when she gets back, and I'd like my head to be clear of the medicine."

Henry got to his feet and leaned over to kiss her on the forehead. "I love you, Nyola. Always remember that."

"I have always known that, Henry." She gazed up at him with such love in her eyes. "Just as I have always loved you . . . and always will."

He held her gaze for just a moment, then turned and walked away. If he stayed there any longer, he'd be sobbing like a baby, begging her to stay. It was bad enough he carried the guilt of not being a good provider . . . of not being able to get her the expensive medical care that might well have saved her life. That guilt ate him up night and day. It was what drove him to work the sluice and pan until his body was wracked with pain. Guilt was a tremendous motivator.

"But it wasn't enough to make me stop seekin' my own way," Henry muttered, heading for the front door.

"Did you say something?" Caeden asked from the table.

Henry had forgotten all about Caeden. "It wasn't anything,"

he called over his shoulder. He wasn't about to explain to this young man that his life choices were the reason his wife lay dying. He wasn't about to speak that truth to another soul. It was bad enough that Nyola knew it. Knew it and forgave him anyway. Sadly that only made the guilt feel worse.

# 6

*W*ith the cooler temperatures of September, Emily found herself in much better spirits. Jake had been right. Autumn was definitely upon them. It was amazing how different the weather was from just a few weeks earlier. Now the mornings were crisp and chilled, while the days were quite mild. Rains came off and on, but nothing overly discouraging. If possible, it seemed that things actually greened up just a bit before changing into a riot of colors.

The hens were laying with regularity, Bonnie-Belle was giving copious amounts of cream-rich milk, and the garden had turned out a nice variety of vegetables. Over all, Emily felt a sense of peace, given the time they'd remained in one place. She tried to be thankful for the past year. A year was usually as long as they ever stayed anywhere, but her father had assured her that they weren't going to pull up stakes and leave anytime soon. Of course, the bad came with the good. Her mother didn't have long to live, the cabin was cramped, and Emily was still no closer to figuring out what God had in mind for her life. In fact, she wasn't at all sure she was any closer to figuring out what God was all about.

Days earlier Mama had asked Emily to sit and have a long talk. Emily could still hear her mother's insistence that Caeden Thibault would play an important role in Emily's future. Emily didn't want to make her mother feel bad, so she tried her best to seem accepting. Mama had told her many times over that she had prayed for Emily to find a husband. Now Mama was growing weaker by the day, and the only man to come around was Caeden Thibault, so naturally she was certain he fit the bill.

Emily had thought to apologize to Caeden. Mama mentioned having spoken with Caeden about her belief that he was to marry Emily. What a horrible thing to put on his shoulders! Perhaps that was why he'd been gone so much of late. Emily knew firsthand from their earlier conversations that her dreams and Caeden's were as far apart as the east from the west. He wasn't at all suited to be a husband, much less a husband to a woman who wanted to put down roots so deep she could never be moved again. But it was much too pretty a day to ponder all these overwhelming and discouraging things, so Emily forced them from her thoughts.

"I will be happy today," she vowed.

Humming a tune in the kitchen, Emily arranged her extra eggs in a basket with some freshly churned butter. Millie would be delighted with the goods, and it would get Emily that much closer to paying off the pig Millie was keeping for her. Then in just a few weeks they would butcher the pig and smoke the meat for winter eating. Emily had never taken on such a task, but Jake Hoover promised to swing by and help, and that was good enough for her. For once her world seemed almost right. Father had even mentioned seeing Kirk Davies in Utica and assuring the younger man that he was in no way interested in selling. To her father's surprise, Davies hadn't argued the point. They all hoped that would be the end of that.

Leaving the basket on the counter, Emily slipped into her outdoor clothes. A quick check of the pocket assured her that her pistol was ready at hand should she have need of it. It gave her a small amount of satisfaction knowing she might even be able to shoot a rabbit if the opportunity presented itself. They hadn't had rabbit for some time, and it would sure make a tasty treat.

She pulled on her hat, then headed to her mother's room. "Mama? I'm heading over to Millie's. I won't be long. Do you have everything you need? I don't want you trying to get up on your own again."

Her mother smiled weakly and gave a slight nod. "I'm just going to sleep a bit. You take your time. I'll be just fine."

Emily went to her mother and kissed her gently on the cheek. "I love you, Mama."

This brought a bigger smile to the older woman's face. "I love you too, Emmy. You are my pride and joy, and I thank God every day that He picked me to be your mother."

Emily nodded in the bittersweet knowledge that their time together was very short. "Guess He knew we'd need each other." But if He truly knew that, why would He take her from Emily now?

*I still need her, Lord.*

Stuffing her emotions down deep, Emily turned for the door. "I'll be back soon."

She returned to the front room and grabbed the basket. She tried hard to keep a positive spirit. There would be time enough to mourn her mother's passing once she was dead. No sense crying buckets of tears over what might or might not happen that day. Time alone would tell when her mother's hour would come, and until then, Emily was determined to enjoy the days they had.

Millie's place seemed deserted when Emily arrived at the door. She glanced around the tiny town and wondered if anyone was still in residence. Millie had told her that a good number of men had sold out to Kirk Davies and moved on. She had also figured that by first snow, she and the Carvers might be the only ones left. The deafening silence of the small town seemed to suggest she was right in her assessment.

"Millie?" Emily called out as she entered.

The old woman padded out from a back room. "Emily, it's shore nuf good to see yo. What yo got dere?"

"Eggs and butter." Emily hoisted the basket onto the counter. "I wanted to make a payment for the pig. Oh, and later I'll have some things for his slop."

Millie grinned her overly toothy smile. "That little pig is de best fed in de county. Yo's gwanna have a nice fat porker by butcherin' time."

"That's what I'm hoping." Emily waited while Millie fetched a bowl to put the eggs in. "It looks like you were right about everyone pulling out. I didn't see a single soul out there. Just empty cabins."

"Still a half dozen or so of us," Millie said, taking great care to transfer the eggs from the basket to the bowl. "Jake won't ever leave dis part of de state, so I reckon he'll be round from time to time. Dere's Zed, Jim, and One-eyed Tom. I don't 'spect Tom to stay around. He's not de type to winter out here in de middle of nowhere."

"Still, it's a far cry from last year, when there were over two hundred people living here." Emily waited until Millie had removed the eggs before reaching into the basket for the two crocks of butter. "I remember all the excitement and how everyone was sure this was going to be a big strike."

"Didn't last long with dat thought," Millie countered. "Folks were up and gone by dis time last year. Post office opened in June and closed down in September. I doubts it ever gwanna open again."

"It's a pity. I really like it around here. I wasn't at all certain when we first arrived, but I do find it quite peaceful now. Nothing like some of those mining camps we were in back in California."

"Still, a gal like yo needs a man and a place of her own."

"You seem to do just fine without a man around," Emily said, smiling.

Millie laughed loud and long. "Yo's got that right. I do jes fine. But I's old and yo's young."

The door opened, and to both of the women's surprise, Jake Hoover entered with a bolt of red calico tucked under one arm and his pack under the other.

"Afternoon, ladies. Howdy do."

"Landsake, you look a sight. You scraped de beard from yo face and done cut yor hair." Millie surveyed him a moment, then nodded. "Makes yo look almost human."

Jake laughed. "I had my picture taken in Lewistown. Figured it was about time. Never know when a fellow might leave this world, and he ought to leave something behind."

Millie chuckled. "A fella don took my picture last year." She leaned toward Emily. "Made a good trade for it too. I keeps it in back and sometimes I jes look at it and wonder at how a little box could make such a thing." She turned back to Jake. "But I'm guessin' yo ain't here for such things as pictures. Yo got an ornery look to yo, Jake Hoover."

"You'd best treat me right, Millie Ringgold, else I won't be leaving this here present with you." He dumped the bolt of cloth on the counter, then nodded toward Emily. "Good to see you, Miss Emily. Those candles ready?"

"They are, Jake. I finished the last of them two days ago. You can stop by anytime to get them." Millie was busy examining the fabric and didn't seem to even notice that Jake and Emily were in the room.

"Well, given you used your own time to make 'em, I figure you oughta let me pay you somethin'."

"You gave us that bear meat, and you're always generous to give us venison and elk. I think you've more than paid your share." Emily picked up her basket. "Maybe if you sweet-talk Millie, she'll let you have some of that butter I just gave her."

"Oh, yo shouldn't be tellin' him dat. Now he'll jes nag me." Millie cackled like she'd just told a great joke. She took up the bolt of cloth and hugged it to her breast. "I'm thinkin' yo's tryin' to get on my good side, Jake Hoover."

"Well, if that's the side where you keep the whiskey, then you're right."

They both broke into laughter at that comment, and Emily moved toward the door. "I'd say you two have some dickering to do, so I'll just be on my way." She couldn't help but smile to herself as she closed the door behind her. She liked these people. They were honest and down-to-earth, and there wasn't a pretentious bone in their bodies. That meant a great deal to Emily.

Making her way around the back of Millie's building, Emily's pleasant thoughts were interrupted when a man pushed her against the wall and tore the hat from her head.

Kirk Davies grinned down at her like she was the first-prize lamb at the fair and he'd just taken possession. "You sure are a pretty thing. Why you hiding underneath that hat?"

"So lewd characters like you will leave me be." Emily tried to push him away, but Davies would have no part of it. Instead he put his hands up on the wall, either side of her, and leaned in. His breath smelled of beer and cigarettes.

"You wouldn't begrudge a fella a look now, would you? Or maybe a little kiss." He moved toward her mouth, and Emily stepped down hard on his foot.

He let out a yell and backed away just enough that Emily moved to skirt past him. Davies was undeterred, however. He caught hold of her arm and pulled her back. "You ought to learn to be nicer. No tellin' where a little kindness might get you with me." He leered at her.

"I don't want anything from you. Not anything at all. Furthermore, I'm not going to stand here and be pawed by you."

He chuckled. "And what are you going to do about it?"

She was just about to pull the pistol from her pocket when Jake Hoover appeared. "Well, there you are, Miss Emily. Oh, looks like you lost your hat." He bent to pick it up, and Davies backed away with a watchful eye. "I hoped to catch up with you to tell you that I have a rooster for you."

She took the hat from him and snugged it back on her head. "That would be wonderful. We can talk over the price when you have time."

"No problem. We can figure it while I walk back to the cabin with you and get those candles."

She nodded, relieved that she wouldn't have to have a showdown with Kirk Davies. "I'd be happy for the company." She moved off in the direction of her cabin, not even waiting to see what Davies might do or say. Jake didn't even bother to acknowledge the scowling younger man.

Jake followed close at her side. It wasn't until the cabin came in view that Jake spoke. "I didn't really mean to get the candles. I just figured Davies was up to no good. Saw him nosin' around the store and figured he might be waiting to cause trouble."

"You were right on that account. I'm grateful for you step-ping in when you did. I thought I was going to have to pull my gun to persuade him of his blunder."

Jake shook his head. "That's one mean fella. I heard tell he beat a man to within an inch of his life over in Lewistown, and all for Davies thinkin' him a card cheat. If you pull that pistol, you'd best be ready to use it."

Emily had often wondered if she could truly shoot a man. In the various places they'd lived, she'd seen a lot of men shot—usually brought on by drunken brawls and claim jumping. "I think in Kirk Davies' case, I would have little trouble."

"I agree. I'll be glad when he moves on."

"Hopefully, that will be soon. He's already managed to buy out most everyone around here. Surely his boss will find a way to be happy with that. Pa saw him in Utica a few days back, and while Davies made a point of trying to get the claim, he didn't argue when Pa told him no."

Jake shrugged. "Some folks are never happy. No matter how much they have or how good things get." He stopped, and Emily did likewise. "I'm gonna go on now. I'll be by one of these days for the candles. Right now I got a few other things to tend to. I'll bring you that rooster when I come for the candles."

Emily smiled. "You're quite welcome to stick around and join us for supper. Once Pa finds out what you did for me, he'll want to reward you."

"Didn't do it for that reason. Can't abide a mean-tempered man who pushes folks around. Especially ladies. No, I need to get on. I gotta get over to the dike and check on a few things."

"Well, all right. I can always bake you another batch of cook-ies. You've certainly earned them."

"You always know just how to sweet-talk me, Miss Emily." He winked and then marched off toward the trees. "Cookies for rescuin' a lady in distress. Makes me think I should do more rescuin'."

Emily smiled and wasted little time crossing the short distance to the cabin. She didn't think Davies would have been foolish enough to follow them, but she didn't put it past him. She glanced back over her shoulder to look down the trail. She saw nothing, but she shivered just the same.

7

The first snow of the season came on the fifteenth of October. It was nothing more than a light sprinkling that left the ground and trees looking as if they'd been showered with confectioners' sugar. The look was charming and glittered like diamonds in the sun, but it also left everyone with a sense of urgency. Winter would soon be upon them, and winter in Montana was nothing to take lightly.

Emily knew from having weathered several winters in Montana that this could mean anything from bone-chilling temperatures and snow to overcast days of darkened gloom. Not that there weren't sunny days, but it was never warm. Especially inside a small cabin. Having sized up their readiness for the colder months, Emily realized they hadn't laid in nearly enough wood, straw, or hay. She had thought to speak to her father on the matter that morning, but he was up and out of the cabin before she had fully awakened.

*There won't be money for all that we need.* Emily dressed in her heavy layers of duck and wool. *Why can't Pa see how hard this is on us? Doesn't he care?* If she were judging solely on his actions, Emily would have to say no. But she knew her father's heart. He really did love and care about them. She knew he would fight to the death for her or her mother, but gold fever kept him from understanding the full impact of his dreams on those he loved.

She had thought about discussing it with Caeden, thinking that perhaps as a young man of higher education he might have ideas for what Emily could do. However, Caeden had been gone for some time—off doing the work he'd pledged to do for the government. He'd taken down his tent more than three weeks ago, telling Emily and her father that he needed to cover some territory to the south of them. He promised to return before completing his tasks, but Emily couldn't help but wonder if her mother's comments to him had frightened him away. If so, it was probably for the best. She could hardly blame the man if he was put off by a declaration that God intended him to marry Emily.

Drawing on her coat, Emily decided to put her concerns aside. There were plenty of chores that needed her attention. She added a knit scarf to her usual ensemble before making her rounds. She checked on the chickens first and threw out some feed. The rooster Jake had brought fit in nicely with the hens. He assumed his role with great authority. Maybe too much authority, for he always seemed to challenge Emily whenever she appeared. She'd taken to arming herself with a broom when visiting the nests.

Next she went to milk Bonnie-Belle in the little lean-to. Given that the cow was due to calve again in January, her milk production was on the wane. Emily knew it would just be a matter of time before she dried up, and then they'd be stuck using canned milk until the calf was taken to market.

"Hello, girl." Emily patted the bovine with tender affection, then reached up to take down the milk pail and stool from the wall pegs. "I don't know about you, but I prefer this chilly weather to that awful summer heat." Bonnie-Belle lowed as if responding. Emily gave her a bit of fresh hay, then sat down to the job of milking. She liked this time of quiet contemplation. It allowed her a few moments to focus only on God. By her own admission, she'd not been overly faithful in praying or reading the Bible.

"Father, I don't always do what I'm supposed to do. We both know that." She sighed. "I want to have faith like Mama, but I'm just so weak at times. I get pretty discouraged and afraid. You've always provided, and I know I sound like an ungrateful child, but I'm worried. I know it's a sin to worry. Mama says that to worry is to doubt you. I don't mean to doubt you, but I doubt other people." She bit her lower lip momentarily. "I especially doubt myself."

She leaned her head against Bonnie-Belle's warm flank. "Lord, I'm so afraid that life is slipping away from me. You've heard me say it many a time, and I suppose it's not worth saying again, but I can't help myself. You know how I long for a home of my own and a husband. I want to make my own family and be a part of a real town. I want a church to attend and a friend, maybe several. Mama says you can do that and so much more. I want to believe that."

In all of her life Emily had only known a few people she could call *friend*, but even then they were more like acquaintances than bosom buddies. She had never felt she could confide in any of them. Not like she confided in her mother. Mama had told her that one day she would have a dear friend to whom she could tell all of her secrets and woes. So far, however, that hadn't happened, and Emily remained guarded with everyone she met.

"I know I shouldn't be so concerned with my own desires

when Mama is so sick. Forgive me for my selfishness." She gave
another heavy sigh and continued milking until Bonnie-Belle
was dry and Emily's hands were aching from the cold. She patted the cow as she got to her feet.

"You've done us good, old girl."

Emily hoisted the milk pail and the milking stool. "I'll see
you again tonight." She put the stool back on the wall and
then made her way out of the lean-to and back to the house,
bucket in hand.

With all of her animal-related tasks complete, Emily busied
herself with kitchen chores. She poured the milk into a crock
to let the cream rise to the top. She then began preparations
for making bread. She hoped to bake a dozen loaves. Jake was
coming soon with her pig, and together they would butcher it.
Emily had promised him more bread and cookies, as well as
some preserves she'd put up the month before. Not only that,
but she'd agreed to take on some mending for the man. Barter-
ing and trading for goods was something Emily prided herself
in. Having grown up with money being scarce, swapping kept
them from doing without. At least most of the time.

It was late in the day when Emily spied Caeden coming from
over the hill. Her heart skipped a beat. He was so dashing and
handsome. She'd been busy chopping wood and used his return
as a good excuse to pause in her duties. With all of his goods
and tent strapped to his back, Caeden resembled a peddler. The
thought brought a smile to Emily's face. If Caeden Thibault
wanted to be a traveling salesman, he would no doubt make a
good one. He had a determination to succeed at whatever he
did, and she found that quite appealing. *I wonder if anything
would stop him.*

"Welcome back." She hefted the ax. "There's some stew on

the stove if you're too hungry to wait for supper. It's left over from lunch."

He smiled. "I might sample it to warm myself up. I wasn't expecting to wake up to snow quite so soon."

"It probably won't last, since it was just a dusting. Last year it came and went until finally in late December it snowed and pretty much stayed until spring."

"I'll be long gone before that happens," he said, pulling his pack from his back.

Emily frowned but turned away quickly and pretended to be completely engrossed in the next piece of wood. She set it on end, then brought the ax down with all her strength. The ax stuck, and Emily lifted both it and the small log and brought both down once again against the stump. The wood split nicely. She took both pieces and added them to her pile. "I'm going to have to get busy putting aside more wood. We don't have nearly enough for winter." She glanced at the small pile of logs her father had assembled. "This is the last of it."

"I can definitely help with that," Caeden offered. "I'm not too bad at chopping and sawing, if I do say so myself."

She made the mistake of looking back at him. His casual manner, windblown hair, and familiarity left Emily almost breathless. *It wouldn't take much for me to fall for such a man.*

Emily pushed such thoughts aside. "Were you successful in your search?"

"I was. A few more weeks and I'll have all of the information needed."

"And then you'll go back to Washington, DC?" She tried to sound as if it didn't matter what he did.

"Yes." He deposited his things on the ground and stretched. "Let me get my tent up, and then I'll take over that chopping after supper. Maybe tomorrow we can head into the trees and see about getting additional wood. Do you suppose your father would let us borrow that ornery mule and cart?"

"I'm sure he would." Emily watched as Caeden began to unfasten the ropes that held his things together. "Can I help?"

Caeden shook his head. "This won't take long. Why don't you go on inside and warm up, and I'll join you in a few minutes."

That seemed like a good idea, so Emily put aside the ax, then gathered up some of the split wood and headed for the house. She relished the warmth of the cabin and hurried to deposit the logs in the woodbox near the stove. Next she checked on her mother and found her still sleeping. Mama slept more and more these days. She rarely ate anything and only took a few sips of water. The doctor had told them this was how it would be in the final stages of her life, but Emily tried hard to ignore it. She wasn't ready to say good-bye.

"I wish we had more time," she murmured, looking down at her mother's peaceful face. *I don't know how I will ever face each day without you here to encourage me.*

She left the room quietly and went to the kitchen to start preparations for supper. A great sorrow washed over her as she thought of her mother's impending death and Caeden's return to Washington. She had some decisions to make regarding her future, and the answers would not come easy. Mama encouraged, almost insisted, that Emily plan to leave the area and strike out on her own. Emily wasn't at all sure what her father would think of such a thing, but she had been giving it serious consideration. The idea of returning to the Bozeman area appealed to her, but so did thoughts of heading farther south to Colorado. She had enjoyed their time in that part of the country, and the winters weren't nearly as fierce.

"Whatever I decide, it'll be hard to follow through unless I find some way to finance it." She looked around the room and shook her head. "And that doesn't look as though it will happen anytime soon."

Caeden assembled his tent behind the lean-to as he'd done on that first day. He stashed his gear inside and then made his way to the cabin. For weeks now Nyola Carver's words had haunted him, and he found it almost impossible to stop thinking about Emily. Nyola felt certain he was intended to become Emily's husband, but he was just as sure that such a thing would never happen. So why was it so hard to dismiss the idea?

Mothers trying to marry him off to their daughters was nothing new. Caeden had been the object of such talk for as long as he could remember. But in his case, it was the mothers of wealthy families who were after him, always on the lookout for ways to benefit the family coffers. Marriages among the rich were arranged with meticulous planning.

Pausing at the cabin door to clean his boots, Caeden couldn't help but think of Catherine Arnold. She had been intended for him from the time he was eighteen. Her father was his father's business associate, and the man had plans for becoming a full-fledged partner in the Thibault business affairs. Of course, Caeden's father had no such plans. He used Bishop Arnold just as he did anyone he deemed capable of furthering his desires. And while it might be perfectly acceptable to marry his son to Arnold's daughter, Archibald Thibault would never let an outsider partner in his business. It was something Arnold never comprehended.

Catherine Arnold, however, seemed to understand her role and played it with flawless precision. She was always the picture of perfection. Graceful and elegant in all of her manners and dress, Catherine would have made almost any successful man a good wife. Caeden shook his head. "But she's not for me."

He hadn't meant to mutter the words aloud. He gave a quick glance around to make sure no one had overheard him. No sense in having to explain. Satisfied that his boots were as clean as he could make them, Caeden gave a light knock and pushed open the door. Ever since his first encounter with Emily he was far more cautious about just barging in—even when expected.

The aroma of baking bread filled the air and mingled with the welcoming scent of stew and coffee. The homey fragrance caused Caeden to consider how very little it took to please him and give him a sense of peace. Back in Albany he had lived in a twenty-room mansion and had never known the sense of belonging he got here in this poor man's cabin.

"I put a bowl of stew on the table," Emily told him. She poured coffee into a mug. "I have some coffee too."

"Sounds good," Caeden said, taking a seat. "I'm sure this will do the trick in thawing me out."

Caeden enjoyed the small meal, then immediately went to work on his journal. He had made continuous notes while surveying various mining claims. He'd secured soil samples that required closer inspection, and he had to be certain that their origins were correctly noted. He finished up just before Emily began to set the table for the evening meal and moments before Henry Carver stomped into the house in his boisterous manner.

"Mighty cold out there!" He caught sight of Caeden. "Good to have you back with us."

"Good to be back. I hadn't expected snow so early. Makes sleeping outdoors less than cozy."

"Well, you're welcome to sleep inside tonight."

Caeden shook his head. "No, I'll be fine. I have some warm gear. I have a little heat stove I can use if things get really bad."

Carver began a long conversation about his day at the sluice. He felt the show of color was good and that it proved it was only a matter of time before he would be able to dig out and wash enough ore to make his fortune.

Supper passed much too quickly. Emily said very little, but this only caused Caeden to watch her more closely. He found it impossible to keep his mind from drifting to thoughts of her—who she was and what she wanted out of life. He thought too of her mother's declaration and wondered if maybe, just maybe, there was something to it. Hadn't his own mother felt confident of God's direction? There had been many a time she had said as much, and Caeden had seen her follow through to a positive outcome. Perhaps Nyola Carver truly had heard something from the Almighty. He knew he was on dangerous ground, but Caeden felt almost helpless to keep his mind from its deductions. Emily was a beautiful young woman, and she had captivated his imagination in a way no other woman had ever done.

After a leisurely game of chess with Henry Carver, Caeden excused himself and made his way outside. The cold night air made a sharp contrast to the warmth of the cabin. He pulled his coat collar up and trudged on to the woodpile. No doubt chopping wood for a while would warm him up and clear his mind.

However, when Caeden finally went to bed, he tossed and turned. He slept, but fitfully, and several hours before dawn he shot up, almost certain someone had called his name. Only silence filled the night. Still uneasy, Caeden pulled on his boots, then grabbed his coat. Outside it was still dark. He could smell woodsmoke from the Carver cabin. Everything remained quiet, but he had the feeling that something wasn't quite right. Caeden reached back into his tent for his rifle. He searched around the outside of the house, and then as he came near the path to the river, he spied the glow of firelight where no fire should be. *Maybe that Davies fellow is back and is camping on the Carver claim.*

Caeden headed down the path, crossing the distance in no time at all. What he found left him uncertain what to do. No one was in sight, but the sluice and small shack where Henry stored his tools was afire. He had no bucket and no blanket. The best he could do was return to the cabin and alert Henry and get help. He raced back up the path and pounded on the cabin door until he heard Emily call out.

"Who's there?"

"It's me, Caeden."

She opened the door and looked at him in surprise, noting the rifle in his hands. "What's wrong?"

"Your father's sluice and shack are on fire. I need a bucket or blanket to beat it out."

She nodded and immediately hurried to the kitchen. She tossed him a wooden bucket. "I'll get Pa."

Caeden didn't wait. Instead he ran back to the work site to see if he could at least save Carver's tools. He put the rifle aside and had carried three buckets of water to douse the burning shack when Henry Carver and Emily finally arrived. Henry had another bucket, and Emily carried a thick wool blanket and a lantern. Together they worked to keep the fire from spreading to any of the dried grass. It was a difficult job, but after about half an hour all that remained were smoldering pieces of charred wood.

"How did this happen?" Emily asked. Her tone was one of utter disbelief. "You didn't leave a fire going here, did you, Pa?"

"No. The ground hadn't froze hard yet, and I didn't even make a fire here yesterday."

"Then someone . . . someone must have set it."

Caeden couldn't blame her for her shock. She looked so small, almost childlike, wearing just her nightgown, the huge canvas coat, and boots.

He shook his head and refocused on the destruction. "I don't know. I was sleeping, and then something woke me up. I thought maybe someone was messing around, so I got up to take a look. I didn't find anyone around the cabin or the lean-to, and that's when I noticed the fire down here."

"Good thing you did," Henry said, shaking his head. "Could have been a lot worse."

"But, Pa, your tools and sluice." Emily held the lantern aloft for a better look. "I doubt any of this can be salvaged."

"The metal of the tools should survive." Her father shook his head again. "I'll just have to whittle out some new handles or see about getting some on credit from the store in Utica."

"I'd be happy to extend you the money," Caeden said.

"I'm obliged," Henry Carver replied. "But I already have an account at the store, and there's no sense in owing two people."

"Who would have done such a thing?" Emily asked, finally lowering the lantern. Then she answered her own question. "Kirk Davies. I'll bet he did this to try and force us to leave."

Her father shook his head. "I suppose you could be right. Guess I'll have to speak with the marshal when I'm in Utica."

Emily frowned. "What do we do until then?"

"I guess we go back to bed. Tomorrow this should be cooled down, and we can sort through what's left and usable," her father said. Caeden could hear a tone of defeat in his voice.

Emily handed the lantern to her father, then reached to the ground for the smoky blanket. "I suppose you're right. We'll have plenty of time come light to figure out what to do next."

The trio started back up the path. It was only as they reached the top of the rise that Caeden spied the cabin. It was on fire, and no small blaze either. It was engulfed in flames, as if someone had poured kerosene over it and struck a match.

Emily screamed, and her father took off running, calling out for Nyola. Caeden raced after him, knowing that if he didn't stop the old man, he'd try to go into the cabin to retrieve his wife. Caeden reached him just as Henry rounded the south wall of the house.

Caeden took hold of the older man. "You can't go in there, Mr. Carver. It's too late."

"My wife is in there!" He pushed at Caeden's hold. "I have to try."

"You can't." Already the roof of the cabin was caving in. "We don't know how long it's been burning, but you can see for yourself no one could live through it."

By this time Emily had joined them. She looked from her father to Caeden, her eyes begging him to save her mother, but Caeden felt certain Mrs. Carver was already dead. Not knowing what else to do, he slowly shook his head, hoping she would understand the impossibility of it.

Emily bit her lip and sank to the ground. Caeden released Henry, praying that the man wouldn't try to do something foolish and leave his daughter an orphan. Carver paced in front of the burning cabin, but he didn't attempt to go inside. The roof caved in, and one of the walls began to lean inward. It wouldn't be long before there was nothing left.

"We saw de fire glow" came a woman's voice from the darkness. "What happened?"

Millie Ringgold and several men emerged from the shadows. Millie crossed to where Emily sat on the ground. She said nothing but put her hand atop Emily's shoulder. The men joined Henry, and Caeden could see they were contemplating what to do next. They had brought shovels, and it was agreed that they would manage the fire rather than try to extinguish it. If they could contain the burning to the cabin alone, then at least the animals and lean-to might escape damage. No one spoke of the fact that Mrs. Carver was still inside the inferno, but everyone seemed to know.

A loud *whoosh* of wind came as one of the glass windows blew out. In turn the air seemed almost immediately to be sucked back in, as if the blaze were drawing a breath. The walls began to collapse one by one. The old dry logs were like so much kindling, and the fire easily consumed the cabin. Thankfully there was little wind.

By first light the blaze had died down. Smudged with soot and ash, the men stood staring at what was left of the cabin. Caeden knew there weren't adequate words to express his sorrow for Emily and her father, so he said nothing. Nyola Carver had spoken to him about a merciful and loving God, but to Caeden's way of thinking, this was neither merciful nor loving. Where was God when that kind old woman was burning alive?

He took several steps back, wondering what he should do. There was nothing left of the home the Carvers had enjoyed. Caeden thought about riding to Utica to buy a wagonful of goods for them and then thought better of it. Henry Carver needed to stay in charge. The man had already lost everything else. He'd wait and see what Carver wanted to do.

Emily and Millie joined him where he stood, but no one seemed inclined to speak. The shock of it all was too much—the pain too deep. Caeden watched as Henry and his friends were talking among themselves. He moved to join them to see what he might do to help.

"Someone clearly set the fires," Caeden heard Henry say. The older man turned and looked back at his daughter. "That Davies fellow is no doubt responsible for this. I didn't tell Emmy, but Davies told me he'd make it so's we had no choice in the matter."

"Yo can stay at my place. I gots plenty of room," Millie said as she and Emily joined the men.

"I ain't leaving Nyola." Henry's tone left little doubt that his mind was made up.

"They can stay with me in my tent," Caeden offered. "It's small, but I think we can all squeeze in."

Millie looked from Caeden to Emily, then nodded. "I 'spect that's best. I's gwanna go fetch yo some blankets and when it's full-up light, we can see what yo wanna do."

And with that it was decided. Caeden doubted any of them would truly sleep, but he managed to talk Henry into resting so as to renew his strength for the task ahead.

❦

Emily found herself wedged against the tent wall and her father's well-muscled frame. Caeden took his position on the other side of her father. She hadn't believed it would be possible to sleep, but hours later she awoke with a start to find herself alone. For just a moment Emily couldn't remember where she was or why. Then the events of the night came to mind like a bad dream, only this time the nightmare was real. She sat for several minutes in the silence of the morning. There were chores that still had to be tended to, but Emily couldn't bring herself to move.

Everything smelled like smoke, and her nightgown and coat were marked with soot and ash. Her hair had come undone from its braid, and out of habit she reached up to comb her fingers through the long brown mass and plait it into order. This routine act allowed the tiniest bit of normalcy to return to her life, but it did nothing to offer comfort. How could it? Her mother was dead, and everything they'd ever owned was gone. Emily didn't even have a change of clothes.

She finally dragged herself from the tent. The morning was a little warmer than the day before, but even so she was grateful for her coat. She walked around the lean-to and up to where the charred remains of the cabin stood. There was nothing left. Mama was gone and everything was burned to ashes.

Emily hadn't cried the night before, and even now she felt the shock too great to even contemplate sorrow. She knew the pain would pierce her numbness soon enough, but for now all she could do was ask the same question over and over. Why?

"Your father went to Utica."

She turned and met Caeden's serious expression. "Did he . . . what about . . . my mother?"

"We took care of her just before he left. We . . . uh . . . wrapped her in a blanket. Your father plans to get some lumber to build her a coffin."

Emily nodded. She walked toward the remains of the cabin. "Do you suppose anything is salvageable?"

"I've been going through some of the debris. I found a few metal things that survived. The bathtub, a couple of pans, and the coffeepot. Of course, the stove is there, as you can see."

Emily disregarded the possibility of danger and made her way into the ruins. She looked around for herself. They had never had much, but now they had even less. She spied the tin in which she had stored her little blue rocks. She picked through the debris and pulled it from the ashes.

"What's that?" Caeden asked, coming alongside her.

She shook her head. "I'm not sure I even know." She opened it to reveal the stones. "These were pieces of rock that clogged the sluice. They were pretty, so Pa thought I might have some purpose for them. I've been collecting them ever since."

Caeden took the tin from her and examined the pieces. "Do you know what these are?"

Emily shrugged. "Jake says he thinks they're gemstones."

"He's right. I believe these are sapphires. They might very well be valuable to the right buyer."

"Don't tell Pa." She turned to him. "Please. Jake said they're having someone examine the rocks, but I don't want Pa getting his hopes up. Especially now that all this has happened. Another disappointment might be the end of him."

"I won't say anything, but since I'll be heading to Great Falls in another couple of weeks, do you mind if I take this with me and have it analyzed?"

Emily shook her head. What did it matter if he took the tin and the pebbles inside? Everything else was gone. "Take it."

She walked away, not at all certain where she was headed. All she knew was that nothing was ever going to be the same— nothing would ever be right.

# 8

Nyola Carver's funeral was held the next day. It was a small affair with a half dozen Yogo residents joining the family. The tiny cemetery held only a few graves, but now Emily's mother would be a part of that memorial forever.

Emily had watched her father work outside Caeden's tent late into the night to ensure that the small coffin was ready. Caeden, too, had held vigil with her, and his presence comforted her in a way she'd just as soon forget. Despite what her mother desired for her, Emily couldn't see leaving her father anytime soon. He was too broken—too grieved.

Dressed in a gown Millie had once accepted from someone in trade, Emily tried to keep her emotions under control. She could see the tears in her father's eyes, the misery in his expression. He blamed himself, even though they both knew it wasn't his fault. At times like this even comfort from the truth seemed very inadequate. Mama was still dead, and whoever was responsible was still running free.

*Kirk Davies is responsible.*

Emily chided herself for being so judgmental, but she felt

confident Davies had committed this heinous act. No one else stood to gain anything. With their home and few possessions destroyed, Davies would be certain the Carvers would give up and leave the area. However, the man didn't know her father. If they had to camp outside in two feet of snow, Emily knew her father wouldn't leave until he was good and ready to move on.

In the absence of a preacher to speak words over the body, Emily's father recited the Twenty-third Psalm. He spoke a few words about the woman he had loved and of her generous nature and loving spirit. They sang one verse and the chorus of "Shall We Gather at the River?" and then her father led them in prayer. It was all so short and simple. It didn't come anywhere near to lauding the many talents and kindnesses of Emily's mother.

After her father concluded the prayer, the Yogo men helped lower the small casket into the ground, with Caeden working respectfully alongside them. Earlier he had mentioned to Emily that her mother's great faith had bolstered his own in a small way. The words touched her heart. Mama was good at encouraging people to have faith. She would have been pleased to hear what Caeden had to say.

As the men began to shovel dirt over the coffin, Emily pulled on her old coat and walked away to gather her thoughts. She saw the Utica marshal ride up and wondered if her father had reported to him all that had happened, and if Kirk Davies had been found and charged.

Putting aside her desire for isolation, Emily made her way to the man before he could even dismount. "Marshal, have you arrested Kirk Davies for murdering my mother?"

Her blunt words took the lawman by surprise. "I beg your

pardon?" He climbed down from his horse but continued holding the reins.

She crossed her arms. "You heard me. No one but Davies was trying to force us to give up our claim. He has to be the one who set those fires."

"Do you have proof of that?" the mustached marshal asked in a tolerant tone.

"I know he threatened us and no one else has." She narrowed her eyes. "Arrest him, and if you threaten him enough, he just might confess."

The man shook his head. "Can't do it that way. There's such a thing as due process and the need for evidence before an arrest. I have to have hard facts and proof, not assumptions."

"So he gets away with murdering my mother," Emily said, her voice rising in protest. "He probably didn't know she was even in the house. I doubt he knew of her existence, but it was murder just the same."

"I understand how you feel, Miss Carver, but you need to stay out of it and let me do my job. I came to offer my condolences and to speak to your father about the matter. I assure you, I will do what I can to get justice for your mother."

His words rang hollow in Emily's ears. She was sure that neither he, nor anyone else, could truly understand how alone she felt.

She took herself off to a small gathering of trees and sat down on the ground to think. Leaning back against the trunk of an aspen, Emily closed her eyes. The day had warmed up and would have been pleasant under other circumstances. A flock of geese honked loud and long as they passed overhead. It was an all-too-familiar sound this time of year as they flew away to escape the winter cold.

Emily gave a heavy sigh. Everything and everyone seemed to

be deserting her. She thought of her mother no longer suffering from her physical maladies. Emily could only hope that she'd died in her sleep from the smoke rather than in the flames. It grieved her to no end to imagine Mama burning to death.

She tried to pray, but her heart ached so much that Emily couldn't find the words. She didn't doubt God's existence or His sovereignty, but she could not understand His allowing something so heinous to happen to a woman who loved Him so dearly.

"I'm not sure I even know how to keep the faith without her." Emily glanced to the sky. "Why, Lord?"

The question of why—many whys—continued to haunt her. Why had their lives taken this turn? Why did her mother have to die? Why were there no answers?

Emily didn't know how long she had sat under the golden leaves of the aspen. She knew that Millie had invited everyone to come to her place after the burial. She wanted to offer them a good hot meal and would no doubt try to talk Emily's father into staying at her boardinghouse. Emily almost prayed that her father would accept the offer, but in her heart she knew he wouldn't. He was a proud man and did everything possible to refrain from being under obligation to any man . . . or woman.

Sticking her hand deep into her coat pocket, Emily felt the reassuring cold metal of her pistol. She didn't like to think she could kill another person, but the idea of threatening Kirk Davies into admitting the truth was something she considered. Of course, Pa had always told her that if she ever drew a gun on another person, she'd best be ready to pull the trigger and end their life. Guns were something never to be toyed with.

The thought of dealing with Davies burned into her thoughts. He deserved to die. Deserved her wrath and that of her father. But what if Davies hadn't set the fires? What if he wasn't responsible for the death of her mother? She shook her head. How could it be anyone else? No one else held them a grudge. No one else had threatened to chase them off the property no matter what it took. It had to be Davies.

Getting to her feet, Emily knew she would have to put aside her desire for revenge and focus instead on what they were going to do now. Cold weather would soon set in, and they could hardly winter in a tent. Not only that, but Caeden and his tent would soon be gone. What if Pa didn't take Millie up on her offer of a free room? What then? Emily supposed she could always take the room and let her father sleep wherever he chose.

Emily walked slowly back to the burial site. She saw the fresh mound of dirt and small wooden cross that marked her mother's grave. Her father had made that cross just this morning. She stared down at it for a long time.

*Nyola Carver*
*b. 1840 d. 1895*

Such a small showing for the life of such a good woman. Would anyone who found this grave in the future wonder at the person buried there? Would anyone guess that she had been a strong woman of God with a generous heart and loving nature? Emily sank to her knees and reached out to trace her mother's name.

"I wondered where you'd gotten off to."

She looked up to find Caeden watching her from a little ways off.

"I had to be alone—to think."

"And what did you figure out?" He stepped to where she was on her knees and squatted down.

Face-to-face she could see the dark intensity of his eyes. "I haven't figured out anything. I asked the marshal if he'd arrested Kirk Davies, but he told me there wasn't any evidence that he had set the fire."

"That does make it hard. Unless the man confesses or brags around town about it, it would be hard to make a charge stick."

Emily drew off her scarf and tied it around the cross. She hated that the grave looked so plain and had no flowers. At least the red scarf would add a little color.

For a time neither of them spoke, but finally Caeden broke the silence. "I'm really sorry about your mother, Emily. I know what it is to lose a mother. You can be proud that your mother died knowing how very loved she was. You and your father treated her so well."

"How did you say your mother died?"

The question seemed to surprise him. He looked at Emily for a moment, then dropped his gaze to the ground. "I believe it was from a broken heart. She'd borne up under my father's tirades and criticism all of her married life. She was never good enough as far as he was concerned. It didn't matter that she was a gracious hostess and loving mother. It didn't matter that she never let a bad word about him leave her mouth. He killed her the same as Davies killed your mother."

"Why was he like that?" Emily knew the topic was painful to him, but she felt almost an urgency to pose the question.

"Because he only cared about himself. He drank too much, raged too much, and demanded his own way—too much. Archibald Thibault cared only about himself and the money he could make. He took mistresses, robbed entire families of their fortunes, and crushed the businesses of his rivals. He was a hard and ruthless man . . . and I will always hate him."

"But why did he drink so much? Did something happen to him that he drank to forget? Was he in pain?"

112

"I honestly have no idea. And frankly it doesn't matter. He hurt everyone with his drinking, and knowing the reason he drank wouldn't make it right."

She heard the anger and bitterness in his tone. Her mother had always said that hatred ate a person up from the inside out. It would eventually taint how they looked at life and would separate them from God.

"It's because of him," Caeden continued, "that I want nothing to do with marriage and family. I couldn't bear to imagine myself turning out like him."

"But you're nothing like that." She met his gaze and forced a weak smile. "You're a good man. You care about the people around you. You would never strive to hurt people that way. Not only that, but you don't drink."

"Maybe not right now, but who's to say what I might become, given the responsibilities of a wife and family?" He shook his head and stood. "I couldn't bear it if I caused that kind of pain."

Emily too got to her feet. "But don't you see? The fact that you care about not causing pain makes me confident that you could never be that way. You took your traits from your mother. Her faith and love taught you to look at life differently. You'll make someone a wonderful husband one day." She hadn't meant to say as much as she did. Would he think her forward, perhaps suggesting they might have a future together?

She lowered her gaze to the cross once more. "I should find my father." She didn't wait to hear his response but made her way to Millie's.

⁂

Caeden watched her go. He wanted to say something about her comment—wanted to question her as to whether she was implying that he might make *her* a wonderful husband. Her mother's words were ever on his mind, yet surely Emily wasn't suggesting anything along those lines. She had never thrown herself at him or acted as some young ladies do when trying to get the attention of a possible suitor.

"Thibault!"

He turned around and found the marshal making his way toward him. Caeden didn't reply. The marshal closed the distance and reached inside his coat. "Been lookin' for you. This came for you in Utica." He thrust an envelope into Caeden's hands.

It was from Bishop Arnold. He stiffened. Dealing with that man and his nonsense was far from Caeden's desires. "Thank you."

"I wonder if I might talk to you a minute."

Nodding, Caeden stuffed the letter into his inside coat pocket. "What can I do for you?"

"I was wondering how much longer you'll be in the area."

"Not long. A week, maybe two. The other members of this geological team are to meet up with me in Havre by the first of December. I figure to get there plenty ahead of time to finish putting my records in order."

The marshal stroked his mustache, and while Caeden had shaved clean that morning, the action almost compelled him to scratch under his nose. "I'm worried about the Carvers. This has been a hard blow, and they are both convinced that Kirk Davies is responsible."

"Well, he seems the only likely suspect." Caeden shoved his hands into his pockets. "The man did threaten them, and he wanted to force Henry Carver to turn over his mining claim. Seems to me it would at least bear checking into."

The marshal stiffened, and his expression turned stern. "And

I will. I know my job. I'm just wondering if maybe you could keep an eye on Mr. Carver and his daughter. Especially the daughter. She seems all worked up about this, and I worry she'll try to take it on herself."

Caeden nodded. He was worried about the same thing. He knew she carried a pistol with her all the time, and now with what had happened, Caeden wasn't at all doubtful that Emily might use it on Davies.

"I'll stick around as long as I can."

"Thank you. That's all I ask. I'm heading back to Utica. I was told Kirk Davies took an old shack not far from town. I intend to pay him a visit. If anything else happens here, get word to me as soon as possible."

Caeden wondered at the man's ability to help from so far away but said nothing. He waited until the marshal had gone before pulling Arnold's letter out of his pocket. He ripped it open and read the first few lines. His anger mounted with each additional line.

*I managed to learn from your uncle that you are in the area of Great Falls. I will be in Great Falls, Montana, on the twelfth of November. I will expect to meet with you there at the railroad hotel. We have a great deal of business to discuss, and it's imperative that you join me. Time is of the utmost importance.*

It was signed *Bishop Arnold* and dated the thirtieth of September. No doubt the boardinghouse where Caeden had taken residence in Great Falls had forwarded the letter to Utica. He had given them that destination should any mail come for him.

Caeden stuffed the letter back into the envelope, determined to ignore the summons. He had very little use for his father's former business associate. He knew Arnold was desperate to get Thibault's money to help fund his political ambitions. He was also desperate to marry his daughter to Caeden.

Caeden's first thought was to ignore Arnold's summons, but then he wondered if the man wouldn't just follow him to Utica and then to Yogo City. Of course, that would require a great deal of effort on Arnold's part. However, he was making a trip all the way to Montana, so the effort had already been made. Apparently Arnold was desperate enough to hunt Caeden down, and that only served to cause greater concern. If only he could get a wire off to his uncle and question what was going on. But that would require a ride to Utica. Unless, of course, he could pay the marshal to take care of it.

Either way, it was going to be an unwanted interference in his plans.

# 9

The days seemed to drag by and grow colder. Caeden knew he would soon have to leave if he were to meet Arnold in Great Falls, but he didn't feel he could leave with the Carvers' future still so uncertain. Emily had spent several nights with Millie, but Henry continued to share the tent with Caeden. Not that he minded, but it wasn't a permanent solution, and no one knew this better than Henry.

When they'd awakened that morning, Henry had muttered something about getting a tent of his own, which gave Caeden a thought. Since he was heading back to Washington, DC, he could just leave his tent behind. He'd explain to Henry that he had no use for it. Surely the old man would see the sense in that.

Caeden was still shaving and contemplating how he would approach the matter when he heard the sound of men and horses approaching. He quickly finished his task and dried his face before going in search of the noise.

To his surprise, as well as Henry and Emily's, it appeared that the men of Yogo had decided to bring the Carvers a new cabin. Well, not so new. They had managed to put the small, well-worn cabin on two large sledges. Where they'd ever come up with those was a mystery. There were two teams of horses with four large draft animals to a team.

Henry was the first to greet them. "What's all this?"

Jake Hoover led the way. "How do, Henry—Miss Emily. Millie reminded me that we have dozens of these old shacks just sitting around empty. Figured we might as well bring one to you as to let it go on unused. Where'd you like to have it?"

For a moment it looked like Henry might refuse the offer, but Caeden was relieved to hear him accept. At least he and Emily would have a roof over their heads.

"Let's set it up in front of where the old cabin was." Henry pointed to an area that had been worn down from people coming and going.

"You heard him, boys," Jake said, turning back to help.

Caeden stepped forward. "What can I do?"

"Nothing just yet. We'll get the cabin in place, and then we'll have to get it off the sledges. And Millie's bringing up a wagonload of goods. We'll need your help with all the unloading."

Caeden stood beside Henry and Emily, watching the men maneuver the teams. It took nearly an hour before they had the cabin positioned where Henry wanted it. After that the real work began.

"All right, now," Jake said, "it's gonna take all of us to get it unloaded off the sledges, but it won't take long."

All the while Emily stood off to one side, watching in silence. Caeden couldn't help noticing her. Since the funeral she hadn't bothered to wear her multiple, shapeless layers. Instead she wore a simple wool skirt, blouse, and shawl. All three had been gifts from one of the men, whose wife had died the summer before.

*I wonder if she's ever had anything new.*

The thought surprised him. He remembered his sisters and

their shopping sprees. They would return home from several days in New York City and insist on showing off their new clothes immediately. Caeden tried to imagine Emily in a new gown of pink silk. He thought she'd look very nice in pink. Perhaps a pale shade of rose. He decided then and there that when he was in Great Falls, he would buy her some new clothes. He didn't really care whether others would think such a gesture appropriate. He would do what his heart was telling him.

"All right, boys," Jake declared. "Let's get this thing set in place." The men, including Caeden, took their places, while Jake explained how they would go about the unloading process.

After wresting the cabin from the sledges, the men stood back to survey their work. Jake had been right; it had taken very little time to unload the cabin. The men were still congratulating themselves when Caeden saw Emily make her way inside. He couldn't stop himself from joining her there.

"What do you think?" He looked around the single empty room.

"I'm not sure what to think," she said, shaking her head. "It certainly will be better than sleeping outside under the stars." She smiled, and Caeden smiled back. "I'm very touched that the men thought to do this," she said.

"They seem a good bunch. I heard one of them say they took up a collection of goods to help furnish the place, and Millie's bringing it up. For folks who have so little, they are very generous."

"Most of the people I've met in mining towns have been good folks. There aren't always a lot of hours to socialize, but there's always a sense of community—of neighbor helping neighbor." She walked to one of the empty window spaces. "We'll need to board this up to keep out the cold and the critters."

"That shouldn't be too hard."

She shook her head. "No, not too hard."

"Has your father decided if the old stove still works?"

She nodded. "He said with just a little work it will be fine. And if not, I'm sure he'll figure out something. I haven't minded cooking outdoors, but when the snows come it will be much more difficult."

"Are you certain you can't talk him into wintering in a town? Even Utica would afford you better supplies and comforts."

"But there's no gold to be mined in Utica," she replied, her tone dispirited. "There'd be no work for either of us in that small of a place, and without work there'd be no money for supplies and comforts."

"I wish your father would let me give him the funds he needs. I have more than enough."

"He's too proud for that." Emily moved back toward the only door. "He likes to see to things himself. Frankly, I'm surprised he's been willing to accept the help everyone has offered today."

"Perhaps he sees where pride has gotten him in the past." Caeden followed her outside. There was no chance for her to respond as Henry Carver joined them just then.

"Well, what do you think, daughter? Will it get us by?"

Emily touched her father's arm. "It will suit us just fine. We'll need to board up the window, since there's no glass or oilcloth to use. And we'll need to get that old stove moved over."

"The fellows are going to do that just now. I was coming to get Caeden in case we need the extra hand."

"I'm happy to help." Caeden glanced toward the western skies and noted the gathering clouds. "Looks like some weather is moving in."

"It's going to snow," Jake Hoover said, coming up behind them. "We'd best get busy. We need to have this place in order before a storm moves in and causes us all grief."

They worked for the better part of the morning assembling

everything. Three of the men, including Henry, cleaned up the old stove and made certain it was working, while some of the others brought in very rough pieces of furniture.

By the time everything was arranged, the one-room cabin looked adequate, but certainly nothing more. Caeden remembered how his stables back home were in much better shape. Larger too. He pushed aside the thought. It wasn't helpful to compare this little cabin to the previous one, nor to any of his property in Albany. Obviously this was the best that could be done for now. Even so, it bothered him a great deal to see Emily looking so pleased. All of her life she'd had to settle for whatever little bit came her way, be it clothing or housing. Caeden frowned as he realized how obsessed he was with providing better for her. What was happening to him?

The men gathered outside, and when Jake mentioned he was heading to Great Falls the next day, Caeden announced his own plans.

"I'll be leaving soon myself. I have an appointment in Great Falls, and then I'm to meet the rest of the geological team and head back to Washington."

Henry looked at Caeden and nodded. "It's been nice havin' you around, but I know you have your responsibilities. You're always welcome to come back anytime."

Caeden caught sight of Emily's face. She looked upset. Was it because of his announcement? He didn't want to think that he was the cause. After all, she'd known all along he would be going as soon as his work was completed.

"We could just ride over together," Jake offered.

"I can't go right away. I still have some loose ends to tie up." Caeden glanced again at Emily, but she'd disappeared back into the cabin. "I'll be taking my horse back to the stable in Utica and then catching the stage, but thank you for the offer."

Jake shrugged. "Company on the trail is always nice, but certainly not necessary." He extended his hand to Henry. "I'll be back around in a month or so."

Henry shook his hand. "Be glad to see you then. You're always welcome here too."

One by one the men left. No doubt they would return to their endless search for riches. Caeden couldn't imagine living the life they lived. He liked moving about and having his freedom, but there were far too many unknown factors in the lives of these men.

"You've made some good friends here, Mr. Carver."

"Now, Caeden, I thought we agreed you'd call me Henry. Don't go gettin' all formal just because you have to go."

"Henry." Caeden smiled. "The folks around here are very generous. I must say I've never seen such good will. Seems strange that folks who have next to nothing should be so willing to part with it in order to help someone else."

"That's been my experience in every place I've ever lived," Henry replied. "I think poor folks are always giving to one another. They appreciate the situation better than someone who has great wealth. Still, it's hard to be on the receiving end."

"I'm glad you allowed for their help." Caeden paused, looking back at the cabin. "It would have been awfully hard on Emily if you hadn't."

"That's the only reason I accepted. I've put that girl through enough."

Caeden didn't want the older man to dwell on his regrets. "Having had money all of my life, I've never been in want. But, in so many ways, you here are all richer."

Henry glanced heavenward. "I remember when we were back in California. We were living in a small mining town, and the folks there were some of the best I've ever known. Once when a man was injured in a cave-in, everybody pitched in to see that he and his family had food to eat. They even worked his claim in their spare time. It wasn't much, but they did what they could."

Caeden tried to imagine the same of the people he knew back in Albany. Oh, there were certainly good folks there. His uncle and mother had been examples of great generosity. But while his wealthy neighbors and friends might have put in a few dollars to assist the poor and sick, he couldn't imagine any of them bothering to go work in someone else's place.

"I guess the only truly bad times were those when claims were disputed or someone insulted someone else. Drinking was always an issue for some. I know you understand the problems that can cause."

Caeden nodded. "All too well."

"That town in California was the only time I had to resort to violence." Henry looked at Caeden and shook his head. "There was this man—a boy, really. He was the meanest, most foul-tempered young man I'd ever met. He seemed to take pleasure in causing other people pain. When he wasn't cheating folks at cards, he was drinking too much and threatening the lives of those around him. He'd been responsible for the deaths of three men, but somehow he managed to escape justice."

Caeden could see that Henry was notably upset by the memory. "You don't have to tell me about those kinds of men. My father was just like that. In fact, it wouldn't surprise me if my father had killed as well."

A light snow began to fall, and Henry turned up his coat collar. "I figure it's good for me to remember from time to time. I don't resort to violence often. Things got out of hand that day. The man tried to force a family off their claim. He threatened to kill the husband and have his way with the wife and then kill her too. He even threatened their two children. He had no respect for the law. He pulled a gun on them, and when I went to intercede, he shot me."

"He shot you?"

Henry met his gaze. "Shot me in the arm, then turned his gun back on the family. He was going to kill one of the little ones to force the father to give in. I couldn't let that happen, so despite my wound, I picked up a shovel and hit him over the head. He fell to the ground and his head struck a rock. He died instantly."

There was great regret in Henry Carver's voice. Caeden touched the older man's shoulder. "You undoubtedly saved their lives."

"That's what everyone said. They called me a hero. I can tell you, I didn't feel much like a hero. I'd caused a man to lose his life."

"But he'd nearly taken yours and would have taken theirs. You did what needed to be done."

"I know, but there hasn't been a day I haven't lived with regret. He was young and maybe could have changed if he'd lived. I've always wondered if it couldn't have been handled some other way."

Caeden himself had those same doubts and regrets. He'd always wondered what would have happened if he'd remained at home to support and defend his mother and sisters. Would his mother have lived longer? Would his sisters have married for love instead of their father's will?

"But it serves no positive purpose to live our lives focused on regrets." Caeden wished he could take his own advice. Many had been the time his mother had shared that same sentiment, but Caeden could find little consolation.

"I know you're right. Nyola used to tell me the same thing. She was a wise woman." He glanced off in the direction of town and the tiny cemetery. "I always appreciated that about her. She had a way about knowing things. She would pray on a matter and tell me what she thought the Lord was directing, and you know what? She was always right. I used to feel a little jealous about her closeness to the Lord. 'Course, she told me a person's closeness to the Lord depended on them seeking Him. They needed to yearn to know Him better. That hit me deep, and I always tried to read the Bible every day after that and spend time in prayer."

He gave a sigh and looked heavenward again. "'Course, the Bible burned in the fire." He sighed again and his shoulders slumped. "I know Nyola's with God now. I know she's out of pain, and that's all I ever wanted." His voice broke. "But I miss her. I miss her so much, and I honestly don't know what I'm going to do without her."

Millie Ringgold brought them supper that evening. Caeden couldn't remember ever having black-eyed peas before, but he found the flavor to be quite delicious. Especially given the healthy portions of bacon that had been cut up and cooked with the peas. There was also some corn bread and molasses, as well as hot coffee that Emily made on the newly restored stove. As their appetites were sated the conversation turned to Caeden's impending departure.

"We've enjoyed having you here with us," Henry began. He toyed with his coffee mug. "I am sorry you had to endure so much. In all this last year we haven't had as many troubles as we've known in just the last few months."

"I was glad to be here to help. I enjoyed getting to know each of you. Mrs. Carver as well. I won't soon forget this family and the love that you showed one another. I never believed such a thing really existed until I experienced it here."

"Surely there are other loving people in your life besides your mother," Henry countered.

"My uncle is a good man. If not for him, I'm certain I would have turned out worse. I used to escape to his house several blocks away. He always knew the right things to say and do. He usually got me busy with something so I couldn't just sit around complaining or raging." Caeden smiled at the memory. "He's the only reason I will one day return to Albany."

"What about your sisters?" This came from Emily, who had been unusually quiet throughout the evening.

Caeden met her gaze. Her chocolate brown eyes seemed to search his face for answers he was somehow hiding. "My sisters are married with families of their own. They really don't need me around." He didn't add that because they were forced to marry men of their father's choosing, Caeden feared the worst. Seeing them unhappy would only stir up a desire in him to intervene.

"But I'm sure they miss you. Weren't you close growing up?" she asked.

"We were. We were bound together by fear, if nothing else. We used to worry about making our father angry. He thought nothing of hauling off and beating me when I did something he deemed wrong, and with the girls it was only slightly different. He used to hit their hands with a ruler until they were swollen. More than once he slapped them full across the face—even when they were very young."

"How terrible." Emily's words were barely audible.

Caeden didn't like the direction their conversation had taken. "It was, but we needn't focus on that. I've made my own way, and they've made theirs. I'm hopeful that they know a better life now."

"Well," Henry said, pushing back from the table, "the time has come for me to get back to work. I need to cut some wood. Tomorrow I'll need to bring down some trees. Want to come and help me?"

Caeden smiled. "It would be my pleasure."

Henry got up and walked to the door. He took up his coat, then glanced back at Emily. "Do you have enough water, or should I fetch you some? Snow's made things slick, and I could save you havin' to make a trip down to the river."

"I have plenty," Emily replied. "Don't be too long at it, Pa. You know the temperature has turned pretty cold, and I don't want you working up a sweat and then getting chilled."

He smiled and waggled his finger at her. "Now, don't go thinkin' that with your ma gone you can boss me around like she did."

Emily gave a chuckle. It was the first Caeden had heard since her mother's death.

"Not that it ever did her any good," Emily replied as she began to clear the table.

"Your ma knew what she was gettin' when she married me." Henry pulled on his coat and then reached for his hat. "She was no fool, your ma. She was never taken in by all my smooth talk and good looks."

Caeden smiled at this, and from the look on Emily's face she found it just as amusing. "Get on with you now, Pa. I've got work to do."

Henry laughed and opened the door. Caeden had thought the cabin drafty and cold, but when the wind whipped in from outside he realized the little place wasn't so bad. The wood stove was keeping it quite bearable.

Once Henry was gone, Caeden found himself wanting to speak to Emily about his trip. He didn't know why, but she seemed to have distanced herself from him since the funeral. Up until then he had thought they were getting along rather well.

She cleared the last of the dishes from the table and put them in a pan of hot water that sat atop the stove. Returning to the table, she nodded toward Caeden's coffee mug. "Are you done with that?"

Caeden glanced down at the half-full cup, then nodded. "I'm so stuffed I can't finish it."

She said nothing but reached down to take it. For reasons beyond his understanding, Caeden reached out to cover her hand with his own. Emily startled and pulled away so quickly that the mug overturned, spilling the contents onto the floor. Before she could do anything, the bare dirt of the floor had soaked it in, and little remained for her to wipe away.

"I'm sorry. I didn't mean for that to happen," she said.

Caeden leaned back in his chair. "I didn't mean to surprise you. I suppose I just wanted a few minutes to talk to you . . . alone."

She looked at him oddly for a moment, then reclaimed her chair. "What about?"

"You. I wondered what you plan to do now."

For a minute Caeden wasn't sure she'd heard him. Her expression was one of perplexed consideration. "I'm not entirely sure," she finally said.

"Maybe you should consider heading to Great Falls too. There are probably jobs there you could get. I know you mentioned wanting to go off on your own. I think your mother wanted that for you too. I could arrange something for you. Get you set up in a boardinghouse."

Emily gave him a tolerant smile. "My mother wanted a great many things." She got to her feet. "I'm sorry. I really don't have time to talk. I need to get the dishes done."

"I could help. I know how to dry dishes quite well." He stood and all but challenged her to refuse his help.

She offered him a little nod. "Very well." She went to the stove. "There's a dish towel in that box to the left of the stove."

Caeden went to the box and found the towel. He positioned himself to take the wet dishes from Emily and continued the conversation. "Emily, I know you are probably very confused right now. Give it some time. I didn't mean to suggest you should rush into anything."

He thought about Mrs. Carver's desire that he should marry Emily and wondered if she had ever told her daughter this. He figured it was likely, but he couldn't know for sure without asking her. Now he wanted to raise the matter but had no idea how to bring it up.

"Sometimes it's hard to know what's right," he murmured instead.

"Yes. Yes it is." She handed him a wet bowl, and he dried it and secured it in the box.

Caeden was getting nowhere. Emily had completely shut herself off from him. Finally he gave a long sigh and fell silent. If he brought up the matter of marriage and her mother's wishes, it might only serve to cause more pain. Emily had loved her mother and respected her thoughts and wishes. How could Caeden possibly tell this beautiful young woman what her mother had told him and that she was wrong—that he was not the husband God had sent for Emily? Especially when he was beginning to wish he was.

# 10

An icy rain fell that night, and as sleet hit the roof of the cabin, Emily tossed and turned on her pallet. At one point when the wind picked up, she heard her father get up and go outside. When he returned a few minutes later with Caeden in tow, she realized her father had been worried about him weathering the storm in the tent.

When once again the room was dark and the cabin quiet, Emily drifted off to sleep only to find herself in one dream after another. Some were good and some bad, but when she awoke the next morning, she felt more tired than when she'd gone to bed.

Her father and Caeden were gone for most of the day getting logs to chop into fuel for the winter. Emily made certain there was something for them to eat and hot coffee to drink. She had no way of knowing exactly when they might come inside to warm up and rest, but she wanted to be ready. What she didn't want was to focus any attention on Caeden's impending departure.

Outside the sun was shining, and despite the colder temperatures of the night, the day didn't seem so bad. Emily busied herself with anything she could. She cleared a path through the icy snow so she could reach the animals. After this she tended the animals, seeing to it that all were fed and watered. She considered moving the chickens into the cabin but decided to hold off. It wasn't that cold yet. She went to check the box in the lean-to, where she had put vegetables prior to the fire. With the weather colder, it made for a nice way to store them. They would no doubt go through those rather quickly, however, and then she had no idea what they would do for food. All the vegetables and berries she'd canned had been in the cabin and were destroyed in the fire. The wonderful supplies Caeden had generously donated and her dried herbs were all gone too. Even her mother's Bible had been lost.

She returned to the cabin and sat down at the crude little table, wondering how they would ever get through the winter. Perhaps she should get firm with her father and insist they move to Great Falls as Caeden had suggested. She could surely get work at a hotel or laundry, maybe even a restaurant. She wasn't a bad cook, so maybe someone there would hire her. But even as she thought about this, Emily knew she'd never convince her father.

"He's such a stubborn man."

Emily sighed. There was always the possibility of going to Great Falls without him. The idea intrigued her for a moment. Caeden had offered to take her and set her up in a boarding-house. Once there in the city perhaps she could gain employment and send money to her father to see him through the winter. It was worth consideration. But Emily knew even as she contemplated the matter, it would go no further. She couldn't leave her father just now. Not after he'd lost everything else.

Three days later, Emily awoke early. She knew why. Caeden was going to leave that day. He wasn't leaving them in want, however. He had worked feverishly with her father to lay in a large supply of wood for the winter months. Then yesterday he and her father had ridden to Utica, where Caeden bought an entire kitchen-full of supplies and even a few other much-needed items. When they returned, Emily had been aghast at the amount of goods Caeden had purchased, but she was even more surprised that her father had willingly accepted the donation.

She donned her coat and warm knit hat that Millie had given her and slipped from the house while her father was just stirring. There was no sign of Caeden being awake, as the tent flaps were still tied shut. Emily was glad. She had no desire to see him off this morning. She had set out bread and ham the night before and knew that her father could easily make the coffee when he found her absent. That way she could stay away from the cabin until Caeden was gone, and she would never have to say good-bye.

Emily took up the two buckets she used for hauling water and headed down the path to the river. Her father and Caeden had put together a little lean-to for her father's panning tools. If the cold of the morning got to be too much, Emily figured she'd make her way there and wait until she was sure Caeden had gone. Hopefully no one would bother to look for her.

When she reached the river, Emily turned one of the buckets over and sat down. Here and there ice had formed, but as was usually the case, the river ran free. Jake told her the river wouldn't freeze solid because it was always in motion. She watched the rippling water flow past her, wishing she could flow away just as easily. There were so many questions she needed answered, and yet answers seemed so unreachable.

*Mama would tell me to pray.*

And in truth she had tried, but for reasons she didn't understand, it only made her feel worse. She was certain her lack of faith disappointed God, and the more she thought of that, the harder it was to pray. And the harder it was to pray, the more confused Emily grew.

Caeden's image came to mind, and Emily chided herself over and over. She had known better than to get close to this stranger. She had warned herself at every turn not to care about him and certainly not to lose her heart to him. So why had she allowed herself to fall in love with him anyway?

No doubt it was just infatuation. At least that's what she told herself over and over, hoping it would ease her misery. Once he had gone, Emily assured herself she would forget him and everything would return to its proper order. Somehow, she just couldn't bring herself to believe it.

Maybe her mother's prayer that she marry Caeden was coming true, despite her best efforts to resist her growing attachment to him. She thrust that thought aside. It was simply impossible for her to believe that God would ever answer such a prayer. Her mother had to have been wrong. A man from Caeden's background would certainly never consider marriage to an uneducated, poor daughter of a failed gold miner.

Tears came unbidden and streamed down her cold cheeks. With her mother dead, the loneliness threatened to eat her alive. She had found comfort in Caeden's presence, but now that would be taken as well. She buried her face in her hands. Somehow, she had to find a way to get through this.

Once she started crying, Emily found it impossible to stop. She cried for her mother's death and the emptiness her passing had left. She cried because of her father's stubborn determination to strike it rich and all that it had taken from her and

Mother. And she cried for all the dreams that would never be fulfilled. Dreams of sewing a wedding dress with her mother. Dreams of a house and a white picket fence. Last of all, Emily allowed herself to weep for the sadness of losing Caeden and the love she would have liked to have shared with him.

*Oh, God, please help me to bear this pain—this sense of loss. I cannot go on under its weight.*

"Emily?"

At the sound of Caeden's voice, Emily's head shot up. She met his eyes, then shook her head and buried her face again. She knew he wouldn't just go away, but she couldn't stop crying, even to shoo him off. Why did he always have to find her like this? She had never been given to tears, even as a child. But ever since Caeden had come into her life, it seemed that crying was all she ever did.

Much to her distress she felt him sit down beside her, and when he moved to put his arm around her, it was too much. Emily broke into sobs as he pulled her close. Couldn't he understand that this only made the pain worse? Even so, she couldn't find the strength to move away.

She had no idea how long he held her as she cried. The last few months had been harder on her than all the twenty-three years before. For the first time in her life she felt utterly hopeless. Her body shook hard as she sobbed out her misery, causing Caeden to tighten his hold all the more.

As the tears began to subside, Emily searched her heart and mind for a way to excuse herself from Caeden's arms. She knew he would question her about the tears, no doubt wondering if they were over him. But Emily figured there were plenty of things she deserved to be crying about, and the fact that he was leaving her forever didn't need to be mentioned among them.

She willed herself to calm down, and only then did she realize how tightly she was clinging to Caeden. He felt warm and safe, and while she longed to stay where she was, Emily knew she had put herself on thin ice. She tried to straighten and pull away, but Caeden held her fast.

"It's all right to cry," he soothed, his voice low, "after all you've been through. Would you like to talk about it?"

Emily attempted to wipe her face on her coat sleeve, but Caeden put a handkerchief into her hand instead. She met his eyes and saw a wealth of concern there. It was impossible to look away. With their faces only inches apart, Emily knew Caeden was about to kiss her. She wanted that kiss more than her next breath, but bells began to clang a danger signal in her brain. If he kissed her, she would be forever lost. He lowered his face to hers.

"Leave me alone!" Emily pushed him away with all her might. Caeden looked at her in shock as he fell off the bucket. "You have no right to . . . to . . . ." Her words wouldn't come. "You have no right." She got up and put some distance between them.

"I'm sorry," he said, getting to his feet. "I didn't mean to offend you." He dusted off his backside, still shaking his head.

Emily immediately regretted her angry tone. "It's not important. I'm the one who's sorry. I should never have acted that way."

"What way? Heartbroken?"

She sobered at the word. If she was honest with him about her feelings, it would serve no purpose. "I miss my mother." It wasn't a lie, but neither was it the truth of why she'd acted as she had. "But that's no excuse for acting in such a wanton manner."

His lips twitched, and his expression changed to amusement. "That was wanton?"

Emily crossed her arms. "I've never allowed such a thing to happen. I wanted to shoot Kirk Davies for less. Had I not been mourning my mother's passing and the changes that have taken place, I would never have allowed you to . . . to . . . hold me."

He took a step forward, then stopped. "You did nothing wrong, and neither did I. I saw you crying and wanted to offer you support. I've come to care deeply about you and your father."

Emily bit her lip to keep herself from declaring that she too had come to care deeply for him. If she told him about her feelings and how her heart was only now realizing just how deeply she loved him, it would ruin everything.

She chose her words carefully. "I appreciate that you care. I know Father has been very touched by your generous nature . . . as have I. I'm very thankful for what you've done."

His eyes narrowed, and his usual serious expression returned. "I didn't do it for thanks."

"Oh, I know that." She could see she had offended him. Maybe it was for the best. "I didn't mean to suggest you did. You are by nature a very giving man, and we won't soon forget your kindness."

"No I'm not."

Emily shook her head in confusion. "What?"

"I'm not a generous or giving man by nature. I'm a hardened skeptic who, until meeting you and your father and even the other people in this area, believed most everyone to be rather self-centered and offensive. So don't applaud me or give me undue praise. I did what I did because you were first kind to me. Your father offered to show me the way to Yogo City and to let me pitch my tent on your claim. He told me I could take my meals with you and never once asked me to contribute to those meals."

Emily considered his words for a moment. He was clearly upset by her comments and her attitude toward him. She hadn't meant to alienate him.

"I do apologize, Caeden. I'm afraid you just caught me at a bad time. Losing my mother was something I knew would happen, but I wasn't prepared for her to die in an act of violence. Losing everything I owned was something I never thought much of, because I didn't have much to lose. However, it bothered me in a way I hadn't anticipated. I suppose I took more comfort in those things than I realized." She tried to think of how else she might keep him from even contemplating whether his departure was part of the reason for her tears. "I've never cared overmuch about the possessions, but . . . well . . . I had lived longer in that one cabin than anywhere else. It was as close to a real home as I've ever had."

"That cabin wasn't your home," Caeden said, holding her gaze. "You and your mother and father made it a home. If you'd ever once been without them and their love, you'd realize that."

⁕

Caeden knew he'd upset Emily by his actions. He'd been a fool to even think about kissing her, but there she was in his arms. So sad. So vulnerable. He was a complete heel to act as he had. Even so, he knew Emily had wanted him to kiss her. He could see it in her eyes, so why would she not be honest with him about it?

She had already turned away to gather her buckets. How could he hope to explain his feelings to her when he didn't understand them himself?

"Let me do that." Caeden followed her to the river's edge.

He took the buckets from her and filled each one. "I'll carry them back for you."

Emily looked at him for a moment, then nodded. She started up the icy trail with Caeden following close behind. His thoughts churned and refused to let him put the matter to rest.

What if he had completely misread her response? Perhaps she truly didn't feel anything for him. It was possible that in her grief and vulnerability, Emily had been unprepared for his advance.

Caeden let out a sigh and shook his head. He was no better than Davies, who'd tried to forcibly impose his will on Emily. It hadn't been his intention to act in such a manner, but something had happened to him when he held Emily in his arms. Something that made him want to protect her—to love her.

They reached the cabin, and Caeden quickly entered to deposit the buckets. Henry was standing over the stove pouring himself a cup of coffee. He threw Caeden and Emily a broad smile.

"I see you found her. Coffee's ready."

Caeden put the buckets down. "I'm afraid I need to be on my way. I've appreciated your hospitality, and if I have a chance to come this way again, I hope I might be welcome again."

"Of course you'll be welcome," Henry replied, "but I can't be sendin' you off without something to eat."

"I'll eat in Utica. I have business to settle up there and then the stage to catch. I'm afraid I've already taken too much time."

He wouldn't allow himself to look at Emily. He worried that his comment might hurt her by suggesting she hadn't been worth the time. He worried too much about everything associated with Emily. It was time that he stopped this nonsense and got on with his job.

"You're always welcome here, Caeden Thibault, but I think

you already know that." Henry crossed to where he stood and extended his hand. "It's been a pleasure knowin' you."

"Likewise." Caeden shook the older man's hand and then turned and headed for the door.

He left to finish loading his horse with all the gear he'd brought. There was so much he wanted to say to Emily, but he knew it would be foolish. They were just two people who had happened to cross paths and enjoyed each other's company. It happened all the time, to hear people tell it. Caeden tied down his saddlebags and frowned.

"But it's never happened to me . . . until now."

# 11

The small cabin seemed even smaller without Caeden around. Emily wasn't sure how that could happen. It seemed logical that losing a person from such a tiny space would make that room seem bigger. But it was just the opposite.

Her father quickly put himself back into the routine of panning for his fortune while Emily tried to figure out what to do with herself. Without her mother to care for, her days seemed empty. She baked and cleaned and even mended some of the donated clothes they'd received, but it was never enough to keep her mind occupied. At times she would go with her father to dig up dirt to be sluiced. Unfortunately, she found it sometimes awkward, even painful, as they both seemed to be trying hard not to say or do anything to remind the other of their loss.

Thinking about Caeden was something Emily was determined not to do, but her heart had other thoughts on the matter. She found herself at the most inopportune times remembering something he'd said or did. Mostly, she couldn't forget what it was like to be in his arms—so safe and warm.

Once when she'd been about fifteen, Emily remembered asking her mother what it felt like to fall in love. Her mother had considered the question for a moment and then replied, "It feels like your insides are being pulled to the outside. You can't think clearly because all of your thoughts are about the person you love, and you wonder if you'll ever be able to feel whole again—without them."

The memory pierced her heart. "Then I'm in love," she whispered to no one.

Falling in love with Caeden had been the last thing on her mind—the last thing she had ever intended to happen. All of these years she had guarded her heart with great care. She had dressed in a dowdy fashion to disguise her figure and looks, and she had avoided men at all costs. To her way of thinking, Emily had built a rather tidy wall between her and the possibility of love. So how was it that one young man could come along and completely knock down her fortress?

"Yo at home, Miss Emily?"

At the sound of Millie's voice, Emily immediately opened the cabin door. "This is certainly a surprise." She stepped back. "Come on in."

Millie carried a bundle, which she handed over to Emily. "Some folks done heard 'bout de fire and left dese for yo."

Emily took the offering to the table and spread it out. There was a man's shirt—stained, but otherwise in good shape. There was also a pair of long underwear, which she was certain her father would appreciate. Last of all there was a woman's blue calico blouse.

"This was very generous of them." She held up the blouse for size. It looked perfect. "I wish I could have thanked them."

"I done tol' dem yo'd be mighty glad to have dem." Millie grinned her toothy grin. "Oh, I gots yo sumptin too." She reached into her pockets and drew out two cans of peaches. "Thought yo pa would like to have dem."

Emily smiled. "He will. Caeden purchased quite a few things for us before he left, but peaches weren't among them."

"Dat young man's shore gwanna be missed."

Emily put the blouse back with the other things and got to her feet. "I have some coffee. Would you like a cup?"

"Shore. I's feelin' the cold in my bones."

"Pa said the same thing. I don't know how much longer he'll be able to keep mining. He's still so convinced that he'll strike it rich, so he keeps on trying. I think he's unwilling to face the truth."

"I'm 'fraid I agrees with him. I'm shore der's gold to be had. Dat's why I keep workin' at it too. But I'm thinkin' dat ain't de problem now."

Emily brought Millie the coffee and caught the knowing look on her face. The older woman seemed to understand exactly what the problem was. Turning back to the stove, Emily poured herself a cup and hoped Millie would just let the matter be. She didn't.

"I figures yo be missin' Mr. Caeden."

Emily didn't want to lie, but neither did she want to admit her feelings. "He was a great help to us. Pa was able to lay in quite a bit of wood for the winter with Caeden's help. He will sure be missed."

Millie took a sip of coffee, then fixed Emily with a stern expression. "Yo gwanna miss him for mo' dan dat. Yo can't be losin' someone yo love and not feel bad."

❧

Great Falls was just as Caeden had remembered it. The bustling of the small city was nothing compared to those back east, but it seemed a world of difference from Yogo City and Utica.

He had arranged to arrive a full day in advance of Bishop Arnold and checked into the railroad hotel, hoping for a chance to have a hot bath and sleep in a real bed. However, once he'd had the bath, his stomach changed his mind about sleeping. He was starved and realized he'd had very little to eat since leaving Utica.

He dressed in his clean shirt and pulled on his jacket. His casual manner of dress would never have worked at the finer dining tables in Albany, but here he knew he'd be excused. He liked that about Montana. It seemed no matter a man's state of dress, he was welcome just about anywhere.

The downstairs restaurant wasn't at all busy, so Caeden found himself quickly seated and served. He ordered a thick steak with all the trimmings and sipped on a cup of strong coffee while he waited. And all the while he did what he'd done since leaving Yogo City. He thought of Emily.

He'd been unable to get her out of his mind, and even as he'd dozed on the stage, it was her image that filled his dreams. Caeden tried to rationalize that he was just worried about her and her father. He cared about them. He could easily admit that much. They had been good to him, and he had enjoyed their company. That was all there was to it, he reasoned. But his heart told him otherwise, and the battle that ensued threatened to steal away all pretense of peace.

*I can't be in love with her. I can't think about marrying her. It would be disastrous. We don't want the same things.*

"Thibault. I didn't expect to meet up with you until tomorrow."

Caeden looked up to find not only Bishop Arnold in his fine gray wool suit, but his daughter Catherine as well. She looked quite pretty in a traveling suit of plum and a blouse of shimmering gold silk. She smiled at him with a look that suggested she knew she was beautiful and that he had noticed.

Getting to his feet, Caeden knew he had no choice but to invite them to join him. It wasn't what he wanted, and he even thought for a moment of telling them he was just leaving. But, of course, the waitress would surely comment on his meal, and that would reveal his lie.

"Won't you join me?" He offered Catherine a chair, then reclaimed his own as Bishop Arnold settled in opposite him.

"This is most fortuitous," Arnold began. "We came in only this morning."

Caeden nodded and motioned the waitress to the table. "We have two more for supper," he explained.

The Arnolds inquired about their dining choices and settled on ham steaks, potatoes, and creamed peas. Catherine requested tea, while her father nodded toward Caeden's cup.

"Bring me coffee. Black." He ordered rather than requested it, and the waitress looked surprised.

Caeden felt sorry for the woman. "I'd like another cup as well, if you would be so kind. And please bring some cream."

The woman smiled at him. "I'll bring it right away." She hurried from the table and disappeared into the back.

Caeden had no desire to pretend to be glad at Arnold's summoning. He decided he would push the older man to get right to the point. "So what is it you need of me?"

Arnold seemed surprised. "We needn't talk business just yet. Catherine would never forgive me if I didn't allow you time to share about your adventure here and when you plan to return home to tend to your father's industries and business affairs."

Catherine leaned closer to Caeden. "You have been sorely missed." She lowered her face just a bit and looked up at him through thick lashes. "We haven't seen much of you since your father's passing. I hope you have plans to return for the holiday season. I would very much enjoy attending the Christmas parties with you."

Caeden shook his head. "I have no plans to return to Albany except to put my father's estate on the market. My uncle will see to the details of that, however, so I doubt I'll be there more than a few days."

Her very perfect mouth formed into a pout. "But that would be perfectly awful. Surely you will take time out to see your sisters and spend Christmas with your family."

"I have no plans for that." Caeden looked to Arnold. "Is that why you've summoned me here? To ensure that I accompany Catherine during the Christmas season?" He knew his words were harsh and could see that he'd offended Catherine, but he honestly didn't care.

The waitress returned with drinks and cream. Caeden added a liberal amount to his coffee and waited for Bishop Arnold to continue. With any luck at all he could deal with all of this tonight and be free of the man. And his daughter.

"There's no need to be hard-hearted," Arnold replied. "Catherine naturally wishes to be with the man she plans to marry. As for me," he said hurriedly, no doubt to give Caeden no chance for protest, "I have critical political matters to discuss. Next year is an important election year, and we need to ensure that the right people get into office."

"The right people?" Caeden gave the man a hard look. "I presume you are including yourself in that matter."

Arnold laughed. "Exactly true. But, of course, my political ambitions have long been known. Your father knew of them and approved them heartily. He knew it would be most useful to have a senator who was also a good and trusted friend."

146

"Given his way of doing business, I'm sure that was true." Caeden saw the waitress approaching with plates of food and waited until she had set them down and was gone before continuing. "I would remind you, Mr. Arnold, that I am not my father. Nor do I have any interest in politics."

Catherine sat by quietly as she'd been trained to do, but it was obvious she held great interest in the conversation.

"Caeden," Bishop Arnold began, "since your father's death I have felt a certain obligation to . . . well . . . watch over you and ensure you make sound choices and business decisions. I know your father would have wanted you to be a community leader. Thibault Industries have greatly benefited New York, if not the world. Yours is a name to be revered and honored. Men will look to you for advice and direction."

"My father's name was more feared and dreaded than revered and honored," Caeden said, cutting into his steak. "It's a name I have long considered changing. As for my father, I don't really care what he wanted."

Arnold looked at him as if he'd gone mad. "I am certain you jest. It's your youth that has given you such thoughts, although I know that you and your father did not always see eye to eye. I often encouraged Archibald to give you a long lead so you could experience the world and the frivolities that so interest young people. However, I also assured him the time would come when you would mature and desire to follow in his footsteps."

"Well, you were certainly wrong on that account. I want nothing to do with my father's footsteps. If I were to follow anyone, it would be my uncle."

"Ah yes," Arnold said, looking most uncomfortable, "Jasper Carrington."

Caeden's uncle had never had use for Arnold and made no bones about it. He thought the man underhanded and devious, and Caeden agreed. When his father announced that Caeden would wed Catherine Arnold, it was Uncle Jasper who had calmed Caeden's rage. He'd reminded the eighteen-year-old that no one could force him to marry anyone he didn't want to marry.

They ate in silence for some time. It seemed to Caeden that the mention of his uncle and his own unwillingness to desire power were things Arnold could not deal with easily. As far as Caeden was concerned, the matter was closed. If this was what had brought Arnold all this way, then he could just return on the next train.

Catherine Arnold poured cream into her tea and stirred it in such a delicate manner that the spoon made no contact with the china cup. Caeden thought her a very beautiful and gentle woman, but he had no interest in becoming her husband.

As if realizing that Caeden was thinking of her, Catherine smiled at him. She seemed delighted just to be in his presence. Touching her hand to her blond hair, Catherine's green eyes never left his. "Travel has definitely left me feeling rather unkempt." She lowered her hand and picked up her fork once again. "But I wouldn't have missed a chance to see you again. I must say the vast outdoors seems to agree with you."

Caeden knew she was trying hard to calm the tensions between him and her father. He thought on the matter only a moment before giving her a slight smile. "I find that I prefer the frontier to the overly crowded eastern cities. People are less concerned with their appearance out here. They practice great kindnesses that I've never witnessed in New York. I very well might settle here."

"Nonsense," Arnold interrupted. "It would be foolishness, and you know it. Honestly, Caeden, I cannot allow you to destroy your future. Nor can I stand by and let your bad feelings for your father tear apart the empire he built."

Caeden fixed him with a hard look. His eyes narrowed and he leaned forward slightly. "You, sir, have no say in the matter."

Arnold looked shocked. He recovered quickly, however, and beamed Caeden a smile. "I do apologize. I sometimes let my zeal get the best of me. I only want the very best for you, son. It is my desire that you and Catherine would know wealth and prosperity all of your lives. If you so dislike running the industry, you should consider allowing me to work as your manager. I know the business quite well, having been your father's associate for so very many years. I realize you hold your uncle in high esteem, and I would not wish that to change. However, while he might well advise you on future decisions, he knows very little about your father's work."

Exhaustion began to take the fight out of Caeden. With his appetite satisfied, he longed only to crawl into bed and sleep.

"One thing you must understand," Arnold continued, "this next political election will change the country. William McKinley is much needed to see our great nation thrive. His campaign manager, Mark Hanna, is even now soliciting donations to secure McKinley's election."

"You mean buy it, don't you?" Caeden folded his napkin and placed it aside his plate. "As I mentioned before, I have no desire to entangle myself in politics."

"But there is so much at stake." Arnold sounded almost frantic. "You need to understand. The Democrats have nominated that repulsive William Jennings Bryan to become president. Bryan stands fast on his support of a free silver inflationary economy in order to benefit the farmers and laborers. Never mind how that will destroy the owners of the industries that employ those laborers and buy those farm goods. We must act on this matter to be sure that Bryan never comes to power. Surely you can see that."

Caeden suppressed a yawn. "Right now I am able to see very little."

"Father, I am quite exhausted myself," Catherine said, reaching out to touch her father's hand. "Do you suppose we might retire and continue this in the morning?"

Her father smiled and patted her hand. "Of course, my dear. I do apologize to you, and to you, Caeden. It was thoughtless of me to insist we discuss this tonight. What say we meet here again for breakfast after we are well rested?"

Caeden wanted to refuse but knew that to do so would only cause delay in getting to bed. "Very well. I will meet you here in the morning." He got to his feet. "Now, if you'll please excuse me."

Catherine nodded, and Bishop Arnold stood also. "Good night," the older man said. "I will look forward to our conversation tomorrow. I'm sure after a comfortable night's sleep you'll see things differently."

Caeden knew that sleep wouldn't change his mind, but he said nothing. Instead he crossed the room to the waitress and handed her enough to pay his own bill. He wasn't about to pay for Arnold's too.

# 12

*C*aeden arrived early at the restaurant. He'd spent a restless night worrying about Emily and her father, and dreading what was yet to come with Arnold. He thought it most unfair that his first night back in a real bed should be so lacking in peace and sleep. He suppressed a yawn and picked up the newspaper he'd purchased.

The front page boasted an ad that offered fall and winter overcoats on sale for as little as ten dollars. Ten dollars would have fed the Carvers for a month, if not two or three. There were also ads for new wagons and carriages, as well as one for a company that would buy furs. Most of the news articles dealt with issues related to the state. Nothing in particular caught Caeden's attention, and without realizing it, he was once again thinking of Emily Carver.

Despite her cynicism at times, Emily was one of the most content people he'd ever known. She had so little, yet even when she'd lost all of her earthly possessions, she didn't complain or rage at the unfairness of life. She simply took it in stride. Her sorrow came in losing her mother. It was a hardship to have everything else stripped away, but it was the death of her mother that Emily mourned. Caeden loved that about her. People were always more important than objects. Pity his own father couldn't have felt that way.

Caeden also loved that Emily cared so deeply for her father. But then, he was coming to realize that he loved a great many things about her. And there was the problem. He loved her. He loved her simple nature, her love of family, and even her faith. The few times they had spoken about God, Caeden had been reminded of his mother and her trust in the Almighty.

Caeden's thoughts turned to ponder Nyola Carver's declaration that God had sent him to be a husband to Emily. Her faith was even stronger than that of her daughter, and as Henry had stated, Nyola seemed able to figure out God's direction not only for herself, but also for her loved ones. Could that truly be the case? Did God honestly speak to people in this day and age?

He was still pretending to read the *Great Falls Tribune* when Catherine Arnold approached him. He could smell her floral-scented perfume before he saw her. He lowered the paper and met her gaze.

"Good morning, Caeden. Did you sleep well?" She smiled sweetly and flashed her green eyes at him in an alluring fashion.

Caeden put the newspaper aside and then got to his feet. "Good morning." He helped her into a chair. "I slept well enough. Where's your father?"

"He's coming. He had something to take care of and said he'd be with us shortly." She pulled off her gloves. "I hope you don't mind. I thought it would be nice to have a few minutes to talk with you alone."

"I see." Caeden picked up his coffee cup and drank. He had no desire to make small talk with Catherine, but he saw no way out of it.

"I know Father can be heavy-handed with his desires, but you must understand that he really does care about you."

"Let's not play games, Catherine. He cares about my money. That's all. He wants us to marry because he believes it will give him access to the Thibault fortune."

Catherine looked down at her bare hands. "I suppose there is some truth to that. However, I . . . well . . ."

The approaching waitress silenced anything else Catherine might have said. The woman deposited a platter of eggs and another of sausages before hurrying away from the table. Caeden saw that Catherine was surprised by the amount of food.

"I hope you don't mind, but I took the liberty of ordering a hearty breakfast for all of us."

The waitress returned with a plate of biscuits and a bowl of gravy. "If you need anything else, just let me know. Coffee is in the pot, and the cream and sugar are there beside it. There's butter and jam as well."

Caeden looked at Catherine. "Do you wish to have tea this morning?"

"That would be nice, thank you." She looked at him as though he'd hung the moon and stars.

"Would you please bring hot tea for the lady?" The waitress nodded and once again disappeared.

"Help yourself." Caeden took up the platter of eggs. "I think we should eat while it's hot. There's no telling how long your father's business will keep him."

Catherine took a portion of the eggs. "I'm sorry about last night. Father has been worried about a great many things."

"No doubt." Caeden gave himself a healthy serving of eggs, then replaced the platter and picked up the plate of sausages. Again he offered Catherine first choice, but she shook her head.

"I've never really cared for sausage." She picked up a biscuit. "This will suit me just fine."

Caeden finished serving himself and waited for her to continue. He was certain she wanted to convince him to help her father and marry her. But he wasn't going to marry her. Not now. Not ever. The sooner she understood that, the better off they'd both be. He started to speak on the matter, but Catherine once again commented.

"There is something I would really like to tell you," she began. "I think it might be useful to both of us."

He raised a brow and halted his fork halfway to his mouth. "Do tell."

She toyed with the biscuit, pinching off a piece and buttering it. "Father has always had his plans, and he has never considered that anyone would dare stand up to him. You have quite vexed him with your ability to think for yourself. I'm not sure why he never saw your strength prior to your father's death. I certainly did."

"Your father only sees what he wants to see." Caeden popped the forkful of eggs into his mouth.

"Be that as it may, it's important for you to know that I am not of the same mind."

Caeden's curiosity grew, but just then Catherine spied her father. "Oh, there's Father now. I suppose this talk will have to wait."

She sounded almost perturbed, but Caeden couldn't imagine obedient little Catherine Arnold showing anything but the sweetest nature. She had been amply trained by her father to simper, pout, and smile upon his command.

"Sorry for my delay," Arnold said, taking the seat opposite Caeden once again. "I'm glad to see you didn't wait on me."

"Help yourself. I thought the least I could do was buy breakfast." Caeden had only done so to hurry their mealtime together, but he could see it put Arnold in a positive state of mind.

The man smiled and gave a nod. "Most generous of you. This will allow us to discuss matters undisturbed."

Caeden steeled himself. He was determined to not lose his temper. He would hear Bishop Arnold out in full, and then he would excuse himself. He had plans to spend the day shopping for the Carvers. They had no knowledge of it, but Caeden intended to send them a wagonful of supplies, including a beautiful new gown for Emily. It might be unseemly to purchase clothes for a woman unrelated to him, but Caeden didn't care. He wanted her to have something new and lovely. Something no one had ever worn before. Something she could call her own.

"I am hopeful you have given great consideration to what I said last evening," Bishop Arnold began. He piled copious amounts of food onto his plate and dug in almost immediately.

Caeden lifted his coffee cup. "I'm afraid my fatigue left me unable to think about much of anything." He took a long drink of the now tepid brew.

Arnold spoke between mouthfuls. Well, very nearly. At times he didn't even bother to clear his mouth before he droned on. "The situation is one that could very well see this country face another collapse. We're already feeling the effects of the devaluing of silver in '93. It wasn't only the mineowners who took a great loss. This conflict with our monetary system has left many people and their fortunes in jeopardy. Your father was smart enough to diversify his holdings. He invested in so many different areas that you will never need fear a complete loss. That's why I believe it is important that you associate yourself with the political arena and put forth some of that fortune to assure your future."

Caeden met the man's green-eyed gaze. His eyes were very nearly the same shade as Catherine's, but they gave the man a devious rather than attractive look.

"As I said last night," Caeden replied, "I'm not interested in involving myself in politics. As far as I'm concerned that matter is closed."

"But . . . but . . ." Arnold sputtered, "you can't be serious. You have responsibilities."

"And I know full well what they are," Caeden said. "I am nearly thirty years old and college educated. You doubt my abilities and my experience, but I assure you I am well aware of what is happening in this country. I have been out among the people who are suffering most. You should try doing that sometime. Then perhaps you would truly understand what is needed politically and economically."

Arnold seemed momentarily taken aback. He cleared his throat and seemed at a loss for words. Caeden hoped it would end the discussion altogether.

"Now, if that is the only thing you came to discuss, I would like to finish my breakfast and bid you both good-bye. I have a great many things I need to handle here in Great Falls before I leave to join my colleagues in Havre." Caeden picked up a biscuit and slathered it with jam. He gave a sidewise glance at Catherine and could see that she looked worried.

"Of course that isn't the only thing. There is the matter of your marriage to my daughter." Arnold reached out to take another helping of sausage. "While I long understood and accepted your desire to make your own way in the world, as you so eagerly pointed out, you are approaching your thirtieth birthday. You must now consider your marriage."

"There's nothing to consider." He popped a piece of the biscuit into his mouth and chewed very slowly. He knew his

156

words and actions would irritate the older man, but he didn't care. He hadn't come here to make Bishop Arnold happy.

"You are wrong, Caeden. There is a great deal to consider. Weddings do not take place overnight. There needs to be a great deal of planning and . . . financial consideration. You and Catherine cannot have a shoddy wedding."

Caeden poured more coffee, then took a drink. When he'd finished, he dabbed his mouth with the napkin and folded it in a most meticulous manner. Finally he could see that Arnold was about to burst from waiting for Caeden's response.

"You are correct. We cannot have a shoddy wedding or any other kind. I have no intention of marrying your daughter, as I told you long ago and reiterated at my father's funeral. You and my father made this arrangement, not I. Neither of you considered my desires or feelings in the matter, even though I made them quite clear at the time. I also doubt very seriously that you considered Catherine's."

"My daughter knows her place. She does as she is told," Arnold protested. "She respects her father's wishes, knowing that I want only the best for her."

"Well, the best isn't a husband who doesn't love her."

Arnold stared at him for a moment, then laughed. "Is that all that worries you? Love will follow, my boy. You'll see. Catherine will be a most attentive and loving wife, and you will soon learn to appreciate her and love her. I have no doubt of this."

"Well, be that as it may, I refuse to even consider marrying a woman I do not love. A woman whose father I cannot respect."

Arnold nearly choked. He drew the coffee cup quickly to his lips and swallowed. "I am deeply shocked and offended by your comment."

Caeden shrugged. "I don't know why it should come as a surprise. You know my feelings for my father and his way of doing business. As you pointed out, you were his closest associate, and you do business just as he did." Caeden paused for a moment to let the words sink in. He doubted that Arnold would leave the matter lie, but at least he would think twice about trying to hold Caeden's father up as a symbol to be respected and followed.

With great care Caeden folded his newspaper. "I am sorry that you made the trip all this way only to hear what I have told you on other occasions." He looked at Arnold. The man was clearly unhappy. His face had reddened, and he'd finally stopped eating.

Caeden got to his feet. "I do hope, Catherine, that I have not upset you overly much. You are a beautiful woman, and your charms are evident. I am certain you will have no difficulty in landing another potential husband."

"Wait. Wait just a minute," Arnold said. He pulled a piece of paper from his pocket. "I have this in writing. This is the contract your father and I made. You'll see it very clearly states that you will marry Catherine and I will obtain ten percent of Thibault Industries."

Caeden took the offered paper and glanced over it. He then handed it back to Arnold and shook his head. "As you will also see, my signature is nowhere on the contract. Now, if you'll excuse me, I have a great deal to accomplish today."

He left the room knowing that he had not heard the last of Bishop Arnold. It would be wonderful to imagine that the man would accept the truth and return to New York, but Caeden knew better than to count on such a thing. Arnold was too much like his father, and his father never took no as an answer when he was determined to have his own way.

*CRISSOUL*

"They are sapphires," the jeweler told Caeden as he examined Emily's little blue pebbles. "I've never seen such clarity and color on stones found in Montana. They might well be worth a great deal."

"That was my thought as well."

"Where did you say you found these?" The man looked up with an expression that almost suggested hunger.

"I didn't." Caeden knew better than to say a word on the location. He knew without a doubt that should he mention Yogo City, the man would most likely share the information with anyone and everyone. He picked up the stones he'd brought and put them in a small box with the others. After they were secure, he dug out a dollar and put it on the table. "For your trouble."

"Are they for sale?" the man called out as Caeden headed for the door.

"No, I'm afraid not. At least not at this time. I want to have them examined back east before I advise the owner of what to do." It was only partially true. Caeden did want to have the value estimated by professionals back east, but he had Emily's permission to do with them as he thought right. If they turned out to be of great value, as he believed them to be, he would sell them and return with the money. He liked the idea of putting a small fortune in Emily's hands. He could only imagine her happiness at finally seeing her father strike it rich.

Making his way to the post office, Caeden mentally composed a note to his friend in New York City. The man was an expert on gemstones, and he would know exactly what the stones were worth and who might be willing to buy them. Better still, Caeden knew he could trust him.

At the counter, Caeden requested a piece of paper, then jotted a note to the man explaining the situation and that he would return to his home in Albany by Christmas. He told the man that if they proved to be valuable, he had permission to sell them to the highest bidder and to send the check to his uncle's house.

"I'm traveling," Caeden explained to the clerk. "Is it possible to pay for you to package this?"

The man eyed the small box and note. "Of course." He figured the price for postage and packaging, and Caeden paid the man. With that task accomplished, Caeden's next stop was the bank.

The day passed without Caeden running into Arnold even once. He figured that to be very good luck on his part. He could only imagine that Arnold would try once again to corner him at supper, but Caeden was going to have his meal elsewhere. He had no intention of repeating the scene from breakfast.

By evening a light snow began to fall, and Caeden was feeling the effects of having skipped the noon meal. He concluded the arrangements for shipping his purchases to the Carvers, and by six o'clock he was on his way to a rather fine-looking restaurant he'd spied earlier while making his rounds.

Several lavishly dressed women were on the arms of their equally fashionable husbands as they entered the restaurant. Immediately Caeden thought of Emily. He'd found her a lovely gown and hoped it would fit. He'd mentioned to the clerk that the young woman had recently lost everything and would need a complete outfit—including things he might not realize. The woman understood and went to work gathering petticoats and other items Caeden would have been much too embarrassed to ask for.

Other couples were seated inside when a smartly dressed man led him to a small, intimate table in the corner of the room. Caeden took his seat, all the while imagining Emily in that new gown. He would love to see her in it. Not only that, but he would love to show her off. She deserved that, and yet most of her life she had hidden her beauty.

*This is ridiculous.*

He picked up the menu and tried to force such thoughts from his mind. Emily wasn't a part of his plans. He wasn't a part of her plans. They were far too different in what they wanted. Weren't they?

But Caeden couldn't forget how neatly she fit in his arms, nor how those dark brown eyes looked up at him with such intensity of emotion that all he wanted to do was kiss her.

*Why is this so hard? Why can't I put Emily Carver aside as easily as I do Catherine Arnold?*

*Because you don't love Catherine,* a voice seemed to speak from deep within his heart.

# 13

"I'm going to need your help today at the claim," Emily's father announced after finishing breakfast. "We're gonna dig out a great deal of earth before the ground freezes hard. Now that the weather has warmed up enough to melt some of the snow, I need to act fast before the next storm."

"What are you going to do with the dirt?" Emily had no desire to accompany her father to his mining site, but she could see he was determined.

"It's vital that I bring the dirt down to the river, where I can wash it a little bit at a time. I need to have enough to work with through the winter. I figure we'll take the cart and Nellie and make several trips. If you'll help me, I know we can finish by dark."

Emily buttered a piece of toasted bread. "I suppose I can, but I had hoped you would take a moment to hear me out about something."

Her father's brows knit together in confusion. "What's on your mind?"

Emily put the toast aside. "All the old-timers around here say that they think this winter is going to be a hard one. If they're right, I don't know how we can hope to make it through. This cabin is full of holes where the chinking is gone or never existed to begin with. Our little stove can hardly be expected to keep the place dry and warm should the temperatures plummet below zero.

"Even Millie says it's not going to be comfortable for us here. She suggests that if we stay, we should probably board at her place. However, I think we should consider moving to Great Falls. You and I would both be able to get jobs of some sort, and then when the weather warms we could return."

"To find our claim jumped," her father said, shaking his head. "No, sirree. I won't risk it. I know there's gold to be had. The man Davies works for knows it too—otherwise, he wouldn't be buyin' up land left and right. Millie knows it as well and goes out to work her own claims. She believes there's a fortune in the ground just beggin' to be dug up."

"Be that as it may, we can hardly expect to get through a bad winter of cold and heavy snows. We aren't equipped, Pa."

He nodded. "But we will be. See, I plan to lay in more supplies before winter. That's why I want your help. Now, we can't just sit here jawin' about it. We got to get out there and get to diggin'. I know you have your doubts, but I'm tellin' you we're gonna get enough gold to see us through the winter."

Emily knew there was no reasoning with him. She got up and gathered the dishes. "Very well, Pa. I'll help you as much as I can. But I won't pretend to be happy about it. I think we're being foolish."

"Oh, don't be in such despair, Emmy. You'll see. God has always provided for us, and He always will."

But instead of comfort, her father's words only served to add further irritation. Why couldn't God provide by giving her father a different dream that included sensible housing and a regular job?

Fifteen minutes later Emily stood beside the cart as her father harnessed Nellie. She felt the entire situation was hopeless. Why could her father not see reason? How was it that his desire for gold never waned—even when he had nothing to show for it?

"There we are," her father said. He took hold of Nellie's harness and led her forward. "I borrowed an extra shovel last night. With both of us loadin' dirt, it'll take no time at all."

Emily said nothing. She thought instead of Caeden. She missed him despite her good intentions to put him from her thoughts. In her dreams she saw him about to kiss her. And sometimes in her dreams she let him. Of course, Emily had never known a man's kiss and could only guess at what it might feel like.

They arrived at her father's mining site and wasted no time getting to work. Emily had never shied away from hard work, but she found the digging to be tedious. Her arm muscles burned as she continued to hoist shovelful after shovelful of the rocks and dirt into the wagon. Her father said nothing as they worked, although from time to time he hummed a tune or whistled.

*How can he be so happy? How can he possibly go on believing in a massive gold strike? He's spent his whole life looking for a treasure that doesn't exist.*

Emily tried not to be angry about the situation, but she felt like a kettle about to boil over. She tried to remember her mother's encouraging words of how even in this God had a purpose. But to Emily it seemed as if God had played a very mean joke on them.

If God loved them so much, why did they have to endure all this suffering and pain? Why did her mother have to die? Why did Caeden have to leave?

There he was again. Caeden Thibault. She couldn't seem to shake Caeden's image, nor the memory of his arms around her.

"It's turned out to be a pretty mornin', don't you think?"

Emily looked at her father for a moment. He seemed so genuinely content. "Can I ask you a question, Pa?" Emily straightened from her digging. "Don't you ever question if this is what God really wants for you?"

He threw a shovelful of dirt into the cart, then shook his head. "Why should I question it?"

"Because you've been at it all of my life and it's never merited anything more than a bit of gold here or there. Never enough to be useful—not really."

"It's seen us through," her father countered. "How can I doubt that God's hand is in it? He's guided us to each place—of that I'm certain."

"If He's guiding us . . . if He really cares, then why aren't we better off? Why haven't you found your treasure? You always told Mama that you'd one day strike it rich and then we could settle down. We'd live in a real house and have everything we needed or wanted. Now Mama's dead and we've lost everything . . . even her Bible. How can that be God's provision?"

For a short time he just looked at her as if willing Emily to understand. Then his shoulders sagged a bit, and his expression grew sad. "If I quit now, then my life will have meant nothin'," he said in a barely audible voice.

Emily shook her head. "How can you say that? You had a wife who loved and defended you to the very end. You have a daughter who loves you. How can a lack of physical treasure mean that your life has been for naught?"

Her father considered this for a moment. He kicked at the rocks, then finally answered. "I figure it's God's will for me. I have to do what He's given me to do." He looked up. "What's this all about, Em?"

"It's about the utter despair I feel given our situation. I have no idea of how I can possibly help us through the winter months with what little we have. I can't imagine us not freezing to death."

"Have faith, daughter."

Emily threw down the shovel. "I've had faith, but it doesn't seem to matter. I'm not at all sure God even cares about my faith."

Henry Carver had never looked more shocked, and Emily immediately regretted her words. She didn't want to fight with him. Neither did she want to fight with God. Why did she have to feel so out of sorts with everything and everyone?

"I'm sorry, Pa. I know that my words are not what you want to hear."

Emily looked at her father for a moment. She toyed with the idea of just changing the subject. It might be better to give up than to continue; after all, what could she possibly gain by hurting him with the truth?

"Em, you seem mighty unhappy."

She took a deep breath. "This isn't the life I wanted, Pa. This isn't my dream. It wasn't Mama's dream. It's yours. You can't expect me to be happy living like this, going day after day never knowing what disaster might strike us next."

A weariness overtook her, and Emily felt as though she were weighted down. "I never wanted to hurt you, Pa. That wasn't my desire. It still isn't. I just feel so confused right now. Mama wanted me to leave and strike out on my own after she died. She used to try to make me promise that I wouldn't just go on following you from camp to camp."

He nodded. "I know that. She told me the same. I guess I just sort of figured you stayed because you wanted to."

Emily went to him and put her hand on his shoulder. "I stayed because I love you and because I'm afraid of what might happen to you if I don't stay. I don't want you to be alone, but I also don't want this life. I hate it. I hate waking up each morning wondering what terrible thing will befall us today." She let go of him and turned away. "I don't expect you to understand, because I don't understand it myself."

Her father let go of his shovel and put his arm around her. "I didn't know you felt so strong about it. I don't want you stayin' because you feel you have to take care of me. I'm able to see to myself. Of course, I would miss your company. Just as I miss your ma's. Ain't nothin' the same without her."

Emily felt horrible for her outburst. She had tried to pray away her feelings of hate for the mining life, along with those of love that she held for Caeden. Why was God not answering her prayers for contentment and the ability to put aside her own desires?

"I'm sorry, Pa. I should never have said anything, and I regret hurting you."

"I'm glad you spoke your mind. I don't want you lyin' to me, even if you think it'll make me happy." He paused and shook his head. "Truth is always best, and the truth . . . for me . . . is that I don't know how to do anything else. I suppose I could go to work diggin' and mining for one of those big companies, but all of my life I've been certain God had a fortune just waitin' for me. I suppose that sounds foolish given where I am now—old and without much of anything to show for my efforts."

Emily hated the sound of defeat in his voice. "But you have me." She turned and looked him in the eye. "And you had Mama's undying love. You can't say you haven't much of anything to show for your efforts. Many a man lives out his life without love. Just look at what Caeden had to go through with his father. Do you know Caeden told me that he had never thought such love existed before seeing our family? You have a wealth of love, Pa. That ought to count for something."

He gave her a smile, but in his eyes the weariness was evident. "I have been blessed with the love of a good wife and daughter, and it does count. It's all that keeps me goin' some days."

Emily knew she would never change his mind about mining. She knew it would be impossible to force him to change. She sighed and smiled. "I suppose we ought to get back to work. That cart isn't going to fill itself."

*

"We've looked all over for you. You didn't come back to the hotel for supper last night, and we feared the worst." Bishop Arnold looked at Caeden and then exchanged a glance with his daughter. "Did you . . . sleep elsewhere?"

"No. I ate elsewhere and returned to get an early night's sleep. Our business is settled, so I can't imagine what you needed from me."

Arnold smiled. "Well, the fact is there's a dance tomorrow and Catherine had her heart on attending. It's a fancy affair with many important people. I thought it would provide me the perfect opportunity to solicit support for the Republicans."

"You don't need me for that. I have no desire to dance, even if I had the clothes for a formal gathering. Which I don't."

"You are very nearly my size. I'm certain you could borrow some things from me and be just fine. I'm hoping that you'll do this as a favor to me." He held up his hands. "I know you don't owe me a favor, Caeden, but I am appealing to your better nature."

Caeden shook his head. "I don't have one."

Catherine reached out to touch Caeden's arm. "I would so enjoy dancing with you. I have so much to tell you."

She gave him a knowing look, reminding Caeden that she had been about to tell him something at their breakfast the previous day. He did battle with his conscience, thinking all the time of Emily. She so often endured unpleasantness for the sake of others. Couldn't he do the same—especially if it allowed him to finally hear what Catherine felt she needed to say?

"It would help me a great deal," Bishop Arnold interjected. "If you were watching over Catherine, then I would feel free to mingle among the men and solicit their support. Perhaps with their support, the loss of yours won't be so detrimental."

Caeden knew Arnold was trying to make him feel guilty, but it wouldn't work. If he agreed to this, it would be solely for the purpose of hearing what Catherine had to tell him.

"I will agree to accompany Catherine on one condition." Caeden narrowed his eyes and fixed Arnold with a hard stare. "You will from this time forward leave me alone. You will not seek me out for any reason, and you will accept that I've no intention or obligation to marry your daughter."

Arnold nodded. "Of course. Of course. That is perfectly acceptable." He flashed Catherine a look that gave Caeden pause. Were they plotting something together?

"The affair begins at six. I will have a carriage, so meet us here in the lobby at a quarter till. Oh, and I will send the bellboy with the clothes you'll need."

"Never mind that." Caeden wasn't about to wear Arnold's clothes. "I'll purchase what I need." He turned and headed out the doors he'd just come in. Hopefully this ordeal would be the end of his encounters with the Arnolds. But he doubted it.

꧁꧂

The following evening the carriage awaited him just as Arnold had promised. Arnold was dressed in his black evening wear and looked refined. Catherine's attire was hidden beneath a beautiful ivory and lavender cloak, but her blond hair had been arranged to perfection high atop her head. Caeden himself had managed to purchase a black suit—not evening wear, but it would do for the occasion.

They arrived in a crowd of other carriages and people. Caeden glanced at the mansion, noting candles in every window. The three-story house looked quite welcoming, but Caeden reminded himself of what he would have to endure throughout the evening. The large and opulent home of someone he'd never heard of might as well be a prison for the way it made him feel. He wondered why he'd ever agreed to such an affair.

"You look quite wonderful," Catherine whispered as they entered the ballroom. Her father walked sedately ahead of them, nodding and smiling to anyone who would look his way.

"It's amazing what money can buy." Caeden's tone was sarcastic, but he saw no reason to hide his feelings. "I hope you'll finally be able to tell me what it was you wanted me to know."

"I do too," she replied. "But it will have to wait until Father is through introducing us around."

Caeden grimaced. "I hope he'll be quick about it."

Catherine lowered her face and her voice. "Am I that much of a burden?"

He immediately felt bad for his attitude. While he despised Bishop Arnold, there was no reason to feel the same hatred for his daughter. In fact, in days gone by he'd actually enjoyed her company. Guilt stirred his conscience. Catherine was no doubt just as much a pawn in this game as he.

"I'm sorry. Let's start over." He'd said very little to her prior to this, not even bothering to compliment her on the beautiful gown of pale lavender silk. "You look lovely this evening, Miss Arnold. That shade is very becoming."

She smiled a look of gratitude. "Thank you so very much. It's kind of you to say so."

Caeden gave her a rare smile. "I hope you'll forgive my hostile demeanor. As you know, I had no intention of being here, but at least with you I know I won't be bored."

But before Catherine could reply, her father had turned to introduce them to the host of the party. After that it was one introduction after another until the musicians began to play and Caeden was able to whisk Catherine away for a waltz.

"Father will be miffed that we didn't stay," she said as Caeden turned her quite capably in the swirl of other dancers.

"I thought the whole idea of this evening was for me to keep you occupied so that he could see to business."

"Of course that was part of his thoughts."

Caeden frowned. "Surely nothing else involves me."

"Hopefully not."

"You are being rather mysterious. I thought you were going to explain something to me. Something about you not being of the same mind as your father."

Catherine winced, and Caeden realized he had tightened his hold on her gloved hand. "I apologize. I find this setting to be quite distasteful, but that's no call for me to forget my manners—or strength."

"I want you to know that I realize the great sacrifice you have made this evening. However, I do believe it's important. First and foremost, I have no more desire for us to marry than you do." She smiled. "Not that you aren't a fine catch."

Caeden felt a wave of relief in her confession. "And the same is true of you."

"Be that as it may," she continued, "I am going to tell you something that you must not repeat. Father would be livid if he knew I was sharing this with you."

Just then the music stopped. Caeden looked around as the musicians began a new tune, this one a reel. Couples began to take their places on the floor. "Why don't we have some punch? Maybe we can slip into one of the alcoves and speak uninterrupted."

She nodded. Caeden led her through the crowd of people. At the refreshment table he took up a cup of punch and handed it to her. He then directed her to a more private spot across the room. Once they were there, Caeden got immediately to the point.

"So what is it your father wouldn't want me to know?"

Catherine looked almost as if she might change her mind. She took a sip of the punch and wriggled her nose. "It's much too sweet."

Caeden took the cup from her and set it aside. "Go on."

She nodded. "Father is in grave financial crisis. He stands to lose everything."

"I'm sorry about that." Caeden frowned. He wasn't really sorry, but what could he say? "What does this have to do with me?"

Catherine looked out toward the dancers and other people milling around the sidelines of the room. "According to my father, your father encouraged him to make some risky investments. He rather insisted, in fact. However, your father took the money and used it for his own gain. He told Father that the investments had failed, when in fact there had never been any to begin with. Father feels cheated and has threatened to make a fuss about it and tie up you and your fortune in litigation."

"I see."

"Caeden, as I mentioned, I have no desire to marry you. Neither do I have any desire to marry one of my father's old cronies." She lowered her voice. "Which will happen if my father believes I'm not going to marry you."

"I'm sorry about that, but—"

"Please just hear me out." She looked quite uncomfortable. "Because of your father's forceful business dealings, my father is threatened with certain ruin. I know that you aren't responsible for your father's actions, but I would encourage you to find a way to help Father so that he won't seek legal action. That would only prove bad for both of you."

"So what is it you're suggesting?"

Catherine met his gaze, her green eyes pleading. "Tell him that you will marry me and give him a bride-price. I know you don't owe him for what your father did, but you can afford to be generous, and a dowry will solve his problems and keep him from marrying me off to someone else. You can insist that the engagement be long, and then after an appropriate time, you can call it off and tell him to keep the dowry. This will be beneficial to us both."

Unfortunately, Caeden could see that what she said made sense. If he appeased Arnold and sent him back to Albany to collect the dowry, then he would be free of him for the moment. And, as Catherine said, in time they could completely break the engagement.

"I don't like being manipulated."

She let go a heavy breath. "Neither do I, but you know that in this day and age women have no say in their futures. Father will sell me off to the highest bidder and not care one whit that he sends me to a loveless marriage. I know I don't have any right to ask this of you, Caeden, but I am begging you to reconsider and help me."

Caeden didn't like the position he was being put into, but he felt sorry for Catherine. Her sincerity reminded him of Emily. What if Emily were being forced into such a position? Caeden knew there would be no need for consideration. He would help her no matter what.

"I suppose," he began after some thought, "that it wouldn't hurt anything if we pretended to go forward with the engagement. You're right in saying that I can afford to give him money. Furthermore, I will have my uncle look into the situation, and if my father cheated yours, then I will see restitution is made." He could see the relief on her face.

"However, you need to know without a doubt that I will not marry you. I don't want a scene months from now with your tears and pleading that I misunderstood and that you cannot lose me."

She smiled. "I assure you that won't happen. I am in love with someone else. Father knows nothing about him, and that's how I intend to keep it until we have the opportunity to elope. Once we're married he will have no say in the matter."

"So how will I know when this time comes and the engagement can be broken?"

"I will get word to you. I don't intend to let this go on for long. Having you tell Father that you want a long engagement will ease the tension for both of us. In the meantime, I will be able to work things out. I will let you know as soon as possible. I honestly don't think it need take longer than a month—maybe two. I believe by the time you complete your work in Washington, DC, and return to New York, we should be able to conclude this sham."

Caeden gave a reluctant nod. "Very well. I will do this for you."

She surprised him by embracing him. She placed a very quick, chaste kiss on his cheek. "Thank you, Caeden. I know this isn't to your liking, but you truly are a knight in shining armor to me. When shall we tell Father?"

"The sooner the better, I suppose."

"I agree. He's standing alone right now. Come. Let's share the news."

# 14

*B*ishop Arnold looked as if he might burst his vest button. He gave an enthusiastic smile to Caeden and Catherine as he joined them for breakfast the next morning.

"I must say, you two have made me the happiest of men. I knew if I could just get you alone with Catherine you would see her merits. Not only that, but at the party I met a gentleman who has offered me a great investment proposition. He's going to join us." Arnold picked up his napkin. "I am beyond delighted by all that has happened." He reached out and patted Catherine's hand. "This will be the wedding all of New York will talk about for years to come."

Caeden refrained from speaking sarcasm and instead offered Arnold a plate of biscuits. "I don't intend to marry her tomorrow. I prefer a lengthy engagement." Arnold's expression sobered. "You needn't look downcast," Caeden continued. "I intend for you to receive a large dowry upon your return to Albany."

"That's good of you," Arnold said, nodding in approval. He took several biscuits, then passed the plate to Catherine. "And what of the original contract?"

Anger rose, but Caeden managed to stuff it back down. "I had no part in that contract and do not intend to honor it. You will receive a substantial amount of money as a bride-price, but nothing else. I'll wire my uncle, and he will arrange the entire matter. As you know, I am to meet up with other geologists in Havre by the first, and from there I will be headed to Washington to share the findings of my research."

"You will return to Albany for the Christmas season now, won't you? I know Catherine will want to announce her engagement to everyone. In fact, Mrs. Arnold and I will want to host a party for just that purpose."

Caeden frowned. "I don't believe I can be there much earlier than Christmas itself. Perhaps it would be best to wait until after the New Year." He cast a quick glance at Catherine, who nodded most enthusiastically.

"Yes, Father. I wouldn't want to simply announce such an important thing at just any party. I believe we should wait until you and Mother can host a proper engagement affair. Otherwise it will lessen the importance."

"Nonsense. Nothing could lessen the importance of you marrying one of the wealthiest men in New York. However, I do understand Caeden's obligations. We can wait until after the New Year if that meets with your approval."

She smiled and passed the biscuits back to Caeden without taking one. "It does. Furthermore, I would appreciate it if you would refrain from sharing the news with your business associates. I would like this to be a surprise for everyone."

"It won't be much of a surprise. Everyone knows you two are intended for each other and have been for several years."

"I realize that, Father." She reached out and placed her hand atop his. "But I ask that you do this for me."

"Of course. It's hard to deny you anything when I feel this happy."

Caeden took a bite of biscuit. He was glad to have the matter resolved and happy to know that he would keep Catherine from being forced to marry someone she didn't love. What left him less than content was the thought of leaving Emily. As he had told her and the Arnolds, he had no interest in marriage. At least he hadn't when he'd come to Montana. Now, however, he couldn't put Emily from his mind. Perhaps once he'd concluded his business with the government, he would return to New York City, speak with the gemstone expert, and then make his way back to Montana. He liked the area well enough, and if it meant he might be able to properly court Emily, he liked it all the more.

"Oh, here's a man I want you to meet," Arnold declared, getting to his feet. Caeden did the expected thing and rose as well.

"We met last night, and I must say this man has given me much to consider. Caeden Thibault, meet Septimus Singleton." He looked at Singleton. "This young man is the head of Thibault Industries in New York."

Caeden was well familiar with the newcomer's name. "Mr. Singleton." He shook the man's hand. "Won't you join us?"

Singleton seemed more than a little pleased. He quickly pulled out a chair as if fearful Caeden might change his mind. "I am happy to make your acquaintance."

Once they were all seated again, Caeden motioned for the waitress. She came to the table and took Singleton's order before the conversation began again.

"I had the good fortune to connect with Mr. Singleton at the dance last night," Arnold began. "He told me about some investments I might consider."

Caeden figured the investments had something to do with the

mining claims Singleton had been buying. "I see." He continued to eat his breakfast. "I hope they will work well for you."

"I think you'll find it all quite interesting," Bishop Arnold continued. "Mr. Singleton has just come from the same area in which you've been working these last months."

Caeden saw Singleton's brows come together just before he lowered his head to cough. The announcement had obviously made him uneasy.

"I have heard Mr. Singleton's name mentioned in the Utica and Yogo City areas. I believe you've been busy buying gold mines."

Singleton's head shot up. "Keep it down, Mr. Thibault, I beg you. We don't need to announce this to the world." He looked around the room as if to ascertain if they'd been overheard.

"As Mr. Arnold said, I've been around those areas since late summer. I'm a geologist working for the government."

"Singleton is looking for investors," Arnold announced. He poured a healthy portion of gravy over his biscuits. "He cannot shoulder all of the responsibility himself, and given the abundance he's already discovered, I am quite intrigued."

Caeden could see that Singleton looked uncomfortable. "So you believe the claims are that good? In my investigation of the area, I didn't find any large deposits of"—he lowered his voice—"gold."

"It's there, I assure you," Singleton quickly countered. He fidgeted with his napkin. "I have . . . had good results. There is quality ore to be had. I've already made quite a fortune."

"Then why would you want investors?" Caeden smiled. "It seems you would want to keep the profits from this yourself."

"Oh, I do. And I have. However, there will be more than enough to go around once the main vein is revealed, which should be any day now. I'm not a greedy man." He smiled at

Arnold. "Once the main vein is discovered, there will be more gold than one man can manage. Of course, I have already hired several men to assist me in the actual work. I believe good fortune should be shared."

Caeden would have laughed, but that would have spoiled any chance of revealing the man's deception. "I believe there have been several gold strikes in that area over the last score of years. What makes you think you will be the one to finally reveal the main vein?"

"Because I have already taken a large amount of gold from the claims I have." Singleton puffed out his chest. "And I have a nose for these things. I always have."

The waitress brought his food. "Will there be anything else?"

Caeden looked to the others. "I don't believe so. Gentlemen? Catherine?"

They all agreed they were fine. The waitress nodded, then hurried to another table where new guests had just taken their seats.

Bishop Arnold jumped right in. "I'm quite excited about the possibilities."

"Mining is a very uncertain thing." Caeden offered the warning even knowing Arnold wouldn't listen. Singleton quickly dug into his breakfast and ate in silence while Arnold continued the conversation.

"There are risks in every investment. I believe in checking these things out thoroughly, however. That is why I have agreed to accompany Mr. Singleton to Utica."

This took Caeden by surprise. "You have?"

Arnold nodded. "Catherine and I will accompany him on the stage in the morning."

Caeden shook his head. "That's very rough country. Catherine wouldn't be at all comfortable."

181

"I won't leave her here unaccompanied," Arnold declared. "Besides, she's heartier than she looks. I believe she'll do just fine. We'll go there with Mr. Singleton and inspect the mining claim he proposes to sell me. If everything looks good, we'll make a contract."

"And how will you know if it looks good?" Caeden asked, pushing his plate back. "It's not like gold nuggets are just lying on the ground. Do you even know what you're looking for?"

"I will," Arnold said, looking rather perturbed. "Mr. Singleton has promised me that his men will be most useful in explaining it all."

"That's right, you have one man in particular who helped you achieve those claims. I believe his name is Davies. Kirk Davies. I remember the name because I found it most unusual that such a ruffian should bear a name associated with church. I believe *Kirk* is Scottish for such a place, is it not?"

"Be that as it may," Singleton finally joined in, "he's been a great help to me."

Caeden wanted to punch the man in the mouth but held his temper. "As I understand it, he was quite threatening to some of those who didn't want to sell."

Singleton laughed nervously. "Nonsense. He might have pressed to persuade them, but he wouldn't threaten anyone. That's not how I do business."

"Well, I am relieved to hear that." Caeden took up his coffee cup. "So I suppose you are finished with trying to purchase claims in the area."

"For the most part," Singleton replied. He again looked quite uneasy. "I have extended the opportunity to those remaining, and if they wish to sell to me in the future, I will still be open to such an arrangement."

"Caeden, we'd like very much if you would accompany us,"

Arnold said, not seeming to realize his new friend's discomfort. "You know the area quite well, and your geological knowledge would lend itself to a better and more complete inspection."

Singleton looked stunned. "I don't think that's necessary. We wouldn't want to arouse suspicion."

Caeden could see the man was upset by even the possibility of Caeden joining them. "I am obligated to meet my team members and return to Washington." Singleton's relief was evident, but he covered it up by ducking his head to refocus on a cup of coffee.

"But couldn't you have your information delivered to them and join them a few days late?" Arnold asked.

Ideas were already churning in Caeden's head. As much as he'd love to see Singleton proved wrong, he wanted even more to see Emily again. To see her and ask her to wait for him. If he could just have more time with her, Caeden was certain he could settle matters between them.

"I suppose it might be a possibility," Caeden finally answered.

Singleton looked none too happy. "You needn't put aside your plans, Mr. Thibault. I assure you I am able to show proof of the claim's richness."

"I'm sure you can, Mr. Singleton. But the fact is, I have a bit of unsettled business in the area, and I believe Mr. Arnold would feel more confident if I was a part of his decision."

"I would," Arnold assured him.

Singleton nodded. "Very well. Then I shall meet with all of you in the morning. The stage leaves at six." He got to his feet. "It's been a pleasure, gentlemen . . . Miss Arnold." He gave a bow and then pulled some money from his pocket. "This should cover breakfast for all of you." He left the money on the table.

Caeden and Arnold stood. "That's most generous, Mr.

Singleton." Caeden could see that the older man was pleased at such praise.

"It's nothing. I'm happy to do it."

He quickly departed the dining room, leaving Caeden to turn his attention back on Bishop Arnold. "You do realize that a great many swindles are going on where mines are concerned. I am quite certain this man is up to no good."

"Well, the inspection will surely prove that," Arnold said, reclaiming his chair. "I find the entire matter more than a little intriguing. I find the idea of owning a gold mine to be quite exciting."

Caeden could see that the man was already succumbing to gold fever. There was no reasoning with him at this point. Let him go to the mine and see the worthlessness of it. Of course, Singleton would no doubt salt it with enough gold to entice Arnold.

He shook his head, knowing the impossibility of convincing some people that their ideas were bad. "Well, if I'm to accompany you tomorrow, I need to attend to business today. If you'll excuse me." He nodded to Catherine and then to her father. "It would be prudent to refrain from giving any money to Singleton until you have proof beyond a doubt." He started to walk away, then turned back. "You also might wish to buy some wool blankets. The trip by stage can be very cold."

◦⊱⊰◦

Emily had never worked harder than she had in the days since Caeden's departure. As her father predicted, colder temperatures had settled over the region and made digging most difficult. Even at the piles of dirt they had brought down to the river, her father had needed to keep a fire going to make it easier to work the soil.

Each day, Emily saw to the animals and then joined her father at the river washing and sluicing through the dirt they had managed to haul down. Each night she fell into bed so exhausted that she went to sleep almost immediately. It gave her little time to really think about Caeden, and that was just the way she wanted it.

Her father managed to collect some gold, although it was hardly worthy of a celebration. If they were lucky it might provide a month's worth of supplies. Always there were more of the blue pebbles to collect. They irritated her father to no end as they clogged up the sluice. However, Emily couldn't help but think how they might be valuable, and she always cleared the pieces away for her father and tucked them into her pocket for safekeeping. She was once again amassing quite a collection.

Emily suppressed a yawn and looked out over the river valley—what little she could see. There was still snow on the ground, but this morning there had been an ice fog as well, and everything seemed covered in diamond dust. It was quite pretty but made long-distance visibility almost impossible.

Nellie pawed at the ground, causing Emily to reach into the cart and retrieve a nice armful of hay. "Here you are, old girl." She tossed the hay on the ground, then gave Nellie's muzzle a gentle rub. "Eat up, for the winter is coming, and you need to be nice and fat."

Pa laughed and picked up his shovel. "I think if I can get just a little more gold together over the next day or two, we can head up to Utica and pick up some supplies."

"I think that would be wise." Emily thought of the long list of needs. "We definitely should buy more blankets, and it would be helpful if we could get a few canvas tarps for the walls. That would help keep out some of the cold."

"I agree. We'll just see what we can pull out today and add it to what we've already set aside. That way we can better know how much we'll have to meet our needs."

"You aren't going to have needs much longer, old man."

Emily froze. The voice of Kirk Davies was not one she had expected. In his absence she had hoped they were finally rid of him. She sunk her hand into her coat pocket, reassuring herself that the pistol was still there.

"The time has come for you to pay your debt," Davies said, stepping out of the fog. He held a long-barreled pistol aimed directly at her father. His short leather coat gave evidence of another revolver tucked in his waistband.

Without thinking, Emily put herself between them. If need be, she would shoot Davies and keep him from hurting her father.

"Now, isn't that sweet." Davies' sarcastic tone made her skin crawl.

"Emily, you need to leave," Father declared. "I'll settle this alone."

"No you won't. My business is with both of you." Davies surprised Emily by crossing the distance in a matter of seconds. He took her in hand and pulled her tight against him. "Like I said, the time has come for you to pay up."

"Pay up for what?"

Emily could hear the agitation in her father's voice. "Let me go." She tried to pull away, but Davies was much too strong.

He leered down at her. "No, little lady, you're my assurance that this old man will do exactly what I want." He looked back to her father. "You were hard enough to track down, but now that I have you where I want you, I'm going to take my time and enjoy this."

"What are you talking about? I've been here all along. You knew that. Even after someone . . ." He paused and narrowed his eyes. "Even after someone burned down my cabin and killed my wife, I've been right here." Emily saw her father take a step forward, but Davies shook his head, and he stopped.

"You deserved that and more. You killed my little brother in California."

The statement was so matter-of-fact that Emily wasn't at all sure she'd heard correctly. Her father, however, immediately understood.

"So that was your brother. He was quite the bully. Always makin' trouble and shootin' folks. He threatened to kill a man's child. I could hardly stand by and do nothing."

Emily remembered that day in the California mining camp and bit her lip. Davies hadn't come here to buy her father's claim for Singleton as he'd said. That had only been a convenient excuse. Instead, he had come with his own purpose of revenge.

"It doesn't matter to me what he did," Davies said, loosening his hold on Emily. "Fact is you killed him, and now I'm going to kill you."

Emily knew this would be her only chance to intervene. She pulled away from Davies, drawing her pistol. It caught on the edge of her pocket, however, and before she knew it, Davies had taken the gun from her. With a powerful backhand he slapped her to the ground, then stepped on the material of her coat and skirt to keep her from moving. It happened so fast that her father could do nothing to help.

"You can't do this," she told Davies. She rubbed her jaw where Davies had struck her. The pain was fierce. "Your brother shot my father and would have killed that family. It wasn't murder. My father never intended for him to die. He just wanted to stop him."

"Like I said, I don't much care what happened. He killed my brother, and now I'm going to kill him." He pulled back the hammer on his gun. "Say your prayers, old man, and say one for her. 'Cause after I kill you, I'm going to make her wish she were dead."

Emily knew her father, and when he charged forward, she wasn't surprised. She heard the gun go off and did the only thing she could think to do. Taking hold of Davies' leg, she bit his thigh as hard as she could and held on tight. He screamed in agony, cursing her. Emily held on, even though he grabbed a handful of her hair to pull her away. She could taste blood as it oozed through the torn trouser. She had no idea if her father was dead or alive, but she'd make certain Davies never forgot his mistake of messing with her.

"Henry, that you shootin'?" someone called out in the fog.

Davies let go a stream of curses, and Emily felt something hard hit the back of her head. Her jaw went slack as the day grew dark. She fought for consciousness, but the blow was too much. As Davies moved out, Emily fell against the frozen ground.

# 15

*E*mily awoke to searing pain and merciless motion. She opened her eyes just enough to see that she was in the back of a wagon and Millie Ringgold was there beside her.

"Where am I? What happened?"

"Jes yo hush, chil'. Somebody done shot yo pa and nearly kilt yo with a blow to de head. Yo bled a lot."

"Pa? Is he alive? Where is he?" She tried to sit up, but Millie held her fast.

"It's bad. Yo pa is gut shot. Went straight through, but it don't look good."

"Where is he?" Her head was about to explode, and Emily closed her eyes, hoping the pain would ease. It didn't.

"De boys got yo pa in de other wagon. Weren't room in yo pa's cart here."

"I don't remember much." Emily tried to force her mind to sort through the darkness. She raised her hand to her brow, hoping it might ease the pain.

"Do yo know who shot yor pa and hit yo?"

Emily remembered they were sluicing, and Pa said something

about going to Utica. Then someone came. She opened her eyes. "I know we were working the sluice. I remember . . . Kirk Davies. He was there. He must have done it."

"That man ain't good for nuttin'." Millie patted Emily's shoulder. "Don't yo worry none. We'll let the marshal know."

Emily gave herself over to unconsciousness once more, and when she next awoke, she was lying on a bed and her head didn't hurt quite as bad. She looked around the room as best she could without moving her head. It was a small, sparsely furnished room. The bed and the small table beside it were the only things that occupied the space.

She stared at the ceiling and tried to remember the details of what had happened and why she was there. Wherever she was. Image chased after image in her mind, and none of them made any sense. Why couldn't she remember?

"I see yo is awake," Millie said, coming into the room with a glass of something.

"I'm trying to be. Where am I?"

"Doc's place in Utica."

"What happened?"

Millie put the glass down on the table and came to sit beside Emily on the narrow bed. The movement caused by the stocky woman made Emily wince, but Millie didn't seem to notice.

"Don't yo remember? I done tol' yo already. Yo pa was shot, and yo got hit on de head. Yo said it were Kirk Davies who done it."

"Pa? Where is he?" Emily tried to sit up, but Millie pressed her shoulders back down. "Yo ain't gwanna get up. Doc wants yo stayin' down."

"But I have to see my father. How is he?"

"It be bad, Miss Emily. Doc say he has to go to Lewistown. He sewed him up and stopped de bleedin', but he say more has to be done and he can't do it."

"If he's going to Lewistown, then I'm going with him." She looked at Millie. "I have to. He can't go alone."

"Doc won't allow for dat."

"He'll have to. Please go get him."

Millie got to her feet. "I don't s'pose I can convince yo to stay." She shook her head and muttered to herself all the way out the door.

Emily drew a deep breath and forced herself to sit up. Her brown hair fell about her shoulders. She touched her head where the pain seemed the most intense and felt bandages. Just how bad was her injury?

It was only a few minutes before the doctor appeared. "What's this all about, young woman? You need to rest."

"I need to be with my father. How is he?"

The doctor's expression turned grave. "He's not good. I can't do enough for him here, so we're rigging a wagon to take him to Lewistown."

"I need to go with him."

"You need to rest and heal," the doctor replied. "I had to put twelve stitches in your head."

"I understand, but my father will need me there." Emily fought back the urge to cry out from the pain. A wave of nausea washed over her, but she fought that as well.

"Your father won't even know you're there." The doctor came closer. "The bullet went right through him and out the back. It narrowly missed the main artery. Even so, he's lost a lot of blood, and even if he recovers, I doubt he'll ever walk again. The bullet passed very close to the spine."

Emily could hardly bear the news. She had only just lost her mother. How could she lose her father as well? Was this what God had in mind for her future? Where was the comfort that her faith should have afforded her?

"I want to see the marshal before we leave."

The doctor looked to Millie, who had remained in the doorway. "Go get him."

She disappeared, and the doctor turned back to Emily. "If I allow you to go, you must rest on the way and once you get there as well. You won't be any good to your father if you don't."

"I understand, but I need to be close by in case . . . in case . . . the worst happens." Emily forced back her tears. Her head already felt as though it would burst, and crying would certainly not help matters.

"I want you to lie back and rest for now. As I said, we're rigging a special wagon for your father. The jostling could well kill him, so we're making a sort of sling for him to lie in. I don't imagine we'll move him for another hour."

"If the jostling could kill him, why not leave him here?" She didn't like the sound of the risk they were taking with her father's life.

"If he remains here he will certainly die. I'm not qualified to care for wounds like his. So we have to take a chance. The hospital in Lewistown has a fine surgeon. I believe your father's only hope is to get him there."

Emily gave just a hint of a nod. The doctor put his hand on her shoulder. "Now let me help you to lie back. You need to rest. The trip won't be easy for you."

"I don't care."

Before she allowed the doctor to ease her back onto the bed, the marshal entered the room. He gave Emily a nod. "How are you feeling?"

"My head hurts." She licked her dry lips. "But I had to talk to you about all of this."

"What do you remember?"

"Pa and I were working the sluice. Kirk Davies showed up,

and it gets pretty blurry after that. I know he had a gun and that he hit me. I . . . I think . . . I bit him." She put her fingers to her lips and nodded. "Yes, I'm certain I bit him on the leg. I can't remember much else."

"I'm afraid your mind is playing tricks on you," the marshal answered. His tone was more sympathetic. "You did suffer a hard blow."

Emily frowned. "What do you mean?"

The marshal shrugged. "It couldn't have been Davies."

"I'm telling you it was. I know it was." She looked at the doctor and then back at the marshal. A fleeting memory came to mind. "He blamed my father for killing his younger brother. It was when we lived in California."

"I'm sorry, Miss Carver. I know that man pestered a lot of folks in Yogo, your family included. I know you figure he set the fire that killed your ma, and maybe he did. I never found anything to prove that, however. But this time you're wrong. It wasn't Davies."

"You're wrong." She shook her head harder than she meant to and nearly cried out at the pain. "It *was* Davies."

The marshal looked to the ground for a moment and then back to Emily. "It couldn't have been Kirk Davies. I don't know the fella all that well, but Davies was in my jail last night. I didn't let him go until just after they showed up with you and your pa."

Emily felt as though the entire world had turned on its ear. Her stomach churned, and she was certain she couldn't have heard right. "Davies was in your jail?"

The marshal gave a brief nod. "He was. He was brawling yesterday and tore up one of the saloons. My deputy brought him in. I'm sorry, but it wasn't him this time."

The nausea returned. "I think I'm going to be sick." Emily

clutched her stomach as the doctor reached down beside the bed and produced a bucket.

"You might as well go, Marshal. If you would, please send Miss Ringgold back in."

He nodded, his gaze never leaving Emily. "I'm sure sorry, Miss Carver."

⚬⚭⚬

Caeden hated the painful jostling of the stage as it made its way along rutted roads to Utica. He hated even more being wedged against the window due to Singleton's stocky frame taking up a good portion of the seat. Across from them, Bishop Arnold and Catherine sat along with an older woman who was bound for Lewistown. At least they all had seats inside. Caeden knew there were at least two men riding on top with the driver.

When they'd first climbed into the stage, it appeared as though Singleton and Arnold would say nothing more about their venture. However, as the miles clicked by and boredom set in, the two men began discussing details about the mine. Caeden saw the older woman doze off. Her snoring left Singleton feeling safe enough to speak in detail about what Arnold could expect.

Caeden had little desire to share in the conversation and closed his eyes. For most of the trip he pretended to sleep, grateful that the two men seemed quite happy to leave him out of their discussion.

"I believe you can recoup your investment within a month's time," Singleton declared.

"Truly?" Bishop Arnold replied. "That's marvelous. What will be required?"

"Well, after you purchase the claim from me," Singleton began, "you'll need to hire workers and supplies for those work-

194

ers. You'll need shovels, picks, and ore carts. Oh, and mules. You'll need mules to haul the dirt and ore to where the water is so you can wash it."

"Wash the dirt? Why would anyone do that?" Arnold asked. "I thought gold mining consisted of breaking ore out of rock."

"There is, of course, that kind of mining—when a vein is found. We are very close to exposing that vein, but right now we are working the dirt and flushing out the bits of gold hidden in it. It's not that difficult." He smiled. "We can go over the details after you secure the claim. You'll need someone you can trust to run the operation. Of course, winter is a difficult time to mine, but with the right people it can be done. These Montana folks are a hearty bunch, and I don't think you'll have trouble getting men who want to work."

Caeden listened to the man drone on and on. It was impossible to get comfortable, but he finally managed to doze at one point, and his thoughts were all about Emily. He was glad he'd been able to arrange for the freight of goods to leave ahead of his departure from Great Falls. It was possible he'd catch up to the shipment in Utica and could be there to instruct locals on the delivery. He didn't want to be there when Emily and her father received the goods, so his thought was to delay the delivery in Utica until he'd gone.

He'd lost track of the stage stops and changes of horses. All he knew was that from Great Falls to Utica the distance was nearly eighty miles. Eighty miles plus the eighteen to where Emily and her father lived. Nearly one hundred miles altogether. It might as well have been a thousand for all the time it was taking.

At the halfway mark they stopped for the night. The place wasn't much, but it was clean and the food decent. That night, Caeden fell asleep and dreamed of his encounter with Emily and how he would explain his heart and ask if she would wait for him to return. He could see her clothed in the new gown he'd bought her. The dusty rose would look beautiful with her dark eyes and hair. He'd even purchased her a parasol of the same color. He doubted Emily had ever had a parasol. Such a frivolous item wouldn't have been considered important.

The next morning, after a breakfast of watered-down oatmeal and bacon, they were once again on their way. Caeden almost felt sorry for Arnold. The man was so obviously uncomfortable. He'd already complained several times of his miseries in trying to sleep the night before. Not only that, but the food had also caused him great discomfort.

Singleton apparently had wearied of the man's complaints and had engaged the elderly Mrs. Dyson in a conversation about her family in Lewistown. It was to his droning voice, telling her about the time he'd spent in Lewistown years ago, that Caeden drifted off.

"Caeden, wake up," Catherine said, giving his arm a shake.

He opened his eyes and moaned. Rubbing a knot in his neck, he straightened and looked around. He found himself alone with Catherine and the stage at a stop. "Where are we?"

"I don't know. Yet another change of teams. This stop, however, is offering food if you're hungry. Father, Mr. Singleton, and Mrs. Dyson all went inside. I wondered if you wanted to join them. I don't think I could keep anything down. This trip is rather jarring."

"I told you it was rough country." Caeden looked out the coach window at the small house. He feared the meal would be as distasteful as their breakfast and decided against it. He figured he could get something better in Utica.

"I knew it would be hard," Catherine said, trying to shake the dust from her dark blue traveling suit. "I wasn't the one who insisted on coming. I would have happily waited in Great Falls."

"I am going to get down and stretch." He rubbed his neck again. "You should take a walk around as well. I'm sure there are facilities for freshening up."

"Yes," she said, nodding. "I suppose you're right."

Caeden opened the coach door and stepped down. The air had turned much colder. He glanced at the sky and saw a bank of clouds moving in from the south. "Looks like we may be in for snow or rain." So far the weather had been good and the trip uncomplicated. If it started snowing, they could be delayed for days.

He helped Catherine from the coach and offered her his arm. "I'm sure," she said, taking hold of him, "Father will be pleased at this display of intimacy."

"Your father is a fool. There's no gold in those mines. At least not the kind Singleton promises him. He's going to put himself in further debt and have nothing to show for it. It will be his ruin."

Catherine looked quite alarmed. "Are you certain?"

"I am. I know the area and have been studying the mineral potential for months. I just don't foresee a large strike. I could be wrong, of course, but I don't think I am."

She tightened her hold on his arm. "What can we do?"

"I don't know. I suppose once we get there and actually see the mines Singleton is offering, I can share my opinion, but when I gave it earlier no one actually cared. Besides that, if Singleton is the charlatan that I believe him to be, he will no doubt have made arrangements to ensure there is gold in the mine he wants to sell your father. He'll probably go so far as to have actual nuggets lying around."

They reached the house, but Catherine made no effort to

move from Caeden's side. "I don't know what will become of our family if he buys the mine and nothing comes of it." She gave a heavy sigh. "These have been such difficult times. He and Mother fight constantly over money. He's sold off all but one carriage and three horses. He even sold some of Mother's jewelry."

"I am sorry. I wired my uncle to look into the matter between your father and mine. I meant what I said. If I have proof of my father cheating yours, I will repay with interest."

She smiled and gave his arm a squeeze. "You are a good man, Caeden. One day you will make a good husband and father."

Her words stayed with him even after they were once again on their way. Emily had said something similar. Could he be a good husband and father? The only example he'd had was no good. Of course, he'd witnessed other men with their families, but his own was good at putting on a show in public. Caeden knew better than to believe that the person a man was in the midst of his peers was the same man in the privacy of his home.

Doubts began to build, and Caeden found himself questioning his plans to ask Emily to wait for him. She had known life with a loving father. But Henry Carver was also a selfish man to drag his loved ones around in search of a dream that most likely would never come. Caeden had to allow that every man was flawed and full of self-interest. After all, he could claim no less for himself. However, he hated the idea of Emily going on day after day hoping and praying for her father to find the treasure he sought.

*But the sapphires could be quite valuable. And if they are, then Henry will have his fortune—his buried treasure.*

Caeden thought of his mother and her faith that Archibald Thibault could change. Right up until her last breath, she told Caeden he needed to have faith. But Caeden knew it was going to take more than faith to be the man he wanted to be. His anger and bitter heart had kept him closed off and unwilling to give of himself.

*God, I don't know if I can change. I don't know if I can let this hatred go.*

When he realized he was praying, it startled Caeden enough that he sat straight up on the coach seat.

"Are you all right?"

Caeden looked at Singleton. The man looked back at him with concern. Caeden nodded. "I'm fine." He caught Catherine's worried expression. Thankfully, Mrs. Dyson and Bishop Arnold had dozed off.

Caeden settled back in his seat. "I'm quite fine. Just had some disquieting thoughts."

# 16

*E*mily waited impatiently for news of her father. The county farm, or poorhouse as most called it, also served as a hospital to the indigent of the area. The people were kind, and the doctor seemed quite capable. At one point he had even called in a surgeon. The doctor assured her that her father was receiving the very best of care, but Emily found the wait almost unbearable.

Of course, the doctor had great concern for her as well. When they'd first arrived, he had tried his best to put her to bed too, but Emily refused. She insisted instead that they allow her to sit outside the room where her father was being kept. That way should anything happen, good or bad, she would be there at his side. For the next twenty-four hours it seemed there was a constant parade of people in and out of her father's room, but still the doctor would not allow her admission.

Her head continued to throb, but for Emily that pain was nothing compared to the piercing ache in her heart. She had just lost her mother, and now her father lay near death. What would be left to her if he should die? There was no other family.

Emily knew she could turn to Millie, but that would only be a temporary solution. There was no work to be had in Yogo City or Utica for that matter.

The idea of work had crossed her mind more than once. What little she'd heard from the doctor made it clear that her father would be weeks, if not months, in bed. Emily knew she would have to find a way to provide for herself. She pulled Millie's shawl close, wondering only momentarily what had happened to her own coat. For some reason she had been separated from it in Utica.

"I wish you would go get some rest."

She looked up to find her father's doctor studying her with an expression of concern. "Your father hasn't even regained consciousness, and frankly that's for the best at this point. He needs a time of absolute rest in order for the swelling to go down. You could use that time to get some rest yourself."

She stood and waited for the momentary dizziness to stop. "I appreciate your concern, but I want to see him."

The doctor nodded. "Very well. Come with me."

Emily followed him into the room where her father had been since they'd brought him in the night before. She thought for a moment that the doctor had been wrong and that her father was dead. He was so gray and still. She edged closer to the bed.

"The surgery went well. I believe he will recover if we can prevent infection from setting in."

It was the first hopeful thing anyone had said. Emily looked to the doctor. "You believe he'll live?"

The older man smiled. "I am cautiously optimistic. That's all I can be for now. Your father narrowly escaped death. I'm still not at all certain how he managed to make it this far. However, he seems to be made of stronger stuff than I gave him credit for."

Emily nodded. She felt the strain of her injury and the last twenty-four hours taking its toll. Just as her knees buckled, the doctor caught her around the waist.

"You're going to bed now. Doctor's orders."

She didn't argue.

⁂

Waking up in a strange place was most disconcerting. For a moment, Emily couldn't remember where she was or why. The large dormitory-style room was arranged in a neat and orderly fashion. She saw there were two other beds occupied, but several others were empty.

She sat up and slid her legs over the edge of the bed. To her surprise she didn't feel dizzy. Perhaps she was finally starting to heal. Emily allowed herself a moment and then tested her strength by standing. Her head hurt, but the pounding was gone and so too the cloudiness that kept her from being able to think clearly.

She saw a woman at the end of the room. She was dressed in black with a starched white apron. Emily made her way to where the woman worked at cleaning off a tray.

"How are you feeling, Miss Carver?"

Emily was surprised that the woman knew her name. "I am better."

She smiled. "I was beginning to wonder if you'd sleep straight through another night."

"Another night?" Emily looked around her. "How long did I sleep?"

"Probably not as long as the doctor would like." The woman—older than Emily had first thought—smiled, revealing several holes where teeth should have been. "He tends to be strict when it comes to his patients."

Emily knew the only patient who really mattered was her father. "Can you tell me how to find my pa?" She figured if the woman knew her name, she would also know her father.

"I'll take you there. The doctor should be with him." She put the tray aside and led Emily through the door and down the hall. There was no further exchange between them, and for this Emily was grateful. She didn't want to talk about her condition or make small talk. She only wanted to know how her father was doing.

The doctor glanced up when he heard the door open. He beamed Emily a smile. "Come and see who's awake."

Emily saw that her father was looking at her with great concern. "Emmy?"

"I'm here." She rushed to his bedside. "Oh, Pa." She shook her head at the sight of him lying there. "How are you feeling?"

"Been better." He looked at the doctor. "I 'spect he can tell you more than I can."

Emily turned to face the physician. "How is he?"

"So far he's doing well. There's been only a slight fever, and the wound sites look good. I'll leave you two to talk, but, Miss Carver, don't make it long. Your father needs absolute rest—no movement whatsoever. I've given him something to make him sleep and keep him still." He reached toward Emily's head. "First let me take a look at your wound. Sit here." He motioned to the chair beside the bed.

Emily took a seat and waited while he unwound the bandage and set it aside. The spot was tender as he moved her hair. "Your wound looks good, although how that Utica physician managed to stitch it so neatly without shaving off a good portion of your hair is quite beyond me." He stepped back and smiled. "Wouldn't do for such a pretty young woman to be bald. We needn't worry about rebandaging."

She nodded. Once the doctor had gone she looked down at her father. "Now you tell me how you feel, and don't try to lie to me. I want the truth."

Henry Carver gave a hint of a smile. "You sound just like your ma. Honestly, I'm doing fine. I can't feel much below my chest, but the doctor said that's to be expected because of the swelling." Then his expression changed. "But what of you? There's a bruise on your face and a wound atop your head. What's happened to you?"

He didn't remember that Davies had struck her? Of course he wouldn't know about Davies hitting her with the butt of his pistol, because he'd already been shot. "Davies shot you and I bit him. Then he hit me over the head. The doctor in Utica said he put in twelve stitches, but it feels like it might have been a hundred."

Tears came to her father's eyes. "I'm sorry. I should have been better prepared. Since he hadn't been around, I guess I thought maybe he'd moved on."

"Well, here's the strange thing about it all. The marshal in Utica told me it couldn't have been Davies." She stated the information in a matter-of-fact manner. "He said Kirk Davies was in his jail all night and the next day until we arrived in our wounded state."

"I guess I don't remember much." Her father closed his eyes. "Are you absolutely sure it was Davies?"

"Yes." Emily didn't wait for him to ask further questions on the matter. "I know it was him, and I can prove it with that bite. I bit him hard. He must have a good-sized wound on his left thigh."

Her father opened his eyes again. "You stay away from him, Em. He's no good, and if he was responsible for all of this, then he's going to consider us unfinished business."

She didn't want to give her father any reason to worry. "I

don't intend to go looking for him, Pa." At least that much was true. "I do, however, plan to have another talk with the marshal when I get back to Utica." Of course, that wouldn't be for some time.

"Men like him never give up," her father muttered.

"He blames us for the death of his brother."

"He blames me," her father said. "That much I remember. In fact, it's coming back to me. I remember it was Davies. All of this is about punishing me. And all I can do is lie here and not move."

Emily could hear the weariness in his voice. "I promise you, I'll be careful. I'm going to leave you to rest like I promised the doctor. He says you're going to be here for a while. He said your injuries are quite . . ." Her voice broke. She had tried so hard to rein in her emotions, but it was just no use. She fought back the tears, but they came all the same.

"Emmy, don't take it so hard. God's got a reason for allowin' all of this."

She forced herself to regain control. Looking up, she could see her father's worried face. "I'm sorry, Pa. I'm just tired. Everything that's happened has overwhelmed me. I don't understand why God would let it happen. I don't understand where He was when Davies was trying to kill us."

Her father said nothing, so Emily continued. "I know that you and Mama always told me that God would watch over us. You told me that I just needed to put my faith in Him and He would see to all my needs. Well, I trusted Him, and this happened anyway."

"Life's not easy and trouble is just a part of it," her father murmured. It was clear the medicine was taking effect.

Emily wiped away her tears. "It's never been easy. Ever. We've struggled just to exist, and now this. You nearly died. Even now you have a lengthy and painful recovery ahead of you. Where is God in all of that?"

She got to her feet much too fast and for a moment felt the room swim. She drew a deep breath. The rage that had built inside threatened to consume her every thought.

"It's not fair, Pa. It's not fair and it's not right. If this is God's idea of watching over us, then I don't know that I want to put my trust in Him."

"Now, Em," her father began without even a hint of condemnation, "these things are hard to be sure, but that's no reason to get mad at God. Seems to me the devil is due his blame in all of this."

"But God is supposed to be stronger than the devil. God is, after all—God Almighty. Why would He let the devil torment us that way?" She searched her father's face, hoping he might reveal the answer to her questions.

"Why'd He let the devil torment Jesus that way?"

It was a simple enough question, but it took the fight out of Emily. She wanted answers—no, she desperately needed answers. However, it wouldn't do her father any good to hear her continue to rant. Emily drew a deep breath to steady her nerves.

"I'm sorry. I should never have said those things. I'm going to go now. You rest, and I'll come back in a few hours."

"Em, don't give up your faith just because of what happened. If you do, the devil and Kirk Davies win. Just keep that in mind."

She nodded. "I will." For a moment she thought of kissing his forehead, then passed on the idea. The doctor had said he needed to remain perfectly still. "I'll come back as soon as they'll let me."

The moment she stepped from his room and closed the door behind her, Emily lost all control and began to sob. She drew a fisted hand to her mouth as if to force it all back inside—the tears, the emotions, the confusion. Tears blinded her eyes and anger blinded her heart. She didn't want to let the devil or Kirk Davies win, as her father suggested, but her faith was dwindling fast. How could God desert them this way? Hadn't her father and mother always told her that God would watch over her in everything? Hadn't they taught Emily to hold fast to the teachings of the Bible and trust God? Hadn't they taught her to love God with all her heart?

*But how can I trust and love when God allows evil men to do such things?*

She stumbled out the front doors to the building and made her way across the small porch and down the steps. The brilliance of the sun made her close her eyes. Maybe it hadn't been such a good idea to leave.

"Are you all right, miss?"

She barely opened one eye to see who was speaking. An older man was standing next to her with a look of concern. Emily closed her eye again. "I'm afraid I am in a rather weak state. I think maybe I should sit a little while."

"Let me guide you back to the chairs on the porch." He took hold of her arm and turned her around. "Just take it nice and slow. There's a step just before you and then another two."

Emily allowed him to guide her, barely opening her eyes to keep from stumbling up the stairs. Once they were back in the shade of the porch, she found it easier. She opened her eyes and met the man's smiling gaze. "Thank you." She hugged her shawl to ward off the cold.

"Are you sure you wouldn't rather go back inside?"

Emily shook her head. "No. I needed some air."

"Why don't you sit here?" He helped her to a chair and then took the seat beside her. "You look like you've been injured." He motioned to her bruised cheek.

Emily started to nod, but doing so hurt and she stopped. "I was. My father even more so. He required surgery and is now recovering."

"I see. Well, I shall pray for him, and for you. Might I know your names?"

"Emily. Emily Carver. My father is Henry Carver. We're from Yogo City currently."

"My name is Reverend Morgan."

Just then one of the nurses stepped outside with a basket over one arm. "Why, Reverend Morgan, I didn't realize you had come."

"I just arrived," the man said, getting to his feet. "I met this young woman and decided to have a little chat before I went inside to check on Bert."

The nurse frowned. "I'm afraid he passed on early this morning, Reverend."

The man gave a solemn nod. "It's just as we anticipated. Thank you for letting me know."

"He went peacefully," she added. "I'm sure he was comforted by all you said and did for him."

"You are kind to say so," the man replied. "I suppose now I shall have more time to visit with my new friend."

The nurse nodded. "I'm off to collect some supplies from the drugstore. I hope to see you again soon."

The man chuckled. "I'll most likely still be here when you return."

She smiled and made her way down the steps. The reverend waited until she was a little way down the road before he sat back down and turned to Emily.

"So why don't you tell me what happened to bring on such tears?"

# 17

*D*ecisions had to be made. That's what Emily had reminded herself every day since coming to Lewistown.
Unfortunately, making decisions seemed to be the one thing
that eluded her.

"So it's been a week," Reverend Morgan said, sitting down
across from Emily.

"It has." Emily glanced up from the oatmeal and coffee that
had been furnished by the poorhouse for her breakfast. How
she missed the fresh eggs her chickens had produced. She hoped
they were laying well for Millie.

"And how is your father?"

She shook her head and met the old man's pale blue eyes.
"Not much improved. The doctor doesn't know if he'll ever
walk again."

The minister nodded. "I know that must be hard to consider."

"It's more than hard. My father has never been debilitated
in the slightest way. If he can't walk and get around as he did
before, I don't think he'll live long."

"You might be surprised, Miss Emily. A man can usually
find a reason to go on, even with such dire consequences. I've

211

enjoyed getting to know your father. He has a strong faith, and that will help him in the healing process."

"Why? Why should it help?" Her tone was bitter, but he didn't so much as offer a condemning look.

"You have been through a lot, Miss Emily. I know it's been difficult to rest in the Lord. But don't turn your back on God just because things got hard. If you don't put your trust in God, you'll find someone or something else to place it in, and that will never go well."

Emily knew he was right, but she had nursed this grudge ever since the shooting. She hadn't even been able to pray without the words sounding sarcastic and challenging.

She gave a long sigh. "I suppose God is quite angry with me for my lack of faith. I've tried not to be so . . . so . . . rebellious." She looked up, feeling rather sheepish. "That's really it. I'm rebelling—fighting against what I know to be true. Fighting against God."

"We all do from time to time."

"I just don't understand. I pray and pray, but it's like no one is listening."

The old man gave her a gentle smile. There was a tenderness in his expression that made Emily feel guilty. "Never think that God isn't listening. And never think that He doesn't understand how you feel or that He's put you aside. You've done that to yourself. Repentance is up to you. Perhaps you've finally come to that place in life where you can't rely upon your parents' faith, but must accept salvation for yourself." Even with this statement his tone offered no condemnation.

Emily pondered his meaning, wondering if there was something she wasn't understanding about faith in God and what was required of her. She'd sat through a good many church services. Had she missed something?

Reverend Morgan got to his feet. "Keep at it, Miss Emily. Keep praying. God is listening, I promise you. He will answer. Meanwhile, I'll keep asking around about available jobs. Just because I haven't found anything yet doesn't mean I won't."

Emily wanted to believe that God was listening—that Reverend Morgan would find someone to hire her—but it was hard. Maybe the hardest thing she'd ever done. She sighed and focused on her food as the pastor set out across the room to speak to another resident. Maybe she was making it too hard.

*I want to know that you're there, God. I need to know that you care. I need to see proof that you haven't abandoned us. I suppose that's selfish, but I feel so alone. Just when I think I can endure the problems set before me, something else happens and I crumble.*

She finished her breakfast and took her dishes to the tub where they would be collected for washing. Yesterday she had helped with the cleanup and today she had helped to cook. Tomorrow she was supposed to help with the ironing, but she had come to the conclusion that tomorrow she would return to Utica. The only problem was how.

Mulling over that challenge, Emily made her way outside. A cold November wind whipped at her borrowed shawl. Winter was definitely on its way.

Pulling the shawl up over her head, Emily tucked her chin and made her way across the porch. She kept the floor of the porch her focus, and only when a pair of boots appeared before her did Emily lift her gaze.

There she found the most beautiful brown eyes staring back at her. "Caeden." She shook her head and the shawl fell away. "What are you doing here?"

He didn't answer her, but instead pulled her into his arms. For several minutes all he did was hold her close, and Emily melted against him. His strength seemed to bolster her, and a tiny bit of hope crept into her heart. Had God sent him? Had God heard her prayers and sent Caeden as an answer?

Caeden pulled away just enough to touch her cheek. Emily knew the bruise had faded considerably, but it was still visible in hues of yellow and purple. He frowned. "I heard about this." He reached out and gently tipped her head forward. "And this."

Emily straightened. "But I thought you were to be in Havre meeting the other geologists."

"It's a long story. First tell me how your father is doing."

She shook her head and felt tears well in her eyes. "Not so good. He'll survive his wounds, but the doctor doesn't know if he'll ever walk. There was so much damage and swelling that the pressure has left him unable to feel much below the waist. There's a chance this will change when the swelling goes down. The doctor told us to have hope, but I am all out of that commodity. At least I was."

His gaze met hers. "I'm sorry I wasn't around to help. I should have figured Davies would wait until I left and you two were alone again."

"The marshal is convinced it wasn't Davies, because he was supposedly in the jail when the attack happened. But, Caeden, I know it was him. My memory isn't clear on some of the attack, but that much I know. Pa remembers it too." The wind blew hard and Emily shivered.

"Where are you staying?"

"Right here at the poorhouse."

He took hold of her arm. "Come on. I'm going to get you a room and a hot bath at the hotel."

"I can't afford that, Caeden."

"Well, I can and I insist. You were also wounded, and you need to take better care of yourself. You look like you've lost at least ten pounds." He didn't allow her any chance to protest but hurried her down the street.

"I have a room here and it's quite nice. I think you'll like it."

"I have a cot at the poorhouse," she told him. "It's sufficient."

Caeden looked at her with an expression that Emily couldn't quite figure out. He looked both sad and angry. "The hotel is a better place for you." He opened the door and pushed her through. "After I arrange for your room, I'm going to go back to the poorhouse and see what I can do for your father. He'll have the best of care. I promise you."

Gratitude flooded Emily's heart. "You don't have to do that."

"I know, but I want to. What good is being wealthy if you can't benefit your friends?" He smiled. "Now be a good girl and cooperate."

He pulled her with him to the front desk. A young woman appeared and gave Caeden a nod. "Mr. Thibault, I see you're back. What can I do for you?"

"This woman is a friend of mine, Miss Emily Carver. Her father is in the hospital with serious injuries. I'd like to secure a room for her—a nice room—oh, and a hot bath." He took out his wallet and produced several bills. "This should cover things initially. I'll be responsible for anything else."

The young woman looked at Emily and smiled. "Miss Carver, we are glad to have you, but sorry to hear about your father."

"Thank you," Emily said, still uncertain about this new arrangement.

"If you'll just sign the register, I'll take you upstairs to the bath. Then I'll prepare a room for you and bring you a key." She looked over the edge of the counter. "Do you have bags?"

Emily shook her head. "No, they brought us here so quickly there wasn't time to bring anything."

"I'll see to that," Caeden promised.

Her stomach knotted. Emily knew she should refuse all of this and return to the poorhouse. It wasn't Caeden's responsibility to take care of her, and what if he got the wrong idea? What if she did?

"I don't know what to say. I'm grateful, of course, but . . ." What could she tell him? *I'm grateful, but I'm also in love with you.*

"Just go get a bath. I'll be back shortly. We'll have some lunch together and figure out what to do next."

Emily nodded and let the young woman lead her upstairs. Her mind was overwhelmed with thoughts of everything that had just happened.

"My name is Anna," the girl told her. "If you need anything, just let me know." She stopped at a room just off the stairs. "This is the bathing room. We have heated water and fresh towels. There's soap on the counter. The plain one is for men and the scented one for women."

Emily caught sight of the large porcelain bathing tub. She'd never seen anything quite like it. Anna instructed her as to how to get the water and where to leave her towel.

"If you want me to wash your clothes, I can do that as well."

Emily shook her head. "I haven't anything else to wear. As I mentioned, my father and I were brought over here in a hurry. We didn't have time to get any of our belongings." Not that she had much anyway, but there was no sense sharing that with the woman.

Anna stepped back and gave Emily a quick glance. "You look about my size. I'll lend you some things."

"Oh, I couldn't." Emily's protest fell on deaf ears.

"I insist. Your things are in need of a good washing—they're stained with blood. Besides, Mr. Thibault said he would arrange some things for you, so it will only be a short time before you have your own clothes."

She smiled so sweetly that Emily couldn't refuse. "Very well. I am obliged to you."

Anna's countenance seemed to glow. "God calls us to bear one another's burdens. I like being able to help a soul in need."

Emily returned her smile. "You are a very kind woman, and I thank you."

⁂

Emily dressed in the blue calico print gown and marveled at her appearance in the bathing room mirror. Anna had appeared just as Emily had concluded her bath, and she not only brought the gown but undergarments as well. They fit as though they'd been made for her.

The mirror revealed the fading bruise on her face, but it also revealed a look of hope in her eyes that had been absent since the attack. She reached for the damp towel and dried her hair as best she could. It had been most difficult to wash her hair. The nurse at the county farm had tried to help Emily clean away the blood with a wet towel, but her hair still needed a good wash. There was no time to sit before a fire and let it dry thoroughly, so Emily braided it and wound it in a knot and pinned it atop her head, careful to avoid the area with stitches. The finished picture left her feeling feminine and rather attractive. For a moment Emily could only marvel at the reflection.

"Is that really me?"

Anna laughed. "You're very pretty, even with the bruise. Do you want me to show you to your room now?"

Emily shook her head. "No, I need to go speak with my father. My time in the bath helped me to think through some things."

She'd given a lot of thought to what she needed to do. There wasn't any work available in town for her. Reverend Morgan had already spent some time asking around. Utica and Yogo City would be the same, but if she returned to their place, she could sell the animals and see if Millie would buy back the mining claim.

Anna finished gathering the towels. "I'll have your key at the desk downstairs. When you get back, just ask for it and we'll show you to your room."

Emily started to leave, then paused. "If Mr. Thibault returns before I do, would you tell him I won't be long?"

"Of course." Anna picked up Emily's wool shawl. "Here. You'll need this."

Emily wrapped the shawl around her shoulders as she made her way downstairs. She knew it wasn't going to be easy to confront her father about what needed to be done, but she had to try. Hopefully, he would see reason and understand her plan.

ᴄ᷂ᴈᴈᴇᴐ

"You'll do no such thing. I'm still in charge, and I forbid it."

Emily looked at her father with great frustration. "Pa, we have to have money. There isn't any work here in Lewistown and it's much larger than Utica, so I most likely won't find anything there either. If we don't sell out, we'll have nothing."

"And if you do sell our animals and mine—we'll have nothing." His brows came together and he frowned. "Not that we have much, but it's somethin'. I won't have you takin' that away from us."

Emily hated that she'd upset him. With great resignation, she sighed. "All right, Pa. I won't sell things, but I am going back to Utica to confront the marshal about Kirk Davies. Caeden Thibault is back in town, and I know he will tell the marshal all that he observed."

"Caeden was here earlier. Told the doc to spare no expense in fixin' me up. I protested, but he wouldn't hear it. Said that I'd helped him out and now he was returnin' the favor. Seems to me all that boy does is return favors."

Emily thought of all that Caeden had already done for her and all that he promised to do. "Sometimes we have to take a helping hand. It's not always comfortable, but sometimes it is necessary. You need to rest now and let the doctors do what they can to see you on the mend."

Emily leaned down and kissed his forehead. "I love you, Pa. Try not to worry about anything. I promise I won't sell the mine or the animals. I don't know what I will do, but I'll make arrangements as I go."

But in truth, short of letting Caeden pick up the cost of everything, Emily had no idea how she could arrange anything.

# 18

Upon her return to the hotel, Emily learned that Caeden had left her a note telling her he would be back to take her to lunch at exactly twelve. She looked at the large grandfather clock in the lobby and saw that was still another hour away. Something the pastor had said that morning continued to haunt her, and she longed to ask him to explain it.

"I wonder if you could direct me to Reverend Morgan's church," she said to Anna. "I'd like to speak to him about something."

Anna gave her the directions, then promised to tell Caeden where she'd gone if Emily wasn't back in time.

Making her way down the street, Emily wrestled with her father's wishes. The doctor said he would be months recovering. Even so, her father refused to allow her to sell the animals and the claim. No one would be there to protect their interests, however. Surely he could understand that this was a problem. Perhaps the answer was for Emily to return and work the claim as best she could. After all, if Millie could work claims by herself, Emily could surely do the same. Not only that, but she knew the people of Yogo City wouldn't let her starve or go without.

Caeden had already helped them lay in a good supply of wood, so Emily felt certain she could cook and keep warm. Perhaps she would ask Caeden to help her get a few supplies. She hated to further burden him, but he was the only one she could turn to. At least the only one with any real financial ability to help. She could promise to pay him back a little at a time.

At the church Emily climbed the steps and hesitated at the door. Should she knock? It wasn't Sunday, so perhaps the reverend wasn't even there. She tried the door and it opened. Peering into the dimly lit foyer she called out.

"Reverend Morgan?"

To her surprise the man appeared almost immediately. He beamed her a smile and motioned her to enter. "You mustn't stand out in the cold, child."

Emily entered the church, letting the door close behind her. "I hope you don't mind the intrusion."

He laughed. "There's no such thing as an intrusion when it comes to God's house."

The minister led Emily to a small office just off the sanctuary. The room held numerous shelves of books, a large desk, and several chairs. Positioning one chair to face the center of the room, Reverend Morgan motioned Emily to take a seat. Then rather than sit behind the desk, Reverend Morgan pulled up another chair and sat facing her.

"Now tell me why you've come."

Emily twisted her hands together. "I . . . well . . . something you said got me to wondering."

He smiled. "And what was that?"

"You said something about me coming to a place where I

couldn't rely on my parents' faith—that I needed to accept salvation for myself."

"And now you're wondering how you do that?" His question was matter-of-fact, but it hit Emily like a blow.

"I always thought I had accepted salvation. I mean, my mother always taught me to fear and believe in God. She always told me Bible stories and I believed them. I knew about Jesus coming to save us from our sins. So, well . . . did I miss something?" She looked at him with an earnest desire to understand.

With the voice of a gentle father, Reverend Morgan began. "Perhaps you didn't miss something, as much as you didn't realize something. You see, it is important to know and fear God. It's important to believe in what the Bible says and to believe in God. Believing is the start of understanding. However, repentance is the beginning of the eternal."

She looked at him without fully understanding. "Repentance of sin, correct?"

He nodded. "What do you know of it?"

"I know that I am a sinner and that I am sorry for the wrong I have done." Emily considered the matter a moment longer. "Is there more to this?"

"True repentance comes from the heart . . . from a deep understanding that we are hopelessly flawed and full of deception and sin. In the Old Testament you can read of God's requirements for His people when they sinned. Great offerings with the shedding of blood were demanded. It is because life was in the blood, and therefore the shedding of such was required to save people from death due to sin."

"Must I sacrifice an animal for my sins?" Emily couldn't keep the distaste from her voice.

Reverend Morgan smiled and shook his head. "No, my dear child. That has already been done—once for all. Jesus came to this world to act as a final sacrifice—to bear the sins of the world. It is through Him and Him alone that we come to God. In the book of John, Jesus tells us that He is the only way to God—the way, the truth, and the life. Before Jesus came, we were at the mercy of God through our own sacrifices, none of which could offer a permanent solution to our sin. Only Jesus could do that.

"In our confession of sin, we acknowledge our hopeless separation from God, and in our belief that Jesus died for those sins, we acknowledge our salvation as well as our reconciliation to God. Then we must live the life of the saved and redeemed. After all, what good is confession of sin if we simply turn right around and do the same things over and over? We must turn away from sin and strive to be like Jesus, who was perfect and knew no sin until He bore ours on the cross."

"That sounds impossible." Emily felt a deep sorrow overtake her. "I could never be good enough."

"No, nor I. It is impossible for us, but not for Christ. We must put our faith in Him to help us live a life that would be pleasing to God."

"But what if I've been too great a disappointment to God?"

"A disappointment?" he questioned.

She nodded. "For all my doubts and my anger. Oh, and my grumbling. What if God is so disappointed in me and my failings that He . . . well . . . that He doesn't want me?"

"Child, do you believe God is all-powerful?"

"Of course."

The minister smiled. "And all-knowing?"

Emily nodded. "He is God. He surely knows everything there is to know."

"So can you allow that God knew the doubts you would have? Can you believe that God knew long before this time of your life that you would make choices and decisions that were other than He wanted you to make?"

"I suppose I can."

"Then how can He be disappointed in you? Disappointment suggests an unrealized expectation, and if God knows all, then how can He be disappointed?"

"But I've made mistakes."

"And no doubt they gave God sorrow. He grieves for His children, but I find it impossible to believe He is disappointed in them."

The regret ebbed away as Emily began to see the truth. It all made so much sense. God truly loved her, just as He had loved her mother. She looked at the old man and nodded. "I understand. It all seems so simple, and yet I have made it quite difficult in my ignorance. Thank you for helping me to see the truth."

Reverend Morgan reached out and took hold of her hands. "That is the calling of God upon my life. That is why I am here—and why God brought you here as well. Maybe you would like me to pray with you?"

Emily smiled. "I'd like that very much."

After praying with Reverend Morgan, Emily felt as though a weight had been lifted. All of her childhood she had listened to her mother speak of faith in God, and through her, Emily felt she had that faith—that understanding. But in losing her mother, Emily also lost her connection to God. Now that loss was no more. She finally understood what her mother had spent a lifetime trying to teach her.

The wind whipped around her small frame, but Emily hardly felt it. She looked upon the world with new eyes and a new hope. No matter what happened with her father's recovery, Emily knew without a doubt that God would provide and that she and her father would be all right.

Caeden was waiting for her at the hotel when she returned. He held out a brown wool coat. "I thought you might need this. Anna told me she'd loaned you some clothes, but I have purchased some things for you. They're in your room. You will have to see them later, however, because I'm famished and want to go have lunch."

Emily set the shawl aside and then let him help her into the coat. "This is lovely, Caeden." She ran her fingers over the black cording that trimmed the sleeves. "Thank you." She looked into his face but left her thoughts unspoken. There was so much she wanted to tell him, but now didn't seem like the right time.

⁓⁂⁓

"There's something very different about you." Caeden looked at Emily as if seeing her for the first time. "I've never seen you like this."

"Like what?" she asked.

He shook his head. "I'm not quite sure. You're lovely, that much is certain."

Emily laughed. "Maybe it's just that I'm cleaned up. And not just on the outside."

"Meaning what exactly?"

"One of the local pastors here helped me to realize how I needed to make my faith in God all my own. I think for most of my life, my faith was tied to my mother's."

Caeden could have said the same thing for his own life. He knew, however, that Emily had something more to say, and so he waited.

"Reverend Morgan—he's the man I'm speaking of—he spoke in such a way that I could clearly see what was required of me and what was not. I've had such anger at what happened and why God allowed it. My doubts seemed numerous and I feared that God was greatly disappointed in me. But Reverend Morgan reminded me that God knows all and knew the choices and doubts I would have. He told me that God might be sad at me having such thoughts or sins, but that He wasn't disappointed in me, because He already knew ahead of time all about my anger and doubts. And because He knew about them—about the way all of us would make bad choices—He sent Jesus."

Hearing her words, Caeden felt as if his mother were speaking. Many had been the time she had told Caeden that God knew well in advance how things would be in their household. That had only served to make Caeden all the angrier. After all, if God knew, then in Caeden's mind that somehow equated with His approving of it as well.

"I feel such a sense of relief," Emily said, bringing Caeden back to the present.

"I have to say your words strike a chord in me. I too have wrestled with doubt and anger toward God. I might have to go visit your reverend." He looked at her and smiled. "I know I am not the man God would have me to be."

Emily surprised him when she reached out to cover his hand with her own. "It's never too late to be reconciled."

He nodded. "No, I suppose it is not."

After lunch Caeden insisted that they go speak with the doctor. He had wired to New York, asking his uncle to consult with physicians in the area. He wanted to let the doctor know what he had done and that they could anticipate a response soon.

They visited with the doctor and then with Emily's father. Henry Carver was delighted to see that Caeden had returned and was even happier to know he was helping Emily. He assured Caeden that once he got back on his feet he would repay anything Caeden spent. Caeden didn't have the heart to tell

Carver he would never pan enough out of the Yogo claim to cover even a portion of what Caeden had spent, but he did assure the man that repayment wasn't his desire, nor was it his motivation in helping them.

Seeing Emily yawn, Caeden realized she must be exhausted. He felt bad for having kept her from resting. Not only that, but she was still recovering. She should have been put in bed and waited on.

As they made their way from the poorhouse, he apologized. "I am sorry for keeping you out. You should be resting. You aren't even healed yet yourself. I will walk you back to your room, and after you have a long rest we can make plans for the evening. As I mentioned earlier, there are quite a few new articles of clothing awaiting you upstairs. There is a nightgown among those things." He felt a moment's embarrassment and looked off down the street. "It should help you rest easier."

"You are too kind. Really, I'm fine. I've been working at the poorhouse helping with the cleaning and cooking. Tomorrow I'll be helping with the laundry."

Caeden stopped her just before they came to the hotel's door. "No. I won't have it. You need to rest. You haven't even had the stitches removed from your head. If you won't take care of yourself, then I will."

She looked at him strangely for a moment, her face scrunching up just a bit. He thought she might chastise him, but instead she looked away and yawned. "I am very tired, and I suppose there is some truth to what you say."

"You must be ill—you aren't arguing with me." Caeden took hold of her arm. "Come on. Do you have your room key?"

"Anna told me to pick it up at the front counter when I got back."

They entered the hotel, and Caeden had Emily retrieve the

key before ushering her up the stairs. He worried only momentarily that the manager and other patrons might wonder at him attending to Emily, but they would simply have to wonder. He knew his motives were pure. Not that he wouldn't like to kiss her and hold her for a time before letting her retire.

They paused at her door, and Caeden motioned across the hall. "My room is just there. If you need me, don't hesitate to knock. I'll be attending to some business while you nap, but I'll be nearby. You can always send someone for me."

"I'll be fine." Emily unlocked the door and opened it. For a moment all she did was stare into the room.

"Is something wrong?" Caeden asked, almost pushing her out of the way to see.

She shook her head. "Nothing's wrong. I just was thinking, other than at the hospital, I've never slept in a real bed."

Caeden looked at the metal-framed bed. It wasn't anything special, but Emily was looking at it in awe. He felt a sense of disgust at himself and all the wasted privileges he'd known. He had taken so much for granted, never giving them a second thought.

"You've never slept in a real bed?" He felt a surge of protectiveness for her, along with a desire to lavish upon her the finest bed that money could buy.

She turned to him and smiled. Her cherry-red lips drew his eyes as she spoke. "I probably won't be able to sleep for all its comfort and softness."

Caeden lost himself momentarily in thoughts of kissing her. He started to reach out and pull her into his arms when he heard footsteps on the stairs down the hall.

"I'd better go." He all but pushed her through the door and pulled it closed. He was still fumbling to unlock his own door when an older man appeared at the top of the steps and went down the hall in the opposite direction.

Emily had no idea what had gotten into Caeden. Had she done or said something wrong? His abrupt retreat seemed completely out of character.

She didn't concern herself for long on that matter, however. Her gaze fell on the far end of the room, where a small table stood. Atop this were several store boxes and parcels. Emily knew she should lie down, but she went to explore the contents instead. She gasped at the riches found inside. Caeden had bought her a nightgown, as he'd mentioned, as well as an entire ensemble. There were stockings, a new corset, petticoats—one very plain and one quite lacy—as well as a new gown and hat. The final package contained a pair of beautiful lace-trimmed drawers.

She blushed to think of him shopping for her in such an intimate fashion. Perhaps it wouldn't have bothered her quite so much if she didn't have such deep and growing feelings for him.

Several times during their lunch she had very nearly confessed her feelings for him, but something had held her back. Uncertainty had clouded her mind, and fear of rejection had kept her thoughts in check. She could tell that Caeden felt something for her, but what if it were nothing more than a brotherly affection—the concern of one soul for another? After all, he'd arranged for her father to have what he needed as well.

With a sigh, Emily began to unbutton Anna's dress. She felt exhaustion overtake her. It had been such a day of surprises, and it wasn't even over. Who knew what the evening might hold for her.

# 19

When Emily finally awoke, she did nothing but stretch and relish the luxury of the bed. Never in her life had she known anything to feel so wonderful. Not only that, but for the first time since coming to Lewistown, she actually felt rested. Maybe it was because at the poorhouse she had shared a dorm with other women and children. She had been wearied by the cries of infants and the tantrums of the children, while also sympathizing with the weeping of their mothers. Emily had never been able to get comfortable on the old army cot, knowing that anyone could wander into the room at any time. But here—this was different.

She closed her eyes and tried to imagine having a bed like this every night. How wonderful it would be to have a beautiful bedroom all to herself with a down-filled mattress and springs on the bed instead of ropes. Even the growling of her stomach couldn't keep her from her daydreams. However, the knock that came on her hotel door startled her awake and caused her to jump from the bed. She had no robe, so she grabbed up the shawl Millie had given her and pulled it around her.

At the door she called out, "Who's there?"

"It's me, Anna."

Emily opened the door to find the young woman bearing a tray of food. "Come in."

"Mr. Thibault wanted me to bring you breakfast. He said to tell you he's secured passage on the stage and that you have two hours to get ready. He figured you'd want to see your pa before leaving town." She went to the table and shifted the tray, tucking it between her waist and left arm. Next she pushed the clothing to one side.

"Breakfast? Stage?" Emily shook her head. "How long have I been asleep?"

Anna laughed as she placed the food tray on the table with the few remaining pieces of clothing. Thankfully, Emily had thought to hang up the gown on a hook by the door. She hurried to finish clearing the table while Anna uncovered the food.

"You never woke up last night for supper. I came to check on you, but you never even stirred. Mr. Thibault told me to let you sleep. You slept clear through."

"I did that at the poorhouse as well. My injury has no doubt taken more of a toll than I realized. I might have gone back to sleep had you not come." Emily glanced back at the bed. "I must say it was the most comfortable bed I've ever slept in."

Anna nodded. "Papa says ours are the finest in Lewistown. It's why folks always choose our hotel." She pulled out the chair, then picked up the clothing that had been neatly stacked there. "I'll put these on the bed."

Emily nodded and took up a piece of bacon. It tasted heavenly. She savored the flavor and then caught the scent of the hot coffee. She'd never been much of a coffee drinker, but even this beckoned her to sit and dig in.

"I'll be back in half an hour to help you dress," Anna offered.

Emily remembered her own clothes. "Did you manage to wash my things?"

"I did. Would you like me to fetch them?"

"Yes. I have a beautiful new gown, but I can't see wearing it on the stage. Oh, and I've put your gown and undergarments next to my new gown." Emily motioned to the door, where all of the articles hung on pegs.

Anna went to collect her things. She ran her hand over the material of Emily's dress. "This is quite lovely. I think you'll look beautiful in this shade." She gave a little laugh. "I think you would look beautiful in just about anything."

Emily was surprised by her comment. No one had ever said much in praise of her appearance. Maybe it was because for so many years she'd hid herself under layers of dirt and oversized garments.

"You are kind to say so, but you are a beautiful woman yourself. I suppose you have a great many suitors."

The girl's face turned red and she hurried to collect her things. "I do have a beau," she murmured.

Emily suppressed a chuckle. "I was sure you would."

Anna opened the door. "Like I said, I'll be back in a little while to help you dress. Oh, and Mr. Thibault went to buy you a small carpetbag to carry your things in. I'll bring that too, if he's successful. I told him I wasn't sure any of the stores would be open yet, but he said he'd handle it."

No doubt he would. Emily hadn't known much of anything to stand in Caeden's way up until this point. She heard Anna close the door and then turned her full attention to the meal. Fluffy scrambled eggs and fried potatoes were heaped alongside six strips of bacon. Sliced bread had been toasted and slathered in butter, and along with this was a small bowl of jam. Coffee and cream rounded off the meal. It was food fit for royalty.

233

Emily giggled. "I feel like a queen." She put a forkful of the buttery eggs in her mouth. Was there anything quite as delicious as a meal prepared by someone else? It wouldn't be easy to go back to her life in the cabin.

True to her word, Anna returned with the new carpetbag just as Emily downed the last of her coffee. She couldn't finish the entire breakfast, but she folded the remaining bacon and put it between two pieces of toast. Pa would love this tasty treat.

Emily quickly donned her new underclothes, then stood holding on to the metal footboard of the bed while Anna cinched up the corset. "Don't make it too tight," Emily instructed. "I need to be able to breathe on the stage."

Emily went to retrieve the freshly laundered wool skirt and cotton blouse. She paused to admire them for a moment. "You did a wonderful job getting the blood out of these."

"Mama said salt water is the trick." Anna went to work packing Emily's nightgown and new dress into the small carpetbag Caeden had purchased. "Mr. Thibault certainly found you a nice bag."

Emily did up the buttons on her blouse, smiling all the while at the thought of Caeden waking some poor merchant from his bed. "He does have his way of getting what he wants."

"Is he your beau?"

Emily looked up. "What?"

"Oh, I'm sorry. That was much too forward of me." Anna quickly changed the subject. "I put your hat and gloves on the bed." She procured a hairbrush from her pocket. "I didn't think you probably had one here, so I brought mine, along with some hairpins. I thought you might want me to fix your hair for the trip and help you with your hat."

"That was very kind. You don't need to wait on me, however. I can just braid it like I did yesterday."

"It isn't a bother," Anna said, looking at Emily with a most sincere expression.

Emily gave in. "Very well. I will allow you to do that, but you must tell me about yourself. How old are you, Anna?"

"Sixteen," the girl replied. She motioned Emily to retake her chair at the table. "I have three brothers who are all older than me. One of them helps out here at the hotel, but the other two have moved off."

"Have you always lived here?"

Anna freed Emily's messy braid and began brushing out her long brown hair. "My mother was born and raised here. My papa comes from Illinois. His family owned hotels there, and he took his inheritance and came west to make his own fortune. He built a hotel in Billings and then sold it and came to Lewistown."

"Why Lewistown?"

Anna giggled. "Because he'd met my mother in Billings. Her pa had taken her with him on a trip to buy stock. My papa met her and fell madly in love. So when he found out where she lived, he decided that was good enough for him. He came here and built this hotel and married my mother. It was all very romantic, don't you think?"

"I do." Emily winced as Anna's brush came in contact with the stitched portion of her head.

"I'm sorry, did I hurt you? I forgot you had an injury. Your hair very neatly covers the stitches when it's all splayed out like this."

"It smarts, but I think I'm fine. I should be able to get the stitches out soon. Maybe even today."

"Hmmm." Anna stepped back and eyed Emily for a moment. "Maybe it's best if we just leave your hair down for the time. If we pin it up it might be hard for the doctor to examine the wound."

Emily hadn't considered that. "I suppose you're right. Just tie it back with my ribbon, and I'll figure out what to do with it after the doctor sees me."

Anna did as Emily instructed. "There. It's perfect." She held out a handful of hairpins. "Take these with you in case you want to pin it up after you have your stitches out."

Emily took the pins. "Are you certain you can spare them?"

Anna nodded. "I have plenty of them." She looked her hairbrush over and extended it as well. "I have another brush too. I would be very pleased if you would take this for your own."

Emily had never known such generosity from a stranger. "You are quite kind, Anna, but I couldn't. The hairpins and your help this morning have been more than enough to show me what a generous and loving soul you are. I've traveled all over the West, and I don't think I've ever met a young woman with a heart as big as yours."

Anna blushed. "Mama says we're to be kind to strangers because they might be angels in disguise."

Emily laughed. "Well, I'm no angel, but I am a stranger and a very grateful one."

⁂

Caeden accompanied Emily to see the doctor and then to say good-bye to her father. Emily had found the removal of the stitches to be rather painful. The wound site was still a little tender, and it seemed the doctor was a bit clumsy when it came to pulling stitches, and not her hair, with his tweezers. Finally, however, the deed was done and the doctor pronounced her well enough to travel. This seemed to satisfy both Caeden and her father.

"I'll return as soon as I can, Pa." Emily spoke as she worked to wind her hair into a knotted bun. "I need to figure out how I can best work the claim. Otherwise we might never get Caeden paid back."

"I don't need to be paid back," Caeden declared.

"Yes you do," Father countered. "I can't go havin' you take care of us. You have no obligation here, and while I know you're a generous young man, I won't have it said that Henry Carver took advantage. Emmy's a good girl, and she can work the dirt we dug up. I'm sure there's gold to be had. Emmy, don't forget the gold dust I saved in that old medicine tin. You could give that to Caeden."

"I won't take it." Caeden gave the older man one of his stern looks. With his eyes slightly narrowed and his mouth set in a firm line, his expression commanded attention. "Now, enough talk of money. I am very concerned about Emily living alone."

"She can stay nights with Millie," her father suggested. "That way no one will bother her."

Emily listened to the two most important men in her life as they tried to decide her future. Without a word she secured her hair at last and took up the bonnet Caeden had purchased. It was a charming little hat of black velvet, trimmed with a large green feather that had been shaped and pinned to follow the contours of the brim. There were no ribbons with which to tie it down, so Emily used the last two hairpins to hold it in place.

"If you two are quite finished making plans for me, I believe we have a stage to catch."

Both men looked at Emily in surprise. Her father chuckled, but Caeden said nothing and instead withdrew his pocket watch.

"Yes, we need to go," Caeden said, glancing at the watch. "Otherwise, we'll miss the stage."

Emily looked at her father. He still seemed so weak and pale.

"I'll be back as soon as I can, but I have no way of knowing when that will be. Please be good and do as the doctors tell you."

Her father laughed. "Listen to that, will you? I suppose from here on out she'll think she can mother me." He held up the bacon and toast she had decided to leave with him. "I'm going to enjoy this, Em. Thanks for savin' it for me."

Emily could only nod. She found herself dangerously close to tears. Caeden extended his arm and shook Henry's free hand. "I'll make sure she's safely delivered to Yogo City."

"You're a good man and I'm proud to call you friend. Now, get her out of here before she starts blubbering or, worse yet, gives me a list of orders to follow."

Caeden smiled, but Emily couldn't help feeling she was deserting her father. She worried he might take a bad turn while she was away. He might even die, and she'd never know it until it was much too late. She realized all at once that both men were watching her. Offering a smile, Emily leaned down and kissed her father on the forehead. "I love you, Pa."

"I love you too, Emmy," he said.

Caeden escorted her from the poorhouse. "I'm sure he'll be just fine. I've arranged for him to have the best care. Try not to worry."

The wind blew at just the right angle and yanked the bonnet from Emily's head. "Oh no! My hat."

Caeden was already in motion to chase it down. He'd nearly reached it when the wind sent it another ten feet down the road. Without pause, Caeden continued after it while Emily secured her gloves. How handsome he was in his dark black suit. She had so long seen him in work clothes that his more formal appearance left her rather in awe. His broad shoulders seemed all the more pronounced in the trim lines of the coat.

He finally captured the hat and made his way back to Emily,

dusting the bonnet as he walked. When he returned he gave her a sweeping bow and presented the piece as if it were an extravagant gift.

"M'lady."

Emily laughed and took the hat. It hadn't suffered much damage, but she didn't want to put it back atop her head only to have it whipped off again. "I believe I'll wait to affix this until we're out of the wind."

"That is probably wise," Caeden agreed.

Anna had arranged for both of their bags to be at the stage waiting, and the driver was just hefting them to store in the boot.

"Good to have you join us," the driver said, tipping his hat to Emily. "Always a pleasure to have a lady aboard. You're our only one today."

Emily smiled but said nothing. She didn't like being the center of attention, and even now she could see that the numerous gentlemen atop and inside the stage were already watching her closely.

"Pity you don't have those old layers of clothes you used to wear," Caeden said as he helped Emily up into the stage. She suppressed a giggle as she caught sight of the four men in the carriage. They seemed most intent on making her acquaintance.

"You can sit here, miss," one of the men announced. Unfortunately, he was sitting on the side where there were already three, and despite their efforts, they couldn't make space for another, even one as slim as Emily.

The man sitting by himself smiled invitingly and patted the seat. "Plenty of room here." His enthusiasm was quite evident.

Emily took her place but crowded the wall of the stage. Caeden climbed in behind her and positioned himself between the man and Emily, much to the other fellow's disappointment.

Caeden's usual stern expression seemed to act as a deterrent to further conversation, and so the others returned their attention to conversing among themselves. Emily felt her hair and found the hatpins that had failed to hold her hat in place. She positioned the bonnet and resecured it, hoping there wouldn't be another mishap. It was the only ladies' hat she'd ever owned, and she certainly didn't want to lose it.

The trip by stage was surprisingly exciting for Emily. She'd never ridden in a stagecoach before and found the entire matter to be a great adventure. Her enthusiasm became rather contagious, and the men surrounding her strove to answer her questions and share whatever knowledge they had of such travels.

It wasn't until they were nearly an hour into the trip that Emily caught sight of Caeden's scowl and decided perhaps her silence would be better. After all, for someone who hadn't wanted to attract attention, she'd done exactly that with her girlish delight over the trip.

Despite her excitement, Emily leaned back against the seat and closed her eyes. She thought about her return to Utica and her plans for seeing the marshal first thing. It was her intention to learn what had been done about the capture of Kirk Davies. She hoped that by now the marshal had paid him a visit and discovered evidence of the bite Emily had given him.

Of course, it was possible that Davies had fled the area, thinking he'd killed her father. After all, when they left Utica there wasn't much hope that he would live. If Davies had gone, Emily wasn't at all sure what she would do. She wanted justice for her father and mother. She wanted Davies to pay.

Somewhere in her thoughts Emily drifted off to sleep. When the stage stopped for a meal break, she awoke to find she had slumped against Caeden and her head was on his shoulder. She sat up with a start and immediately apologized.

"I'm so sorry." Her voice was barely a whisper, but it caught the attention of her traveling companions.

"He don't look too put out," one of the men commented.

Another grinned and pushed back his felt hat. "I know I wouldn't be."

Still another declared in a most confident voice, "If he is, you can sleep on my shoulder when we get back on the road."

Caeden muttered something under his voice, but Emily couldn't make it out and didn't want to draw further attention by asking. The door opened, and the driver reached up his hand. Emily, being the only female on the stage, decided his action was for her benefit and quickly took hold and let the man help her down.

"Thank you," she said, uncertain what to do.

"The privy is in the back, and the food is in the house. We won't be here but twenty minutes, fellas and miss." He nodded in acknowledgment of Emily. "Don't be wastin' any time. We got a schedule to keep."

Caeden took hold of her arm. "I'll escort you out back, and then we can make our way inside." He lowered his voice and moved her away from the others. "I'm afraid if I don't keep an eye on you, one of those . . . gentlemen will. And worse, they'll get ideas of how to further irritate me."

Emily suppressed a smile. Caeden seemed quite possessive of her, and he hadn't seemed to mind that she'd slept on his shoulder. Perhaps he had more feelings for her than that of a protective brother. Maybe he had fallen in love with her just as she had with him.

Caeden didn't like men ogling Emily. He hadn't been joking when he'd mentioned a desire for her to have her old clothes back. At least then she had been hidden away, to some degree.

All he could do was assert his possessiveness of her and show the other men Emily was off-limits.

Once they were back on their way, Caeden began to relax a little. His actions at the stage stop had made it clear he would brook no nonsense where Emily was concerned. At the table he had given one poor man his fiercest scowl just for handing Emily the salt without her requesting it. The others hadn't missed this, and from that point on they only cast quick side glances at Emily when they thought Caeden wasn't watching.

Even so, Caeden felt a tremendous sense of relief when they finally pulled into Utica. It was late in the day, there were thick clouds overhead, and the light was all but gone. Not only that, but there was a taste of snow in the air. It certainly wouldn't do to try to make Yogo tonight.

"We should probably get rooms at the hotel for the night and then worry about getting you back to the claim tomorrow." Caeden shifted rather impatiently as he awaited their bags. Glancing around, he found himself more than a little aware that Emily was a beautiful woman in a rowdy cow town where the men far outnumbered the women.

*What's wrong with me? I'm acting like* . . . He didn't want to acknowledge the thought. The truth disturbed him more than he wanted to admit. *I'm acting like a jealous, possessive husband.*

"I need to speak with the marshal." Emily looked around. "It's not all that late. Do you suppose I'll find him at the jail?"

"I suppose so." Caeden took their bags from the stage driver. "I'll walk you over."

She didn't say a word, and he wondered if he'd done something wrong. Had he offended her by taking charge?

They passed by the well-lit hotel restaurant where Caeden had first had dinner with Emily's father. Through the big window at the front, he could see that the place was packed. Maybe by the time they finished with the marshal and got their rooms, the place wouldn't be quite so busy.

They hadn't gone ten feet, however, when Bishop Arnold's voice called out in a commanding manner, "Caeden Thibault."

He turned, as did Emily. Caeden had little desire to deal with the man but knew it would do no good to tell him so. Then to his complete displeasure, Catherine stepped from the restaurant to join her father.

"I find your behavior in leaving without a word to be completely unacceptable," Arnold started in. "You accompanied me here to give me your opinion on my mining interests." It was then that Arnold seemed to take an interest in Emily. He looked her up and down, then turned back to pull his daughter forward.

"And to have you desert your fiancée without a word was most uncalled for."

Caeden looked at Catherine momentarily, then turned to Emily, whose expression had gone blank. He knew that look. It was how she handled anything distasteful or surprising. He wanted to counter Arnold's claim and deny his untimely announcement, but Caeden could see the worry in Catherine's eyes and so said nothing.

"We were quite worried, weren't we, Catherine?"

She nodded. "Very much so. But, as you can see, Father, our worry was unwarranted." She smiled at Caeden. "We're glad to have you back."

Caeden tightened his grip on the bags. "I can see that." He looked to her father. "And have you completed your transaction with Mr. Singleton?"

"I have." He seemed to puff out his chest. "No thanks to you. Even so, I'm certain that when you inspect the place for yourself, you'll find everything in order." He lowered his voice to a whisper. "The ore we've pulled out was assayed just today and found to be of the highest quality."

"No doubt." Caeden knew the ore taken from the mine was most likely placed there for just such purposes. Either that or Singleton had an arrangement with the assayer. If there truly was an assayer in Utica. More than likely Singleton had hired someone to play the part.

"Of course it's too dark to go out to the claim tonight," Arnold began, "but in the morning I would like you to inspect it for yourself. I'm quite encouraged."

Caeden shook his head. "And where is Mr. Singleton?"

"He had to return to Great Falls. He has another investor that he plans to bring out here. The man has really been most helpful. He's offered to help me secure a crew to work the mine. He says he has a trusted man who could act as foreman for me."

"And how did you manage to pay for the claim?" Caeden knew it was rude to ask about such matters, but he pushed for an answer. "After all, it isn't like the bank here would have that kind of money on hand."

"I arranged it in Great Falls. I wired my bank in Albany for a short-term loan, and they wired approval to the bank in Great Falls." Bishop Arnold smiled. "Singleton believes I can make back my investment in a month's time. He plans to return at that time and see just how things are going."

Caeden didn't want to make matters worse by telling Arnold that Singleton was probably long gone. He was tired, and he knew Emily was exhausted. No, it would be better to have this conversation in the morning.

"If you'll excuse me," he began and turned to look at Emily. She wasn't there. He frowned and looked back at Arnold.

"The young lady who was with you left a few moments ago.

I presume you were simply assisting her with her bag," Arnold said, narrowing his eyes.

Caeden could only imagine what Emily was thinking. Arnold had announced that Catherine was to be his wife. He'd never had a chance to tell Emily anything about their arrangement. Not that he had thought it would ever be necessary. Now, however, she believed he was going to marry Catherine, and any chance he had of proposing she wait for him might face serious obstacles.

"If you'll excuse me, I need to catch up with her. As you said, I have her bag."

"I was hoping you might have dinner with us," Arnold announced. "Our food hasn't arrived yet. Why don't you join us. We have a great deal to discuss, and I know Catherine has been absolutely pining for you."

Caeden hated himself for not putting Arnold in his place and declaring the farce that he and Catherine had contrived, but he knew it would spell disaster. Catherine would suffer, and Caeden would bear the responsibility and guilt should she be forced into a loveless marriage because of him. Surely he could just explain it all to Emily. She was the understanding sort. Wasn't she?

⁂

Emily stormed into the jail feeling ten different kinds of fool. Why should it be such a surprise that Caeden had a fiancée? Why shouldn't he? He was wealthy and handsome and no doubt quite popular in his circles. How foolish she'd been to suppose he felt something for her.

*He probably sees me—us—as a charity case. He can do his good deeds and feel better about himself.*

Emily's embarrassment quickly turned to anger. "Marshal, I've come to find out what you've done about Kirk Davies."

The marshal looked up in surprise. "I'm glad to see you've recovered, Miss Carver. How's your father doing?"

"He's alive. He may never walk again, but he's alive." She fixed him with what she hoped was her most intimidating glare. "Now what of Kirk Davies?"

"Now, Miss Carver, you probably don't remember since you were suffering from a concussion, but I told you that night they brought you and your pa to Utica that Davies was in my jail when your attack happened."

She leaned down. "And I told you he was there and I bit him. I bit him hard on the thigh after he knocked me to the ground. Go find him and make him show you his left thigh. That shouldn't be so difficult."

"Well, truth is, I haven't seen anything of him."

Emily crossed her arms. "Of course not. I suppose I'll have to track him down myself." She turned to head for the door.

"Now, wait just a minute," the marshal said, coming from around his small desk. "You can't go takin' the law into your own hands." He grabbed hold of her arm and spun her around.

Emily pulled away from him. "Well, it appears someone must. You are most unwilling to do your job."

He frowned. "You need to calm down, Miss Carver. I am doin' my job. Like I told you, Kirk Davies was here in my jail when you claim the attack took place. I don't know him very well, as he was new to this area and kept to himself, but I'm not a liar."

She knew this was getting her nowhere. "If you'll excuse me, I'm quite tired and I've yet to arrange passage back to Yogo City."

"Well, that I can be of help with," the marshal said, sounding quite relieved. "Just follow me out back. Jake Hoover is loading up some supplies. I'm bettin' he'd take you home."

Jake was more than happy to have Emily's company. Despite the lack of light, he was headed to Millie's and knew she'd be glad to see Emily. He helped Emily mount one of his mules and repositioned a sack of flour behind her and one of sugar in front.

He secured a few other items to some of the other mules and then picked up the lantern that had afforded him light.

"If you don't mind holdin' on to this, we'll be on our way."

Emily nodded and took the lantern. Jake took hold of the lead mule's rope and urged the animal forward. He began to tell Emily all about the happenings that had gone on in her absence. Emily didn't much care, and she certainly didn't feel like conversing. Her thoughts were still back on the beautiful woman engaged to Caeden.

Jake questioned her about her father, and when Emily didn't say more than a half dozen words, he broke into a story about a time he'd been shot. Emily barely heard the words as she battled her anger and disappointment. It seemed the only men she had thought to count on were of no use to her. Not her father. Not Caeden, and certainly not the marshal of Utica.

Their progress was slow but methodic. After about four hours Jake stopped. "We can rest for several hours and then go on if you like." Emily's back and neck ached from the hours of stage travel and now her bareback adventure on the mule, but she was determined to reach Yogo.

"If you need to stop, that's fine. But don't do it on my account. I'd just as soon get home."

He smiled. "I figured as much. We'll rest a bit and have us a fire to warm up with and then we'll push on."

Emily definitely enjoyed the fire. She hadn't realized how cold she was. At times like this she longed for her old canvas coat, but she had no idea where it had ended up after her father's shooting.

It wasn't long before they were back on the road and Emily finally felt some of her anger slip away. Jake seemed to sense this too and started posing questions.

"What are your plans, Miss Emily?"

She considered the matter for a moment. "Pa doesn't want me to sell the claim, so I guess I'm going to work it. We dug up quite a bit of dirt prior to his getting shot. I'll work with that for now."

"I can't imagine he expects you to be doin' that."

"I don't know exactly what he expects. I tried to talk him into letting me sell the claim and all the animals. The doctor doesn't know if Pa will ever recover his ability to walk. Pa says he will, and you know Pa. He's just stubborn enough to prove us all wrong."

"Well, just the same, I don't think you should do it. It's not safe for a woman to live out there alone."

"I thought I'd see if Millie would let me stay with her, maybe let me trade chores for rent."

Jake nodded. "I'm sure she'll be happy to. You know Millie cares a great deal about you, as do I, Miss Emily. I'd like to help you out too. I'll go hunting tomorrow before I head off to the ranch. I want to make sure you have some meat."

"Thank you, Jake. I do appreciate what you've done for us over this last year. I know Pa didn't very often pay you, but I'll do what I can to see you're compensated."

"That ain't necessary, Miss Emily. Some folks can pay and some folks can't. I don't want you worryin' about it."

After some time of traveling in the pitch-black night with nothing more than a lantern for light, Emily finally spied the lights of Millie's boardinghouse. She could already imagine the warmth of a fire in the dining room and the comfort of a hot meal.

"Look there, Millie knew I was coming back tonight and stayed up to greet me. She's gonna be glad to see you too, Emily."

"I don't know about that, but I'm glad to finally be here. I'm weary to the bone." The long hours of travel left her unable to even think clearly. Jake helped her from the mule, and Emily took hold of his arm and gave it a squeeze. "You were a godsend, Jake. Thank you for bringing me here."

He laughed and put his arm around her to pull her toward Millie's front door. "'Tain't no trouble. Besides, you know I've got a soft spot for the ladies."

# 20

When Caeden had found the marshal absent from the jail, he'd gone back to the hotel, hoping Emily might be there waiting for him. When he found she wasn't, he secured a room for himself and then went in search of her. After several hours he finally located the marshal, but the news wasn't what he wanted to hear.

"What do you mean she was here, but now she's gone to Yogo City?" Caeden asked the marshal.

"Just what I said. She came here and asked me about Kirk Davies and then she left. Headed back with Jake Hoover."

Caeden wondered for a moment what he should do. To follow them he'd have to rent a horse again, and that would take time. What with it being the supper hour, the liveryman was probably elsewhere eating.

"I'm glad you stopped by, however," the marshal said, pulling a piece of paper from his desk. "This telegram came for you. I went to hunt you down and learned about you heading over to Lewistown to check on the Carvers. I was going to have it sent over with the stage in a day or so, but since you're here, I guess you've saved me the trouble."

Caeden took the telegram and read it. The news wasn't at all what he wanted to hear. His geologist colleagues sent word that he was to make his way to Washington without delay. Apparently there was to be some sort of congressional committee meeting, and he was to give a report based on his findings. His absence would spell trouble for all of them and threaten a research project that was only just beginning. The meeting would take place a week from tomorrow. It didn't give Caeden a whole lot of time.

"Thanks." He stuffed the telegram into his pocket.

He started to leave, but the marshal called him back. "I hope you'll be able to talk some sense into Emily Carver. She's convinced that Kirk Davies shot her pa, but like I told her, Davies was in jail. I'd only just let him go shortly before she and Henry Carver were brought to Utica. He couldn't have been the one to attack them."

Caeden frowned. "It's not like Emily to lie about a thing."

"I don't think she is lying," the marshal countered. "I think that blow to her head caused her to think she knew the attacker. Since so much had happened with Davies prior to that, I think she just let her mind remember him."

"I don't suppose there's any chance to question Davies about the situation."

The marshal shrugged. "If you can find him, ask all the questions you like. I haven't seen him around. I even went out to that old cabin he's supposed to be holed up in, but there wasn't any sign of him. Maybe he's just layin' low."

Caeden perked up at this. "Why would he need to lie low if he's done nothing wrong?"

Again the marshal shrugged. "I would imagine he's heard

about the Carvers and figures folks will blame him. It's just a guess."

"Well, my guess is that he did have something to do with the attack and doesn't want to be too accessible for questioning." Caeden headed once more for the door. "I will tell you this much. If you don't find him, I have a feeling Emily will."

That thought scared Caeden more than he could say. If Emily set out to find Davies and prove that he was responsible for the attack, she would probably get herself killed.

It turned out to be impossible to rent a horse before morning, and when Caeden returned early the next day he had to pay an outrageous price to use the liveryman's own mount. He wasn't in any mood to dicker with the man but made it clear he wasn't happy. Nevertheless, with no other choices available, Caeden paid the price and headed to Yogo.

Exhausted, Caeden tried to keep his mind alert for any trouble on the road. Sleep had been nigh on impossible for him the night before. Over and over he kept seeing Emily's face when Arnold had announced his engagement to Catherine. The matter was simple to clear up, and had she but waited, Caeden could have done just that. Instead, she'd spent the night believing he belonged to another woman.

He pushed the horse to a gallop, knowing it probably wasn't the wisest thing to do. He might encounter bears or other problems. The bay gelding took it all in stride. He seemed familiar with the road, and the chill of the November day made him frisky. Caeden used this to his advantage and gave the horse his head. If he was able to keep up the pace, it wouldn't take but a few hours to reach Yogo.

He arrived without incident in Yogo City just after noon. He didn't bother to stop by Millie's or anywhere else. He rode straightaway to the Carvers' cabin, knowing he'd find Emily there. He had gone over and over the things he would say, but now as he neared, Caeden wasn't at all sure that Emily would even want to hear them. And, even if she did, Caeden couldn't be sure she'd forgive him.

He remembered her recent dealings with the pastor in Lewistown. Emily had been notably changed, and she said it was all due to understanding more about God and His love. Caeden wanted to believe God's love was real, but the pain of his past kept niggling at his spirit. If God truly was love, then why had it been the one thing denied his mother?

*She had your love and that of your sisters.*

His mother had always said how much that love blessed her. Caeden remembered his mother was also quite loved by her own parents and siblings. Not only that, but she had a great many friends, all who adored her.

*But my father didn't love her. He only used and abused her.*

He frowned. "Lord, I want to believe that you care—that you love me—that you loved her. I just don't understand why you let her suffer so. It hurts to remember her pain. It hurts to remember that I could do nothing to make it better."

Emily's cabin was just ahead. Caeden spied smoke rising from the chimney and felt a sense of relief. He drew up to just in front of the shack and dismounted. He felt like a nervous schoolboy. How could one woman so deeply affect his sense of calm?

Caeden tied the horse off and drew a deep breath. There was no sense in worrying about how he'd explain. He just needed to find Emily and get the job done. Simple truth was the best. He knocked on the cabin door and waited.

Emily opened the door dressed in her old clothes and canvas coat. Her eyes widened at the sight of him. "What . . . why are you here?"

"You left without your things last night. I brought them. They're on my horse." He motioned to the carpetbag he'd hooked over the horn of the saddle.

Without waiting for her to speak, he went back to retrieve the bag and brought it to her. "I had hoped to talk to you last night."

"I didn't want to keep you from your friends." She looked down at the ground and then stepped back. "You might as well come in. I need to talk to you about the things you sent."

Caeden stepped into the house and put the bag down just inside the door. There were crates sitting all around the small single room, and all were unopened.

"I don't know what all you purchased, but you must take it back," Emily began. "I can't take advantage of your generosity."

"Nonsense. I bought these things as a way to thank you and your father for letting me stay here."

Emily put her hands on her hips and turned to face him. "You already did that before you left. You bought food for us and helped chop wood. There was no need to send anything more."

"I wanted to." He stepped closer. "You lost almost everything in the fire, and I was moved by the generosity of your neighbors. Those people had little or nothing and yet they were willing to share. That impressed me and also shamed me. I have great wealth and have never practiced even a fraction of their giving."

Emily nodded. "They are good people and so are you. I am certain that had the needs of others been presented, you would have been as lavish as you've been with us."

"Then it's settled. You will keep what I've sent and enjoy it in the knowledge that it gave me great pleasure to do something useful with my money. Besides, it would cost a great deal of money to ship all those boxes back to Great Falls."

She opened her mouth and looked as if she would protest,

but instead she gave a brief nod. "Very well. I don't suppose I will convince you otherwise."

He smiled, feeling quite satisfied with himself. "No, you won't."

"Well then, I appreciate that you brought the carpetbag all this way. I don't have anything in the way of refreshments to offer except for a cup of cold water." She looked at the stove. "Jake's bringing some meat today, and I do have a few eggs and some bread Millie gave me. If you're hungry, I could make you something to eat."

He nodded. "I'd like that. I left so early I didn't get break-fast." He glanced over at the crates. "If you open some of these, you'll find a great deal of food. I bought up enough to get you through the winter as I figured it. There are quite a few canned items." He looked around at the unopened boxes. "Why don't I start opening these while you cook?"

She looked hesitant, but Caeden didn't give her a chance to refuse. Instead he went to the stove and retrieved the poker. "I'll just pry off a few tops and we'll see what's what."

Caeden was halfway through the crates when he remembered his real reason for coming. Trying to sound casual, he brought up the topic of the Arnolds. "Those folks you met last night are from New York. Mr. Arnold was a business associate of my father's. In fact it was Mr. Arnold and my father's idea that I should marry Catherine."

"She's very beautiful. I can see why you would be happy to take her as a wife."

"But I'm not."

Emily turned from the stove. "You're not what?"

Caeden pulled a sack of flour from one of the crates. "I'm not taking her as a wife."

Emily looked confused as her brow knit together. "But Mr. Arnold said she was your fiancée and you didn't correct him."

"No, I didn't. There were . . . there are some extenuating circumstances, and I'd like to explain them."

She turned back to her cooking. "There's no need. You certainly do not owe me an explanation."

Caeden could see this wasn't going to be easy. "I think I do. It's important to me that you know the truth. When I left Albany I made it clear to Arnold that I had no intention of marrying anyone. I saw the wreckage left by my father and didn't want to risk doing that to someone else."

Emily scooped out the scrambled eggs onto a plate, then turned her attention to slicing bread. She said nothing, so Caeden continued.

"Catherine and I were never a part of the decision making. We had grown up together, although she was much younger than I. Still, I never lied to her or told her that I planned to honor the arrangement. She knew I didn't love her."

Still Emily said nothing, but Caeden knew she was listening. He only hoped that she would understand his current arrangement.

"When I went to Great Falls I had a chance to speak with Catherine alone. She told me that her father is in dire financial straits. He was victim to my father's schemes. At least that's what I was told. I have my uncle back in Albany checking on the situation."

Emily plopped two pieces of buttered bread into the skillet. "Do you want me to make coffee?"

Caeden hoisted the large sack of flour and brought it to where Emily stood. "No. Where do you want this?"

She scrutinized the sack for a moment. "I suppose in the corner. I'm not sure how I'll ever keep the mice out of it." She turned back to the bread.

Without waiting for further instruction, Caeden dumped the

sack in the corner and returned to the stove. He hoped Emily would finish with the cooking, then come sit with him while he finished telling her the story.

"I don't have any jam," she said, flipping the pieces.

"That's fine. I'd like it very much if you would join me at the table so I can finish telling you what you need to know."

"I need to know? What in the world would I need to know?" She looked at him without emotion, but rather than wait for an answer, she pointed to the table. "Go sit down." She took up the plate of eggs. "I'll bring this to you in just a minute." Emily turned her attention back to the stove, and Caeden felt he had no choice but to wait. He took a seat and watched her in silence. Just the sight of her made his heart beat faster. Her mother had once told him that God had sent him as a husband for Emily. He hadn't believed it then, but now her declaration seemed quite reasonable. Maybe God really did love him.

In a few minutes Emily placed the plate in front of Caeden. She then drew a fork from her apron pocket and set it alongside the plate. For a moment she did nothing but stand there staring down at the food. Caeden glanced at the plate. The toast was golden brown and the eggs cooked to perfection. "It looks delicious." He pulled out the chair beside him. "Why don't you get a plate and share it with me."

"I've already eaten."

"Then please sit with me, and take off your coat, for pity's sake. You look as if you're about to run away."

She acted as though she would refuse but finally nodded. She hung her coat on a nail by the door, then returned to take a seat at the table. Caeden bowed his head and offered thanks—something he hadn't done in a long time but that suddenly felt very right.

"Father, we give thanks for your provision. Amen."

"Amen," Emily murmured. She looked at him for a moment and sighed.

Caeden lost no time. "Once I knew the situation with Arnold and his finances, I realized he would stop at nothing to see Catherine married to a wealthy husband. Catherine is already in love with someone else, but he doesn't have the large fortune her father would like. She is terrified he will sell her off to one of his old cronies."

"Sell her off? Like a slave?" Emily's tone was incredulous.

"In some ways. Arnold is the kind of man who sees Catherine as a prize to be bartered for. He would find the man who could most benefit his coffers and future plans. Then Bishop Arnold would force his daughter into marriage with that man."

"How awful." She toyed with the hem of her apron, refusing to look him in the eye.

"Yes, it is, but it's very often done among the elite of society. Marriages aren't always about love but rather business dealings." He waited for her to comment, but she didn't.

"So, because Catherine was up against this, we agreed to let her father believe we were accepting of the engagement he and my father had contracted. It's nothing more than a sham, however."

This got Emily's attention. "For what purpose?"

"To buy time," Caeden explained. "Catherine needs time. We will plan for a long engagement. Meanwhile, she hopes to arrange an elopement with her young man. If her father believes she's engaged to me, he won't have any further plans for her."

"How will this help his financial problems?"

"Despite the betrothal being a sham, I'm paying Mr. Arnold a large dowry or bride-price for Catherine's hand. It's a small thing to do in order to keep Catherine from a life of misery. In a short time, after she has the opportunity to put her plans in action, I will break the engagement. If I cancel the engagement, then I will be expected to forfeit the dowry. I alone will bear the shame, and Catherine will still be highly regarded in her social circles. In fact, she will no doubt garnish a great deal of sympathy. More important, she'll be able to marry her true love."

Emily finally seemed to relax a bit. She met his gaze and nodded. "That's quite admirable of you. She's fortunate to have you as a friend."

"Miss Emily, are you home?" Jake Hoover called from outside.

Emily jumped to her feet and hurried to the door. Caeden grimaced. He wasn't through with what he wanted to say, but with Jake there he couldn't continue. Instead he focused on the food she'd fixed for him.

"Well, hello there, Mr. Thibault," Jake said, coming into the cabin with two sacks slung over his shoulder. "I thought you'd gone on your way."

Caeden swallowed. "I was delayed. I needed to speak with Emily about some important matters." He turned his attention back to the food, hoping Jake would finish his business and leave.

"Well, I brought the little lady some elk." He put the sacks on the table opposite Caeden, then looked around the cabin. "Looks like I'm not the only one makin' deliveries."

"Caeden sent this stuff to us. It arrived after Pa was shot and moved to Lewistown. I just found it here this morning. He said it was in thanks for what Pa had done for him."

Jake smiled. "The Lord works in mysterious ways." He looked at Caeden and raised a brow. "It would seem you were mighty thankful."

"I still am." Caeden finished the last of his toast and said nothing more.

Jake seemed to realize he'd intruded and started for the door. He put his hand out and touched Emily's coat hanging there. "I see Millie got this cleaned up for you. Knowing her, she probably cleaned your gun as well."

Emily smiled. "I didn't check, but I was happy to get both back."

"I was sure you would be. Look, I'll check on you again, Miss Emily. Let Millie know if you need anything. She can always get word to me."

"Thank you, Jake. You've been most kind. Once I get organized I promise I'll make you some of your favorite cookies."

Jake hesitated for a moment at the open door. He looked back at Caeden as if ascertaining his trustworthiness. Caeden held his gaze for several moments before Jake nodded and left the cabin. Emily waved from the door and seemed in no hurry to return to Caeden's company. He frowned. This was turning out to be more difficult than he'd expected.

"If you'll excuse me," Emily said, reaching for her coat. "I need to go down to Millie's."

Caeden got to his feet. "Please wait. I have something to say."

Emily was already out the door but paused. Caeden followed her, hoping, very nearly praying, for the right words. His entire future depended on this moment.

"Well?" Emily looked at him and offered him a hint of a smile. She moved away several steps. "What is it you want to say?"

"I . . . I'm going to be gone for some time." Caeden searched for the words, but nothing seemed right. "I wanted to . . . well . . . I wanted you to know that . . ."

He looked at her for a long moment, then did the only thing he could think to do. The one thing he'd wanted to do for a very long while. He closed the distance between them in two long strides and pulled Emily into his arms. Without another word he covered her mouth with his in a long and passionate kiss.

He felt her yield to his touch, melting against him just as he had hoped she might. He deepened his kiss, bending her slightly backward. Her arms went around his neck. Caeden wanted the moment to never end, and Emily seemed to be in no hurry to go. *She does care about me. She wants me as much as I want her.*

When he ended the kiss, Caeden continued to hold her. He knew time was of the essence, but moments like this weren't soon to come back his way. "I love you, Emily." He whispered the words against her ear. "I didn't think it was even possible for me to fall in love, but I have."

He turned his head to gaze into her eyes. She looked at him with eyes wide and mouth slightly agape. Whether she was more surprised by the kiss or his declaration, it didn't matter. Caeden put his hand to her cheek. "I have to return to Washington, and as I said, I'll be gone for some time. I had to come here, however, and ask you if you'd consider . . . if you'd mind . . . waiting for me?"

He wanted to ask her to marry him but worried that the suddenness of the entire situation would cause her to bolt. He swallowed back the lump in his throat. Her silence was killing him.

꧁꧂

Emily could hardly believe what Caeden had just said. Frankly, his entire appearance at the cabin, not to mention the kiss—her first—had been quite stunning. She had cried herself to sleep the night before, hating that the marshal didn't believe her and that Caeden was to marry another. Now with his arm still around her, his thumb stroking her cheek, Emily found structured thought almost impossible. She didn't want to ruin the moment by saying anything. In fact, she would have really liked to hear him declare his love once again.

"Emily?"

She put her hand over his and pressed it to her cheek. "I'll wait."

He smiled one of those rare, heartfelt smiles she had come to love. "I knew you cared for me."

"I do." Her voice was barely a whisper.

He chuckled. "Just remember those two little words. They should come in handy in the months to come."

Caeden kissed her again, this time much quicker. When he stepped back Emily immediately longed for his return.

"I've got to go." He mounted the bay and looked down at her. "I've set up a bank account for you in Lewistown. I know you and your father are ever so self-sufficient, but humor me and draw on the account if you need to. I don't like the idea of you being out here by yourself trying to pan for gold in a blizzard."

Emily laughed. "I'm not that foolish. Still, I did tell Pa I'd try."

"I don't see as you should have to tell him where the money came from—just that you have what you need." Caeden shrugged. "It's not a lie."

For a moment neither one said anything. Emily could see the longing in Caeden's eyes. It matched the feeling in her heart. "You'd best go."

He nodded. "I suppose so." He turned the horse toward Yogo City. "You've changed everything in my world, Miss Emily Carver. I hope you realize that." He gave the horse a nudge in the side and urged him forward.

Emily stood fixed, watching until Caeden was out of sight. Last night everything had seemed so hopeless. What a difference a few hours could make.

# 21

Kirk Davies fought off the dizziness that threatened to put him on the floor. He hadn't felt good in days, and upon waking this morning he'd found it almost impossible to put weight on his left leg.

He muttered curses, most directed at Emily Carver. If she hadn't bit him, he wouldn't be dealing with any of this now. He certainly wouldn't be sitting in a doctor's office in Utica with his leg swollen beyond its normal size.

The doctor, an older man with a no-nonsense approach, entered the room and eyed Davies for a moment. "What seems to be ailing you?"

"My leg. I . . . I injured it and now it's causing me grief."

The doctor felt his forehead. "You're burning up. No doubt it's infected. Drop your pants and I'll take a look."

The man didn't offer to assist Kirk at all, which only served to bring about more cursing. Kirk undid his gun belt but kept it close at hand. He'd learned over the years it was never wise to be separated from his revolver, and he wasn't going to start now.

Removing his pants proved more difficult. His fingers fumbled with the buttons but finally managed the job. He worked the canvas pants down the swollen leg to reveal the dirty bandage on his thigh.

"Get up on the table," the doctor instructed.

Again Davies growled out curses as he fought to keep from passing out from the pain. His pants fell to his ankles and nearly caused him to fall as they bound his legs. With no other choice, however, he gritted his teeth and managed to settle onto the examination table.

The doctor didn't take any great care with the removal of the bandage, and when he pulled it away, putrid pieces of flesh and blood came with it. The stench was almost unbearable.

"You're just about to lose this leg," the doctor declared. "Why'd you wait so long to get in here?"

"Busy," Kirk said, still clenching his teeth. He wasn't about to show any sign of weakness.

"What happened? This looks like a bite. Did you tangle with some animal?"

"I fell off my horse and landed on a jagged piece of wood." The lie came easy. He couldn't very well tell the doctor that Emily Carver had bit him. Word might get back to the marshal, and Davies had worked too hard on his plan to have it all be for naught.

The doctor's expression revealed his skepticism. "I've seen a lot of wounds in my years, but this one still looks like a bite. It might help me if you tell me the truth."

"Look, old man, just patch me up."

The doctor shook his head. "It's not going to be that easy. You're going to have to stay here. I'm going to have to treat this around the clock. Even then, I think we're too late. I may have to amputate."

"You ain't takin' my leg and I ain't stayin' here. Just give me some medicine and bandage it."

The doctor fixed him with the stern look of a father about to discipline his son. "You aren't listening. We'll be lucky if losing your leg is all that happens. You may well lose your life. You've waited too long to get in here for attention. The infection has spread. You see those streaks of red? If those reach your heart you'll be dead."

Davies might have been worried if he believed the old man's words. Doctors were always trying to scare people into doing what they wanted. After all, that's what made them money. He was no fool. He thought about pulling his gun in order to force the man to do what he wanted, but Kirk knew he wasn't well enough to handle it if the old man decided to make a break for it. "Doc, I'll take my chances. Just patch me up the best you can and give me some medicine."

"There's not a whole lot I can give you that will help." The doctor went to a small cabinet and unlocked the door. "I'll do what I can. I'll clean out the wound with carbolic acid. It won't be pleasant, so I'm going to give you a healthy dose of laudanum to ease the pain. It'll make you sleepy." He pulled two bottles, one brown and one clear, from the cabinet.

Next the doctor opened a box on the counter and pulled out rolls of bandages. He brought all of this to the table and set it beside Davies. "I'll need to get some instruments," he announced, then disappeared for a moment.

Kirk knew he had a fever, but he felt chilled to the bone, and every part of his body seemed to ache. He looked down at the clear bottle marked *laudanum* and decided to help himself. He was about to put the bottle to his lips when the doctor returned.

"I don't suppose you'd use a spoon."

Kirk stopped and nodded. "Give me one."

The doctor put down the small tray he carried and handed a spoon to Davies. "Take four teaspoons."

"That all?"

"It'll be enough for now." The doctor placed several instruments in a shallow pan, then poured carbolic acid over them while Kirk dosed himself with laudanum. The doctor took another pan and placed a good amount of bandage material in it and doused that with carbolic acid as well.

Finally he came to Kirk and took the spoon and bottle. "Lie back on the table."

Kirk did as the man instructed and tucked the gun belt in close to his side. The room spun around him, and even when he closed his eyes, Kirk felt as if it were still moving. He heard the doctor fiddling with his tools, but for the life of him Kirk couldn't manage enough interest to look.

"You might want to bite down on this."

Kirk opened his eyes to find the doctor holding a rolled-up towel. For a moment he couldn't remember what the man wanted him to do with it.

"This isn't going to be pleasant, even with the laudanum. You may want to chew on this to keep from yelling." He pushed the towel toward Kirk's mouth.

A hint of understanding permeated the fog, and Kirk took hold of the cloth and clenched the roll between his teeth. Once this was done, the doctor immediately went to work.

Kirk had never known such torture, and in other circumstances he would have killed any man trying to put him through such an ordeal. He cried out against the muffling of the cloth, fiery pain spreading to every part of his body. Just when he knew he could stand no more, a black haze started to cloud his vision and even the sounds of his own cries seemed muffled. After that, he knew nothing.

When he woke up, the doctor had finished and the leg was bandaged. His pants were still down around his ankles, but at least the surgery was done. He looked around the room and saw that the doctor was busy instructing a young man on how to clean the instruments. Struggling to sit up, Kirk again fought the dizziness. At least the pain was less, no doubt thanks to the laudanum.

The doctor looked back at him, then said something to the boy and sent him on his way. "Your wound is very bad, Mr. Davies. I want again to urge you to remain here with me. I can provide you constant care. We'll know soon enough if this has done anything to reverse the infection."

Kirk struggled with his pants. Once he had them up around his knees he slid from the table, careful to put no weight on the left leg. "I'll be fine."

"Very well. I'll send you home with a bottle of laudanum. You're going to need to remove the bandage every two hours. I want you to heat up some vinegar and take a towel and soak it good. Then apply it to the wound. It'll hurt like . . . well . . . it'll hurt. The heat and vinegar, however, will hopefully pull some of the poisoning from the wound."

"Every two hours?" Kirk shook his head, still fuzzy from the laudanum. "I ain't got time for that."

"Then you'll be dead soon and will have no more time for anything," the doctor said with a shrug. "It's your choice."

Kirk pulled on his gun belt and secured it around his waist. "I ain't no weakling. I'll be fine." He tested the leg. The pain was instantaneous and shot up through his hip and gut, but he told himself it wasn't nearly as bad as it had been.

The doctor went to a closet on the far side of the room. Kirk wasn't sure what the old man was doing, but when he pulled a single crutch from the enclosure it all made sense.

"Use this. I'll want it back. You need to keep as much weight off the leg as possible. I'd give you the set of crutches, but I know you wouldn't use them. Men like you never do."

"Meanin' what?" Kirk asked.

"Meaning you like to keep your gun arm unencumbered."

Kirk nodded. "Yeah, you got that right. Don't want to give folks the idea I'm weak. But you just keep your crutch. I want both hands free. What do I owe you?"

The doctor looked at him for a moment and shook his head. "I don't take money from dead men."

The comment struck a nerve with Kirk. The man was determined to scare him, and Kirk wasn't about to give in to fear. It hadn't served him in the past and wouldn't serve him now. Of course, the man could be right. The wound was pretty bad— the worst Davies had ever known. He pushed aside his rising doubts and hobbled to the door. "Your loss. You just wait and see. I'm gonna prove you wrong, old man."

Kirk made his way outside. Utica was fairly busy that morning. There were at least three freight wagons in the street and enough folks milling around to constitute a crowd. His leg burned and throbbed, but Kirk was determined to make his way to the saloon and buy a bottle. The laudanum was tucked safely in his pocket, and that, along with some stout whiskey, would surely ease his pain. For a moment he contemplated whether it was easier to ride his horse or walk. Mounting was a most difficult procedure, and so he decided it would be better to just walk down to the saloon and then back to the doc's.

The barkeep gave him a nod when Kirk stumbled into the dimly lit room. "We ain't open for business. I had some trouble here last night and a lot of cleanin' to do this morning."

"I just need a bottle of whiskey." Kirk tossed down some

coins. "Got myself hurt, and doc wants me to stay off the leg. I need the whiskey to help with the pain."

"Doc's sure been busy this last month what with the Carver shooting. I guess the old man is going to live, though. I heard Doc talking about it when he was in here the other night." He looked at Kirk as if anticipating a response.

Kirk had heard rumors of the old man making it through surgery. He knew Emily wasn't dead. He hadn't hit her hard enough to kill her. Well, he'd get this leg healed up, and then he'd take care of Carver once and for all.

"You gonna get that bottle, or do I need to come back there and get it myself?"

The man either took pity on him or else was afraid Kirk might resort to violence if he refused. He quickly procured a bottle and scooped up the money.

"I could use that bottle back."

Kirk nodded. "You'll get it." He clasped the whiskey to his chest and momentarily closed his eyes. He'd never been this sick in his life, and all he wanted to do was get back to the shack he called home and fall into bed.

He limped out into the sunlight and began the trek back down to the doctor's to retrieve his horse. He drew one ragged breath after another and forced himself to focus on walking a straight line.

"Davies."

He turned and found the one man he'd hoped to avoid. "Marshal."

The other man eyed Davies oddly. "Saw you stumbling there. What seems to be wrong with your leg?"

"Fell off my horse."

"Where'd this happen?" The marshal continued looking at him as if he didn't believe Kirk.

"Up in the mountains. Why?"

The marshal shook his head. "Just wondered. Hate to see a man incapacitated." Kirk started to go, but the marshal spoke again. "I see it's your left leg."

"Yeah, what of it?"

With a shrug the marshal shook his head. "Just noticed it. Got to be hard to mount a horse."

"I'll get by," Kirk told him. The man looked more and more suspicious, and Kirk wasn't about to answer any further questions. Kirk narrowed his eyes and hoped he looked as mean as he felt. "You'd do well enough to get on with your marshaling somewhere else."

He didn't wait for a response but headed for his horse with as little of a limp as possible. Perspiration formed on his brow. The effort was almost impossible, and when he reached his horse, Kirk took a moment to put the whiskey in the saddlebag and regain his wind. With the marshal still watching, Kirk clenched his teeth and lifted his left leg to the stirrup. The pain was excruciating, but he didn't let it show. Instead, he used the bulky muscles of his arms to pull himself atop the animal, putting minimal weight on the leg.

The marshal continued to watch him, but Kirk no longer cared. He knew if he didn't get out of town soon, he just might pass out cold in the middle of the street.

The ride back to the cabin seemed endless, but Kirk tried his best to keep his thoughts on how he'd make Emily Carver pay for what she'd done to him. He'd torment her for a time and eventually kill her. The thought brought him a sort of peace and pleasure. He'd seen to her old man, and now he'd see to her.

As Kirk approached his cabin, a man came out from the

wooded area to the right. He had an ax over one shoulder and was dragging a tree trunk behind him.

"You see the doctor?"

Kirk nodded and reined the horse to a stop. "He cleaned it up and gave me laudanum." With great effort, Kirk kicked his feet from the stirrups and then slid down the side of his mount. The animal was well trained and didn't move. Kirk freed the whiskey from his saddlebag and stumbled toward the cabin.

The other man let go of the tree and ax and came to where Kirk was. He put his arm around Kirk and all but carried him inside. He took Kirk to the nearest chair and helped him to sit.

"He say how long you'd be laid up?"

Kirk met the eyes of the man who was so nearly the identical image of himself that they could have been twins. "Taber, open this bottle. I need a drink."

"All right, but aren't you gonna tell me what the doc said?"

"He tried to scare me into stayin' there. Said I was about to lose the leg. I told him I wasn't gonna let him take it, so I might as well go home. He wasn't happy, but I figure that's because I denied him the chance to make a lot of money and practice his amputating skills."

Taber frowned. "Are you sure you shouldn't have stayed? I've already lost one brother, and I don't like the idea of losing another."

Kirk shook his head. "You ain't losin' me. I'm fine. Just need some rest."

Taber poured them both a whiskey. "And all this trouble from that little Carver gal. Guess she needs to pay for what she's done."

"Yeah." Kirk tossed back the whiskey. "She does, and I've been mullin' over just how to go about that. But it's not just that. The bartender told me Carver is definitely still alive. I think we're gonna have to go to Lewistown and finish the job."

"Don't you think they'll be lookin' for you?"

Kirk shrugged. "I figure we can work out the details while my leg heals. It'll be a while—maybe another week or two. By that time they will have forgotten all about me."

Taber laughed. "Don't count on it. From what you've told me about Emily Carver, I doubt she'll let this go. Maybe we should just take her with us to Lewistown for safekeeping. Maybe if she's with us, the others will know we mean business."

"Like I said, we can make our plans while my leg heals." Kirk groaned and closed his eyes. "Right now I just need some sleep."

Kirk tossed and turned. The pain refused to abate, and he was now beginning to wonder if the doctor had been right. Taber attended to him, bringing a wet towel to cool down the fever, but nothing seemed to help.

"Doc said to soak some towels in hot vinegar and put it on the wound." His voice was barely audible.

"You want me to do that?" Taber asked. The worry in his expression left Kirk afraid of just how bad things were.

"I don't suppose it could hurt."

Taber nodded and went to the stove. The tiny shack rattled and allowed in drafts of cold air as the wind blew hard. "It started snowing a little while ago. Maybe we should think about heading south—after you take care of business, of course."

"Might be I'll have to have you take care of it," Kirk murmured. "It worked once. I'm sure it could work again."

He smiled to himself at the memory of Taber posing as Kirk in Utica. They had come up with the scheme together. Taber would cause a ruckus and get himself thrown into jail as Kirk Davies. Meanwhile, Kirk would go and kill Henry Carver and his daughter. It had nearly worked, and had Kirk not heard someone calling out to Carver, he would have finished the job. But with Taber in the jail, Kirk knew it was best to get out of sight. He'd hoped that the bullet he'd put in Carver would have taken care of the job. It was a great annoyance that it hadn't, but the ruse had served its purpose. The marshal hadn't even bothered to question him about the shooting.

"I'm thinkin' maybe I could go back to the doc and agree to stay at his place. Then you could go and kill Carver in Lewistown and then come back here and nab the woman. You could bring her here and tie her up. I'll no doubt hear about her disappearin' and then I'll know it's safe to come back." He forced a smile. "I'll have my alibi, Carver will be dead, and we'll have our fun."

Taber nodded. "I think you just might have a plan there."

⁂

Albany was much as Caeden had left it well over a year ago, only now it was covered in snow. He had wrestled with his conscience about returning ever since leaving Montana. He had also spent a good deal of time in prayer. His heart toward God had changed little by little. He knew Emily's influence had helped in that matter, but more so, he'd started truly trying to seek God on his own.

The thing that troubled him most, however, was a deep fear that God couldn't forgive him for having turned away. Now as he made his way to see his uncle, Caeden hoped to discuss the matter with him. Uncle Jasper had always been a man of God, and if anyone had the answers, Caeden felt certain he would.

He'd been in town for less than twenty-four hours, but already word had reached him from Catherine, as well as her father. The missives had come separately, hand delivered to his hotel by staff members of the Arnold household. It was clear that Bishop Arnold was still in the dark about the engagement. His letter was quite simple—stating that it was imperative Caeden come for dinner so that they could get the wedding date set and start making plans. Arnold also mentioned a business venture on which he wanted Caeden's opinion.

Catherine's note had been simpler still with just four words: "I've made my arrangements."

It was her signal to him that he could break the engagement. Caeden figured to kill two birds with one dinner appearance. He would show up, and prior to supper being served, he would announce that he'd given the matter great consideration but felt that he must now break their engagement. Arnold would be furious, but Caeden would soothe the man by assuring him he could keep the dowry. Caeden hadn't yet decided what excuse he would use for ending his betrothal but felt certain it wouldn't matter. Arnold would try to change his mind, and Caeden would stand fast and refuse.

Uncle Jasper's butler opened the door to admit Caeden. The black man smiled, quite delighted to see him. "Good morning, sir. Your uncle has talked of nothing but your return. You'll find him in the library."

"Thank you, George. How are you these days?"

George had been a free man all of his life, and for a good portion of it he had worked as Uncle Jasper's butler, although the two were more like friends. "Exceptionally well, sir. Thank you for asking." He beamed Caeden a smile. "It's been kind of quiet without you around."

Caeden couldn't help but smile. This man had taught him a good deal about baseball when they were both much younger. "Hit any home runs lately?"

George chuckled. "Not of late, sir."

Caeden shrugged out of his coat. "Me either, and I think it's a pity on both of our accounts. If I were staying in town longer, I'd have to put together a game just to see if you could still hit those lightning-fast grounders that I could never catch."

George took Caeden's hat and coat. "I'm afraid my days of being lightning fast are gone. I'm more a gentle summer rain these days."

Caeden chuckled and made his way to his uncle's library on the second floor. Caeden knew the way by heart. He'd come here often as a means of escaping his father's temper, and the place was more home to him than the estate on which he'd been raised.

Uncle Jasper was a most distinguished-looking man at the age of fifty-eight. His black hair was peppered with white, but he still bore the appearance of a man ten years his junior. He sat near the fire reading, as Caeden remembered him doing so often in years gone by.

"Hello, Uncle."

Jasper Carrington looked up, his expression one of pure joy. "Caeden, my boy, I thought you'd never make it. How good to have you finally here." He got up and crossed the room. "Let me see how you've fared."

Caeden laughed and embraced his uncle. "As well as anyone can when they've spent the last few weeks in Washington, DC. How are you?"

"Splendid now that you're here. Do tell me you're going to be back for a while."

Sobering, Caeden shook his head. "No. But that's why I wanted to come speak with you right away."

His uncle nodded. "Ah, it's just as I presumed. Have a seat. Have you had breakfast?"

Caeden took a chair and stretched out his legs. "Yes, at the hotel."

"You should have come here to stay. You know you're welcome to be here while you're in town. In fact, I insist."

"It was late when I got back last night. I didn't want to rouse poor George or Mrs. Claremont out of their beds."

"Mrs. Claremont has been housekeeper here long enough to know that people might come or go at any given hour, and George has always welcomed you here. So do say you'll at least have your things moved over while you're here in Albany. Goodness, you are staying for Christmas, aren't you? It's only a week away."

"I am going to stay that long," Caeden replied. He ran his hands down the gray wool of his trousers. "I figure I owe my family that much. But there's a lot I want to accomplish in that time."

"I presume much of that has to do with Bishop Arnold."

His uncle reclaimed his leather wingback chair, a longtime favorite. In all of his memories of Uncle Jasper, that chair figured into most. When Caeden was born, Jasper had been about the same age as Caeden was now. Caeden could remember being quite young and curling up on Jasper's lap to hear a story. Here in front of the hearth, the large brown leather arms would engulf him in a warm embrace. Times here with Jasper were very nearly his only pleasant childhood memories.

"You might as well know," his uncle continued, "Arnold is in a bad way. He came to me two days ago."

"Why? He received the dowry, didn't he?"

With elbows planted on the arms of the chair, Jasper steepled his fingers together. "It would seem the man was duped by someone who sold him a worthless gold mine."

"But I anticipated that. I figured we gave him enough to absorb that loss and keep him afloat for a while."

"Well, it seems he spent a great deal arranging for men to work in the mine and purchasing equipment with which to make his fortune. But, just as you said in your letter to me, the mine is worthless."

"So why did he come to see you?" Caeden fought back the irritation that threatened to ruin his visit.

"He didn't know when you would arrive. He hoped to convince you to give him more money until he could recoup his losses. I told him that it had come to our attention that your father had taken advantage of him in their final business venture and that you wished to return that money with interest. After that, he seemed content and had little more to say. I gave him a check just as you instructed me to do."

"I'm to have dinner with him tonight. He believes it's to set a wedding date, but I intend to break the engagement instead. Catherine sent word that she's ready for me to do so, and I see no reason to delay."

"Bishop won't like that."

Caeden shrugged and crossed his arms. "I really don't care. The man will have to figure out his own way. I pity the family and hope that since Catherine is soon to elope with her true love, perhaps they will be able to benefit her mother and siblings with his income."

"It should be so. The young man in question has just come into his inheritance. A sizable one that was unexpected. It seems his grandmother died and left him everything. It's raised some hackles among his siblings, but I doubt it will cause him too much grief. He should be quite acceptable to Bishop."

"I'm just glad that Catherine can marry for love."

"And what of you?" His uncle looked at him with a knowing smile. "Your letter spoke of a certain young woman in Montana."

"Emily. I have to own that I've lost my heart to her."

"And she's agreed to marry you?"

This brought a grin to Caeden's face. "I didn't propose exactly, but she did agree to wait." He just as quickly sobered again. "But none of this is the real reason I've come today. Besides spending time with you, I hoped to get your counsel. In fact, I have to have your counsel before I can return to Emily and ask for her hand."

"You want my counsel on marriage? You know I've been a widower since before you were born." His uncle shook his head and relaxed his hands. "I doubt I can offer you much wisdom."

"No, not about marriage. About God."

Jasper's expression softened. "Go on."

Caeden looked downward at the ornate Persian rug. "How can a person know if God really and truly forgives him?"

"I suppose because the Bible says that if we confess our sins, He is faithful and just to forgive us our sins. It's one of those things that must be taken on faith. Why do you ask?"

Caeden rubbed his chin thoughtfully. "I guess because I have a lot to be forgiven. Is there a limit to God's forgiveness?"

"If there is, I certainly haven't found it." He smiled. "No, my boy. God's forgiveness is limitless. Just as His love is. What is required of you . . . of all of us . . . is a sincerely contrite heart."

"I spent so many years angry at God. Angry and rebellious and far from righteous." Caeden grimaced. "I'm deeply ashamed of the man I once was."

"And have you asked God to forgive you for these many rebellious and angry sins?" Uncle Jasper's tone offered no condemnation.

"I have," Caeden admitted. It wasn't nearly so hard to confess as he had thought it might be. "I told Him I was sorry for how I'd let my father's bad behavior dictate my relationship with Him. I can see now what Mother meant when she told me God's love was enough for her—that it helped to ease her sadness and kept her from complete despair. I just want to know that I can have that same love."

"You can," Jasper said after a moment's contemplation, "but I can't make you see that or feel it. You have to find that for yourself. It's all about trusting, Caeden. You need to trust that God is who He says He is. You need to believe that His Word is true and never changes. The same God who loved your mother is the same God who loves you. The truth given in His Word to her is the very same on which you can count now."

Caeden let out a heavy breath. For several minutes he did nothing but stare into the fire. After a while he spoke. "Trust has always come hard. I'm not sure I would even know how it felt."

"You trust that young woman of yours, don't you? She has promised to wait for you. You do believe her, don't you?"

"Of course."

Jasper smiled and leaned forward. "How can you be sure she'll keep her word?"

Caeden smiled. "That's easy. I know her. She's a woman of her word."

"Exactly. And as you get to know God better, you'll learn that He is also one to keep His word. Trust comes in time. Trust comes in knowing Him better and better. After a while, you'll know how that feels. There will be a peace that comes to rest in your heart."

That statement caught his attention. Peace. There was a certain peace in his heart. He no longer felt that same restlessness that he'd known in years gone by. He no longer felt imprisoned by the haunting memories of the past.

"There is peace. You're right. I just didn't realize that was what it was." Caeden looked at his uncle in wonder. "It's unlike anything I've ever known before."

"Yes. The Bible calls it a peace that passeth all understanding. In that peace, you will be able to see more and more of God's blessings. And, Caeden, He will bless you. He already has, and you have no further to look than your young lady."

George appeared at the door of the library. "Sir, this letter just arrived for . . . Mr. Thibault." His formal announcement made Caeden chuckle as he got to his feet. "Honestly, George, I'd much rather you call me Caeden and ruffle my hair like you did when I was little than to call me Mr. Thibault."

George said nothing but extended the envelope to Caeden with a wink. Caeden looked down at the writing. He recognized the name of the gem expert to whom he'd sent the Yogo sapphires. Emily's sapphires.

"What is it?" Uncle Jasper asked, coming to join Caeden at the door.

Caeden read the letter, then looked into the envelope again to pull out a check for a sizable sum. He looked up to meet his uncle's curious gaze. "Blessings. God's blessings."

# 22

From the moment he arrived at the Arnold residence, Bishop Arnold tried to get Caeden to join him in his study for a few private words regarding a business venture. Caeden refused, telling the man that he had only one point of business on his mind and it didn't involve a private audience with Arnold. Unhappy at this turn of events, Arnold led Caeden into a large sitting room, where Catherine and her mother were already standing to receive him.

"Mrs. Arnold, I want to thank you for inviting me here this evening," Caeden said, giving a slight bow. "Catherine, you look lovely in that plaid."

Catherine smiled knowingly and brushed down the skirt of the red-and-green plaid gown. "I thought it rather festive for the season."

"Indeed it is," Caeden agreed. "In fact, your entire house looks quite ready for Christmas." Pine greenery and red ribbons trimmed out the fireplace mantel, and a sprig of mistletoe hung over the archway that led into the music room.

"We have entertained several times this Christmas season," Mrs. Arnold replied. "I do so love this time of year."

Caeden allowed Bishop Arnold and his wife ten minutes of conversation and questions about his trip and how he'd fared before clearing his throat to make his announcement.

Arnold gave a chuckle, no doubt believing Caeden meant to discuss the wedding. Caeden did nothing to correct his thinking. Catherine, who had remained fairly silent since Caeden's arrival, watched and waited for him to break their engagement. He had no idea of how she would respond. He didn't know if she would play the woman scorned or collapse in a fit of tears or simply take it all in stride. What he did know was that this was what they both wanted and he couldn't finalize their agreement soon enough.

"I am sorry to say that my coming here tonight is not for the purpose you'd hoped for."

Bishop Arnold's expression sobered a bit. Caeden definitely had his attention. Catherine moved closer to the fireplace—farther from the others in the room.

"I am afraid that I have come to break my engagement to Catherine."

Bishop Arnold opened his mouth to speak, but Caeden held up his hand. "I would rather you hear me out than ask questions."

Arnold's face reddened, but he closed his mouth.

"Catherine and I have long held the opinion that we were not suited for each other, and with that in mind I must end this engagement. While I hold that Catherine is a lovely woman who will make some man a wonderful wife, I am not that man."

"But we have an agreement," Arnold interjected. "You gave me a sizable dowry."

"Which you may of course keep." Caeden saw Catherine's slight smile and just the hint of a nod.

"That . . . that . . . isn't the point. You . . . we were going to push ahead in business together," Arnold sputtered.

"I never agreed to that, Mr. Arnold. I have no intention of joining our businesses or fortunes together. I will refrain from voicing all of my reasons, but I believe they are known to you."

"I demand you give your reasons," the older man countered. "I have nothing to hide. You, on the other hand, may feel a need to keep a great many things from exposure."

Catherine stiffened and lowered her face to gaze into the fire, while Mrs. Arnold looked most uncomfortable. Caeden felt sorry for the Arnold women. None of this was their fault, and any angry retort he might have given was squelched when he thought of causing them pain.

Caeden shook his head. "Mr. Arnold, I am sorry that this comes as such a disappointment to you. I believe it's best if I simply take my leave now." He walked to where Mrs. Arnold stood and lifted her hand. "Thank you again for inviting me to dinner, but I must decline."

She nodded, and Caeden gave her a smile before releasing her to stand before Catherine. "I know what our engagement meant to you." With his back to the others, he gave her a wink. Catherine maintained a sober expression. "I hope that you won't think poorly of me. I do wish you all the best for your future."

"Thank you, Caeden. I appreciate that you came here tonight to release me in the comfort and privacy of my home. I will always remember you fondly." She smiled, and Caeden did likewise.

He regained his stern expression when he turned back to face Bishop Arnold. "Good evening." Caeden headed for the door, where one of the housemaids appeared with his coat and hat.

Bishop Arnold followed close on his heels. "This isn't over. I won't allow you to simply put my daughter aside in such a manner. You gave her no explanation—no understanding of what she's done wrong."

"She's done nothing wrong." Caeden did up the buttons of his black wool coat.

"Then why end our arrangement?"

Caeden looked Arnold in the eye. "Because I do not love her and never will. And any thoughts you had about our becoming business partners of any sort were exactly that. Your thoughts. I would never do business with you, Arnold. You and my father were cut from the same cloth. I couldn't stand the underhanded dealings from him, nor will I put myself in a position to endure them with you."

Arnold's face reddened and his nostrils flared. Narrowing his eyes, he pointed a finger at Caeden. "You slander me and you slander your father. I won't stand for it. I will pursue this in court."

Caeden shrugged. "Do so if that is your wish; however, I would remind you that your finances are quite depleted and can certainly not support a lengthy legal action. I, on the other hand, can withstand any lawsuit you deem necessary for years to come." He turned his top hat in hand and studied it for a moment.

"Furthermore, given your ambitions to align yourself with McKinley's presidential campaign, I would think you'd want to avoid scandal and a public acknowledgment of your business failings." Caeden looked up again and saw that the truth of the matter had finally started to hit Arnold. "And should you press this further, I will make certain to give an interview to every newspaper that asks. That would certainly deter McKinley and his people from wanting you to be a part of their campaign, much less any more important roles. Now, if you'll excuse me, my uncle is expecting me."

The young maid who stood silently at the far end of the foyer stepped forward to open the door. Caeden hadn't thought much of it when she'd admitted him to the house earlier, but it now seemed evident that the loss of money had caused Arnold to dismiss his butler. Yet another example of others suffering for the sins of one.

~~~~~~~~

"Pa, you must listen to reason." Emily put her hands atop her father's shoulders. "The doctor said you mustn't overdo. You need to take your recovery slowly."

While it had been wonderful news to hear from the doctor that her father was now starting to walk just a bit, he had also requested Emily come to Lewistown to force her father to listen to reason. She had laughed at the note mentioning the word *force* where her father was concerned. Henry Carver had never allowed anyone to force him into much.

"I'm feeling better, Em. I can't see just sittin' around. I need to get back to work."

Emily straightened and looked down at her father. "The doctor said that might not be possible. You need to face the truth, Pa. You might never be able to work at mining again."

"Bah, he didn't think I could walk again either. Now just look at me. I'm gettin' better every day. No, sirree, I'll not be defeated by any man tellin' me what I can and can't do."

"But you won't continue to improve if you overwork your body. You aren't young anymore, and you need to give yourself time to recover."

"And I say I can do that better at home. If you won't arrange it, I'll fix it myself."

"And just how would you propose to do that?" Emily pulled

up a chair and sat down. She was exhausted from arguing with her father. "Look, it's nearly Christmas. Why don't we just stay here at least that long? We can enjoy each other's company. After that we can see about arranging for you to travel back to Yogo City."

Her father seemed to mull this over for a moment. "I suppose I can agree to that if you can promise to get me home afterwards."

"I'll go speak with the doctor right now and see what I can arrange."

Emily had rejoiced to hear that her father was making great progress. It was nothing short of miraculous, the doctor had declared, and that too made Emily glad. She had prayed long and hard for her father's recovery, and it seemed God had gone far beyond her expectations. She wouldn't admit it to her father, but she felt almost certain that if Pa thought he could once again work the mines, that was exactly what he would do.

◦⥾⥾◦

Life had never been worse for Kirk Davies. He knew he was close to death—and he feared it. When Taber suggested they return to Utica and see the doctor again, Davies didn't protest, but neither did he believe there was anything to be done. Something told him he wouldn't recover, and the very thought left him terrified. What happened to a person once they passed from this world? Were those religious ninnies right in thinking there really was a heaven and a hell?

"I'm scared, Taber. Never . . . never felt so bad."

"You've got me scared too." The sound of his brother's voice was one of resignation. "We'll be to the doctor in just a little bit." He held fast to Kirk while the two rode double on Kirk's

288

sturdy gelding. Having had no wagon or even a cart to use, this was their only option.

It was seven o'clock and pitch black when they entered Utica. Kirk found himself barely conscious, and every thought was of his impending death. Life had never been fair to him, so he had no reason to believe death would be either. He thought about all the stories he'd heard about heaven and hell. Heaven was for good folks and hell was for bad. He knew he wouldn't have qualified as good, even on his best day. That left him only one possibility, and that was hell.

He'd heard a great many stories about the torment and pain of hell but had never believed them. He hadn't bothered to believe in God either. Seemed to him a man was supposed to be able to tend to himself without some imagined deity watching out for him.

Maybe death was just the end of things. A blank void—a nothingness. If it was, then Kirk didn't figure he had much to fear. After all, if death was the end of it all, then he'd be out of pain and know nothing more. But even this failed to offer him much in the way of comfort.

Maybe, just maybe, the doctor was wrong and there was something he could do to help. Could be he'd learned something more about wounds like Kirk's. It was possible.

Taber pulled him from the horse and carried him to the door of the doctor's house. "It'll just be a few more minutes," he told Kirk. "Just hang on." He kicked at the door and called for the man until the door finally opened.

"What's the . . ."

Kirk raised his head and saw the doctor's face at the door.

"Oh, it's you," the doctor said. "Lasted longer than I figured."

Taber pushed past the doctor. "Where do you want him?"

"I can't do anything for him," the doctor said, shaking his head. "I told him that when I first saw him. If I'd have amputated the leg, he might have had a chance."

Taber placed Kirk on a chair. "I don't want your excuses. I want you to save his life."

The doctor crossed his arms. "This man is going to die. I cannot stop that—it is inevitable."

Hearing the doctor's words was like the pounding of nails into the lid of his coffin. Kirk shuddered and let the words sink in with the finality intended. This really was the end, and there was nothing anyone could do about it.

He closed his eyes. It was almost as if hearing the words had given him permission to let go. "Tab . . . Taber."

His brother knelt beside him. "What is it, Kirk?"

"The doc can't . . . can't help." He strained to draw breath. "Take . . . care . . . of business. You . . . know . . . what to do."

⁘

"I still don't see why you have to leave tomorrow," Caeden's sister Deborah declared. All around them a bevy of children squealed and shouted their pleasures at the wondrous new Christmas toys they'd received. The house hadn't been quiet since Caeden set foot in it that morning, and he didn't believe it would be for some time to come.

"Yes, you should at least wait until after New Year's," Mary, his younger sister, added. "We're to have a very large party and dance. You would be quite welcome. I know there are a great many people who would like to see you again."

Caeden shook his head. "Emily is waiting for me. I've been gone long enough."

"So we don't even get to be a part of your wedding?" Deborah asked, pressing her lips to a pout. "That seems most unfair. I love weddings."

Laughing, Caeden got to his feet. "I'm sorry to be such a disappointment, but you know that I am quite unconventional."

Uncle Jasper laughed. "That he is."

"You're lucky I stayed in town for Christmas. I only did it for you two. Well, and to finalize the sale of the estate."

Mary's husband stepped forward with Deborah's husband close behind. "You were most generous to share the sale with us," he declared. "I know it was quite touching to Mary."

Caeden saw his sister nod. "It was my pleasure."

"It will help me expand my business," Deborah's husband added. "I am most grateful."

"I am glad that it is beneficial to all of you. I'm also glad to be on my own course now, following my own dreams rather than burdened by our father's." He could see a look of agreement in the eyes of his sisters. "Now, let us focus on something happier. I'm quite interested, in fact, to try that Christmas punch you've both been boasting about."

Deborah smiled and came to take hold of his arm. "Then let us satisfy your interest." She led him away from the others to the refreshment table. "I do want you to know that I'm happy. Mary too. We have good lives, and despite having our marriages arranged by Father, we have come to know love. Our husbands are good men."

"I am thankful to know that," Caeden said, turning to touch his sister's cheek. "I was so afraid you would both end up like Mother."

She patted his hand. "Then fear no more. Go instead, and make a wonderful life full of love for yourself. I do hope that in time we will have a chance to meet Emily."

Caeden nodded. "I hope so too, but for now I think we'll

make our home in Montana. I rather like the wide-open spaces. And you could always come and visit."

Deborah looked at him in what could only be described as disgust. "I hate travel and I hate the country. No, I do not plan to make my way to the wilds of Montana. You will just have to return here." She rose on tiptoe and kissed his cheek. "Now, let me get you some punch."

Later that night as Caeden and Uncle Jasper made their way home, his uncle turned the conversation to the future.

"I want you to know that I intend to leave my estate to you. I've watched you handle your own affairs wisely. I've known you to listen to counsel and make good choices. And I've seen you be quite generous with your sisters. I feel my estate could not be in better hands."

"I'm honored, Uncle Jasper, but I would prefer that my inheritance not come for a very long time."

His uncle chuckled. "Well, I have no plans to leave this world, but when I do, I know that everything will be in your capable hands. You've done your mother proud, Caeden. I know she must be smiling down from heaven."

"I like to think that she would be pleased," Caeden replied, folding back the carriage blanket as they came to a stop in front of Jasper's home.

"I'm certain she is. I'm certain she was always pleased with you." Jasper waited until they were out of the carriage to add, "Your father was a difficult man, Caeden. However, I know he was pleased the day my sister gave him a son. Alcohol poisoned his mind, but I believe there was a time when he too was quite proud of you. Think on that, rather than on the man he became and the pain he caused."

Caeden looked up at the lighted windows of Jasper's home. There was something very warm and welcoming about this place. Something he'd never felt for his parents' home, but something he hoped and prayed he would feel in the home he made with Emily.

"I'm done thinking about anything to do with the miseries of the past. I'm leaving that in God's hands . . . where I should have put it long, long ago."

# 23

ow, don't forget your promise, Pa." Emily shook her finger. "You told the doctor you would do as I said so long as he let you come back to the cabin. Now we're here, and you're already starting to be ornery. You're only supposed to be on your feet to get out of bed and into the chair and then again when you return to bed. Next week you can do a little more walking, but you have to take this slow."

Her father chuckled and smoothed out the blanket on his lap. "I can't say as this chair is very comfortable."

"Caeden was very thoughtful to have that wheelchair shipped to Lewistown just for you. If you're all that uncomfortable, I can cushion it with a blanket."

"Not just yet. Maybe later." Her father frowned. "I'm not gonna stay long in this chair. I don't have it in me to sit idle."

Emily kissed the top of his head. "I know, Pa. But I know also what the doctor said. You need to give yourself time. It's barely been a month. If you try to rush things, you'll only cause the healing to delay or stop altogether."

Her father gave a defeated sigh. "I suppose I have no choice."

"Well, it's not like we have to worry overmuch about it. Caeden has provided quite nicely for us." She glanced around the one-room cabin, pleased with how she'd been able to make the place quite cozy with Caeden's gifts.

"I don't like that he's spent so much on us. You know how I feel about charity."

Emily smiled. She knew her father didn't know the half of it when it came to the money Caeden had put out for their care.

"Caeden said it wasn't charity; it was gratitude for what we'd done for him. It gave Caeden great pleasure, and I think that we have to allow that God provided for our needs through him. We can hardly fault God or Caeden for their loving-kindness. Besides, you know what I told you—he asked me to wait for him."

Her father seemed to consider this, then gave a nod. "Have you heard anything from him?"

"Not after that one letter that told me he'd arrived in Washington, DC. I'm sure he's been very busy." Emily tried to sound encouraged and hopeful. "We'll probably hear something soon."

Her father nodded. "Well, I can't imagine he'll stay away any longer than necessary, and when he comes back I'm bettin' he asks you to be his bride."

"Well, that may have to wait." She walked to the stove to check on the bread pudding she'd put into the oven half an hour earlier. Sticking a knife in the middle of the dessert, she pulled it out. "It's done." She took the pan from the oven and set it atop the stove.

"What did you mean?"

Emily looked at her father and shook her head. "I don't understand. I said the bread pudding is done."

"No, when I talked about you bein' Caeden's bride, you said it may have to wait. Why would you say that?"

"Well, there's a lot to consider. After all, you have quite a recovery ahead of you. I'm just glad there's a foot of snow outside. Otherwise, I know you'd be wheeling yourself down to the river to pan." She smiled but could see her father's expression was one of concern.

"You can't be puttin' off marrying just because I'm healing. I won't have you wastin' another minute of your life on my account."

Emily came and knelt beside her father. "Pa, I can't cast you aside in order to marry Caeden. We have to focus on getting you well first."

"I won't have it," her father countered, pounding his hands against his thighs. "Your ma would have my hide if she thought I'd stood in the way of you having happiness with a man who truly loves you."

"But you aren't standing in my way." Emily gave his hand a gentle squeeze. "We're family and we take care of each other. That's what Mama taught me. It won't be forever." At least she hoped it wouldn't. She wanted to be as positive as her father that his recovery would soon be complete. Even so, she wasn't at all sure what she'd do once he was well.

"Well, God's made it clear to me that you've sacrificed enough, Emmy. I'm gonna see you married, and soon."

She laughed and got back to her feet. "Well, first we have to have a groom."

Just then a knock sounded on the cabin door. For a moment she dared to hope it might be Caeden. The knock sounded again as if the visitor was impatient. Her heart seemed to skip a beat as she went to answer the insistent knocking.

Emily opened the door and found the Utica marshal on the other side. "Well, come in before you freeze to death." She hid her disappointment and gave the man a smile.

He took off his hat and kicked his boots against the doorjamb before entering the cabin. "I heard you folks came back while I was away. How are you feeling, Henry?"

"Better every day. I've just been trying to convince Emmy to stop fussin' over me. I'll soon be fit as a fiddle."

"Pa makes a terrible patient." Emily headed back to the stove. "I've got some bread pudding just out of the oven and coffee if you'd care to have some."

The marshal smiled. "I'd like that a whole lot."

"Have a seat at the table. Maybe you and Pa can even get up a game of checkers or chess." Emily hurried to collect bowls for the bread pudding.

"Can't stay that long. Fact is, I came here with a bit of unpleasant news." The marshal took a seat at the table.

Emily turned and could see the look on his face was rather grave. "What's happened?" She feared his news might relate to Caeden and tried to steel herself for the blow.

"Kirk Davies is dead."

Emily's father rolled up to where the marshal sat. "Dead, you say?"

"Yup. He died from an infection." The marshal met Emily's gaze. "An infection from that bite you gave him."

"So you finally believe me." Emily felt slightly vindicated. She let out a heavy sigh. "You almost had me thinking I was crazy." She turned back to the dessert and started dishing bread pudding into the bowls.

"I do apologize for that. The situation is a rather strange one, but I finally have some answers. Davies has a brother who could be his twin. His name is Taber Davies. He was the one who brought Kirk into Doc's place, and that's where Kirk died. Sometime in the night Taber snuck back there and took the body and left. I have no idea where he buried Kirk or where he went after that, but I'm kind of fearful that he may still be around to cause you problems. I wanted to warn you."

Emily put the bowls aside and came to sit at the table. Her knees felt like jelly at the thought of another Davies coming to try to kill them. Her father had been responsible for the death of one Davies brother, and now she was to blame for another. No doubt this Taber Davies would want revenge.

"That's why I wasn't in town when you folks came through. I was out looking for Taber. I even wired the marshal over in Lewistown to be on the lookout."

"Do you suppose he might just give it all up and leave the area?" Emily's father asked.

The marshal shrugged. "I have no way of knowing. Folks suggested he and Kirk had been living in an old shack to the west of town. I checked it out several times since you two were attacked. However, while it did look like someone had been living there, there wasn't anybody there when I arrived. I tried following some tracks to see if I could pick up the direction Taber might have gone, but then that big snow blew in and covered up any sign of direction."

"Well, we will have to arm ourselves."

Emily looked at her father. "We armed ourselves last time and it didn't turn out so good."

"Kirk caught us by surprise. We don't have to let that happen again."

Forcing herself to return to the stove, Emily finished putting a vanilla sauce atop the bread pudding before serving it to her father and the marshal. She didn't want to worry Pa, but she felt almost certain Taber Davies would pay them a visit. With her father an invalid and Emily responsible for the animals and everything else, she couldn't help but wonder how they would ever be safe. Perhaps she could talk her father into moving into Millie's place temporarily.

"Pa, I think it would be wise if we went to stay with Millie. Just until the marshal can locate Kirk's brother."

"I wouldn't let Kirk run us off, and I won't let his brother do it either." Her father's tone left her no doubt the matter was settled.

She returned to retrieve mugs of coffee for the two men. "I hope this is strong enough. You'll find sugar on the table if you'd like." She placed the cups in front of each man.

The marshal looked up, and his expression only served to feed Emily's fears. "I think your daughter has a good idea. You two ought to stay with Millie, or better yet come on up to Utica. We've got a decent boardinghouse and—"

"The answer is no," Emily's father interrupted. "I ain't runnin' away from this. We're forewarned, so we'll be ready for trouble."

Emily could only pray he was right.

"I'm sorry, mister, but the snows have kept the stage from running. Check back in the morning."

Caeden let go an exasperated sigh. He'd been delayed already by heavy storms that left most of the northern states covered in snow. Now he found himself once again helpless to do anything but wait. At least he'd made it this far. Only about eighty miles stood between him and Emily, but it might as well have been eight hundred.

The stage clerk seemed to understand. "I know that Joe hopes to head out to Lewistown in the morning if it doesn't snow more. You can leave your trunks here if you like. I'll see that they're safe and locked up. There's no guarantee, but if I were you I'd come early in the morning and wait around here to see what happens. If Joe does head out, it'll be early. Oh, and you might want to invest in a blanket or two to bring along. It'll be slow going and freezing cold. You'll want to dress warm. Wear boots and gloves. You might be asked to help push the stage if it gets stuck in the snow."

Caeden nodded. At least it was something. "I'll be here. You make sure he doesn't leave without me." He laid some money on the counter. "For your trouble."

The clerk's eyes widened at the generous offering. He pocketed it quickly, as if Caeden might change his mind. "I'll see to it that you have a seat."

With nothing more to be said or done, Caeden made his way through the snow to the hotel where he'd taken a room two days earlier. The waiting was more than irritating. Caeden couldn't shake the sense of urgency he felt. He needed to get back to Emily and assure himself that she was all right—that Kirk Davies hadn't caused more trouble.

*⁊⁊⁊⁊*

Emily startled at the sound of someone outside the cabin. Earlier the wind had blown so hard she couldn't hear anything else. But now there was an unsettling silence, and even the rooster wasn't bothering to crow. Silence except for the movement she was certain she'd heard. She glanced to where her father was sleeping soundly on his cot near the stove. He didn't so much as stir. Emily got up, pulled her coat on over her nightclothes, and moved closer to the door. She heard noise again. There was definitely someone outside. Emily tried to calm herself. It could be an animal.

She bit her lower lip and felt for the reassurance of the pistol in her pocket. Dread settled over her. Could she really shoot a man? Emily swallowed the lump in her throat. If Davies was outside, he'd be there with the sole purpose of killing them. Emily knew she'd have to shoot him. There'd be no firing a warning shot to scare him off. She'd have to level the gun right at him and fire before he had a chance to shoot her.

Drawing a deep breath, Emily tried to steady her nerves. "Lord," she whispered, "give me strength. Give me wisdom. I don't want to have to shoot someone." She leaned against the wall beside the door. "Please, Lord. Please protect us."

She jumped at least a foot when a heavy hand pounded on the door. Emily drew the pistol from her pocket, knowing she was out of time.

"Who . . . who is it?"

The silence seemed ominous, but then a familiar voice called out. "It's me, Miss Emily. Jake Hoover."

Emily sighed in relief and pocketed the pistol before opening the door. "Jake." She forced a smile even though she was still trembling from head to toe. "Come in."

"Mighty cold out there," he said from behind a frost-covered beard. "Glad I grew my whiskers back."

She chuckled. "They have always looked good on you. What brings you here?" Emily glanced over to where her father still slept and lowered her voice. "Pa's still asleep."

Jake nodded. "I only figured to stop in and check up on you, and I do apologize for the early hour. Millie asked me to come. She's worried about you and your pa."

"I have to admit I've got some worries of my own." Emily drew a deep breath. "Did she tell you about Kirk Davies having a brother?"

"She did. That's partly why I came by. Millie wanted me to convince you and your pa to come up to her place."

"I wish we could." Emily moved to the stove and opened the door to throw in some more wood. She motioned Jake to take a seat. "I'll get some coffee on."

Her father began to stir. No doubt he'd come fully awake in a matter of moments. Emily hoped Jake might have the ability to convince her father that leaving this isolated cabin was for the best. She cast a quick glance at Jake and felt a sense of hopelessness. Her father was stubborn and convinced that they could fend for themselves. Ever since hearing about Taber Davies, he'd taken to sitting in his wheelchair with a rifle settled across his lap. Even now, the Winchester rested beside his cot.

Emily put the coffee on, then turned back to meet Jake's watchful eye. "How about some breakfast?" She motioned to the far side of the cabin, where her hens were keeping warm in one of the crates left after unpacking all of Caeden's gifts. "I'm sure to have some eggs."

Jake nodded in an uncharacteristic solemnity. It was as if he could read her mind and understood that his task of convincing them to leave was useless. "That sounds good, Miss Emily."

She returned his nod. One way or another . . . they would get through this. She only hoped it would be without injury or the heavy guilt of having blood on her hands.

# 24

*J*ake had no luck in talking Emily's father into leaving the cabin. He said nothing more on the matter but had assured Emily that he and some of the other men would keep an eye on the Carvers. It was the best Emily could hope for.

She went about her chores in guarded precision, paying the closest attention to the immediate area around the house and the animals' lean-to. Jake had mentioned as he left that being watchful and aware of what they had and where they'd placed it would benefit her most.

"Sometimes," he'd told her, "what's missing is just as important as what suddenly appears. Both can signal trouble."

That evening, Emily fell into bed feeling a little less worried. Whenever she'd started to fear, she remembered Jake's promise to keep watch, as well as God's faithfulness. God had protected them through so many bad situations. She knew He wouldn't leave them now.

The next morning she awoke to the crowing of the rooster. The poor old boy wasn't at all happy to be caged and separated from his ladies, but given his temperamental nature, Emily found it necessary to keep him confined.

Seeing that her father was already awake, Emily helped him dress, then assisted him into the wheelchair. "I'm going out to check on Bonnie-Belle and Nellie. Once I've got them fed and watered, I'll fix your breakfast."

"Don't forget to take your pistol."

Emily was already at the door pulling on her coat. She patted the pocket. "I have it right here."

Her father nodded, but she could see the worry in his eyes. "Don't fret, Pa. I'm doing everything you told me to do. I won't take any chances." She drew on her gloves and then a thick wool cap that her father often used.

She wasn't surprised to find Zed, one of the few miners who remained in the area, coming to call. He carried a rifle ever so casually at his side as he approached the cabin.

"Pa will be glad to see you." She gave Zed a smile. "I'm glad to see you myself. I'm heading out to feed the animals and check on Bonnie-Belle. She's due to calve any day now."

"I'll come along with you," the grizzled old man replied. "Then I'd be much obliged to see your pa and maybe talk you out of a cup of coffee with him."

Emily laughed and gave the old man a nod. "You can talk me out of breakfast too. I put the coffee on and the biscuits in the oven before coming out here. Oh, and I have plenty of eggs. My hens really enjoy the warmth of the cabin, although that old rooster is less inclined to be confined. He's been a real annoyance."

Zed laughed. "Put him out in the snow for a time. He'll settle down soon enough." As if the bird had overheard the comment, he let go a loud crowing that left both Emily and Zed chuckling.

Emily checked Bonnie-Belle and gave her some extra hay. "I

know she'll be glad to have this baby." Emily stroked the cow's neck. Next she moved to the makeshift stall where Nellie was stabled. "Well, hello, Nellie-girl, and how are you this fine day?" She filled the mule's trough with hay while Zed kept watch. It felt so much better to have someone stand guard. Her last act was to break the ice on the water trough. Zed helped her with this, handing her his rifle while he took the ax and made easy work of the situation.

"That ought to hold them for a while," Emily said, exchanging the ax he held for his rifle. She returned the ax to the woodpile, then together they headed back to the cabin.

"I brought water up yesterday while Jake was still here." She started to suggest bringing in firewood now but decided it could wait until after breakfast.

"As I was saying," she continued, "I have plenty of water and just put a pot of coffee on before you arrived. I'm sure it's ready."

She led the way back to the cabin with Zed close behind. It was reassuring to have the men of Yogo City looking out for her and Pa.

Inside the cabin, Emily found her father ever ready with his rifle. He relaxed at the sight of Zed. "Look who's come to share breakfast with you." She took off her hat and gloves and dropped them by the door. "I found him when I went to do my chores." She deposited her coat and then headed for the kitchen.

"Zed, good to see you."

"How're ya feelin', Henry?" The old man didn't seem to even notice the snow on his boots, but crossed the room to where Emily's father sat.

"Doin' better every day. Won't be long before I'm back to pannin' the river. Now come on over to the table and have a seat. Emily's promised me some biscuits and gravy."

"Sounds mighty good. Ain't had that in some time. Been

mostly eatin' on my jerked meat and flapjacks these days." He followed Henry's wheelchair to the table and waited until he was positioned before taking a chair. "'Course, she mentioned some eggs as well."

"You can have both, Zed." Emily held up two cast-iron skillets. "Thanks to everyone's generosity, I have two pans to cook in, plus a stewpot. We're living in high clover."

The men chuckled while Emily turned back to the stove. She was grateful that her father's friends had been so attentive. Her father needed his male companions to keep his spirits high. It was clearly a job that Emily couldn't do—at least not in the same capacity.

The men talked about the mining claims and their glory days while Emily checked the biscuits. They were nearly done. She refocused her attention on fixing canned-milk gravy with ham drippings and diced pieces of ham. She added salt and flour to the mix and stirred until it started to thicken. While this cooked a bit more, she checked the biscuits again and found them nice and brown. Lastly, she fried up four eggs.

Within a few moments she had the meal on the table and was pouring mugs of coffee for her father and Zed. "I hope this is strong enough for you, Zed." She put one of the steaming cups in front of him. "If you need milk for it, I can open a can, but we haven't any fresh."

The old man took a moment to warm his hands on the cup and then sampled it as Emily handed her father his coffee. "Don't need a thing. It's just right. Everything's just right when a fella gets fed by a pretty gal."

Pa laughed. "You got that right. Emmy, sit down and I'll offer thanks."

She did as he asked and felt a sense of peace wash over her. God truly was watching over them, and no matter what happened, she knew He had it under control. She silently prayed that God would see fit to return Caeden to her soon and added a desire for answers regarding her future. Emily might have gone on praying about those answers, but she heard her pa's amen and knew the two men would question her if she continued to bow in prayer.

Lifting her face, Emily smiled and picked up the plate of biscuits. "Help yourself, Zed."

The breakfast passed in a friendly conversation about Emily's young man, the heavy snows, and of course whether or not they would strike it rich come spring. Emily tried not to give in to worry about her future, but the more the men discussed the coming year, the more she pondered what she would do. If Caeden did return and ask her to marry him, she knew the matter would bear some consideration given her father's condition. There would also be the question of where Caeden would expect them to live . . . and even how. Emily knew he'd enjoyed living off the land and traveling from place to place, while she still longed for a house she could call her own.

Zed departed shortly after breakfast, leaving Emily to clean up while her father picked up the Sears and Roebuck catalog Emily had brought back from Lewistown. He thumbed through in silence, but Emily knew he was bored. She tried to think of something—anything she could have him do while seated in the wheelchair. Caeden had supplied them with new things, so fixing stuff wasn't even a needed chore. Even so, Emily knew there had to be something.

Just then a thought came to her. She had planned to kill one of the hens that had never been good at laying. She and her father had talked many times of having a hunger for fried chicken, and Emily knew her father could be very useful in plucking feathers and cutting up the bird.

"Pa, I wonder if I could ask you to help me with something."

Her father looked up in surprise. "What did you have in mind?" He sounded most anxious.

"Well, you know we've talked about butchering one of the hens. I thought I might do that today, but I have plenty of other chores. If I kill the hen, I wondered if you'd pluck her and cut her into pieces. That way I could fry her up for supper. Otherwise it'll have to wait, because I need to wash clothes today."

Her father seemed relieved. "I'd be right happy to see to that. Wouldn't be no trouble at all. In fact, I could probably be on my feet long enough to kill the bird as well."

"No, it's too slick outside. It'll only take me a minute, but the rest would tie me up for some time. I'll see to it as soon as I finish cleaning up." She turned back to the dishes and smiled. Now, if she could just think up something for him to do each day.

o≥§εo

It was nearly evening by the time Emily realized the hour. She'd managed to get their clothes washed and hung on the opposite end of the room, and her father had been true to his word and handled butchering the hen. Emily saw that the job had given him real purpose. Her father's spirits seemed considerably higher when she'd taken the chicken from him.

With the chicken frying in a large cast-iron skillet, Emily boiled a few potatoes to go along with their meal. Checking the stove, she added the last pieces of wood to the fire.

"I need to fetch us some wood before it's dark." She headed for the door and pulled on her coat. She put her hand in her pocket and felt for the pistol. "I'll leave the door open so you can hear me if anything goes amiss, but I'm sure old Jim or Jake will be watching over us."

Her father gave her a nod and checked his rifle. "Don't be long."

"It's too cold out there to be very long at such a task."

She didn't bother with her hat or gloves. Gloves would just make it harder to handle the gun should the need arise. She opened the door and looked out across the hills. The sun had set in a swirl of orange, red, and purple. It was one of the things she liked most about Montana—the sunsets were incredible and second only to the sunrises.

The woodpile was just at the side of the cabin, so Emily felt fairly safe. If someone were hiding out in the trees, they would still have to cross the open space to reach her, and by that time she could have her gun in hand.

She gave one more quick glance at the thick stand of pines before picking up several of the split logs. When her arms were full she hurried her steps back to the cabin and breathed a sigh of relief.

Her father nodded and relaxed his hold on the rifle. "That ought to do us through the night."

"I thought so too."

She put the wood in a box by the stove, then went to close the door. Before she could get it completely shut, however, Emily found it pushed back, and a thickly bearded man took hold of her.

"Evenin', Carvers. Glad to find you at home."

Emily stiffened as the man's hold on her tightened. She saw her father lift his rifle and knew without looking that the man was Taber Davies. Thankfully he held her left arm. If she could just slip her right hand into her pocket without drawing his attention she could reach her pistol.

"I'd drop that rifle over the side of your chair if I were you," Davies commanded her father. "See, I have a gun on your

311

daughter, and I'll put a hole in her. Not a killin' hole, mind you, just one to make her suffer while I put the next one in you."

Emily saw her father's indecision. "You might as well shoot him, Pa. He'll kill us either way."

"Now, that's not a very friendly thing to say." Davies pushed her in far enough to get the door closed behind them. "I never said nothing about killing either one of you." He sniffed the air. "Smells mighty good in here. I think maybe I'll let you feed me."

"And then kill us? That is why you're here, isn't it, Mr. Davies?" Emily turned enough to see his cold blue eyes.

He laughed but kept his gun fixed on her. "I suppose you got me all figured out. But you can never tell. I might like your cookin' so much that I'll just take you along with me once I finish with your pa. I gave Kirk my promise that I'd take care of this matter for him. Promised him that on his deathbed."

"And you blame me for his death, no doubt." Emily saw no reason for pretense. Davies was bent on revenge, and there was no sense in pleading or trying to talk him out of it. Men like Davies were never willing to compromise.

"The doc did say that your bite is what killed him, so you can't very well deny being responsible for the job. Seems between you and your pa you managed to kill off my brothers. They were all I had left of my family." Emily's father moved the tiniest bit, and Taber turned back to refocus the revolver on him. "Now, you'd best do what I said, old man. I don't have a lot of patience."

Emily hoped her father would surprise Taber Davies and just fire right into him, but instead she saw him lower the rifle.

"That's good. Now put it over the side on the floor." Davies motioned with his revolver. "Do it now."

The older man scowled but did as Davies instructed. When

the rifle was on the floor, Davies pushed Emily from his side. "You got any rope?"

"Just the rope I use for the clothesline." She motioned to the clothesline, where the washing hung.

"Get it and tie that old man up."

"He's an invalid. It's not like he can get up and run out of here." Emily hoped Davies would believe that her father was completely incapable of moving from the chair.

Taber Davies grinned. "That's right. I plumb forgot. My brother put you there. It was a real disappointment to him that he didn't finish the job."

Emily motioned to the stove. "If you don't mind, I need to get the chicken off the fire or it will burn." Davies glanced toward the stove and nodded. "Guess we can't have that. Sure makin' my mouth water."

She moved slowly, hoping to keep him from any concern that she might decide to trick him. She moved the skillet to the warming shelf and then slipped her hand into her pocket. Davies seemed no wiser, and it gave her courage that perhaps she could draw the pistol and shoot him before he could harm either her or her father.

"I guess you don't have to tie him up." Davies lowered his revolver just a bit. "I suppose it's enough for him to know that I'll make him sorry if he tries anything."

"I suppose it is." Her voice dripped sarcasm. She kept her distance, hoping Kirk wouldn't give her much thought at all.

"You're a feisty one—that's for sure. Kirk told me you were. He also told me what a looker you were. He didn't lie on that account. Take that coat off so I can see how you're put together."

Emily kept her right hand in her pocket but began to unbutton the coat with her left hand. Just then there was a knock at the cabin door, and all three of them froze. Emily prayed that whoever it was would realize there was a problem and go for help. The knock sounded again.

"You'd better answer it," Taber said in a whisper.

Emily licked her dry lips and nodded. She came around him to reach for the door when Davies buried his hand in her hair and pulled her backward. The action caused her to cry out.

"Quiet," Davies whispered. "Don't try anything or I'll kill your father and then I'll kill whoever is on the other side."

She nodded as much as she could, and he released his hold. He stood behind the door as she opened it just a crack. To her utter horror she found Caeden's smiling face beaming back at her. Before he could say a word, she frowned and shook her head.

"If you're looking for Jake, he isn't here." She swallowed hard, praying Caeden would remain silent. "He left here some time ago and is probably over at Millie's. I'm sure you can . . . find him there."

She hoped he would see the pleading in her eyes. He looked at her oddly, cocking his head to one side. But after a moment he nodded, seeming to understand her plight. Emily quickly closed the door.

"Good," Davies said. "You handled that real good. Now get that coat off."

Emily did as he said. She pulled her left arm out, then let the coat slide off her right arm to the floor, all while keeping her hand and gun hidden in the folds of her skirt. She took a step away from him but kept her focus on his eyes.

"Stay where you are." He reached out and touched her face, then let his hand trail down the side of her throat. "You sure are a looker. I'm gonna enjoy making you pay for killing my brother."

His hand slipped lower and Emily jerked back, causing Davies to just laugh. She knew there wasn't room enough to raise the gun and fire before he could knock it from her hand, so she tried to step back once again.

"I told you to stay put. You might as well get used to me touching you, because I'm going to do quite a bit of it before I'm finished here."

"Leave her alone," Emily's father protested. "I'm to blame for your family's misery. She might have bit Kirk, but he was only there because of me."

Taber turned and looked at Henry Carver before nodding. "That's true enough, but the way I see it, you're both responsible and you're both going to pay. In fact, I think I'll just take care of you right now."

"No!" Emily hadn't meant to cry out and feared it might cause Davies to lash out.

But then without warning the door to the cabin flew back. Taber whirled around to aim his gun at the intruder, but he had no chance to fire as Caeden barreled into his midsection and sent him crashing to the ground. Unfortunately, Taber still managed to hang on to his revolver and struck out at Caeden, catching him in a glancing blow with the gun's barrel.

Zed and Jake rushed in as Caeden fought to regain control of the situation. Emily thought of the gun in her hand but knew it wouldn't do her any good. The men were moving too quickly, and she would never risk shooting one of them.

Taber wasn't deterred by Zed and Jake's appearance. He threw a punch at Caeden, knocking him to one side, then raised his gun to aim. Emily screamed, but the shot that was fired came from Zed instead of Taber. She watched as a crimson stain spread across the front of Taber's gray coat. He sank to the floor without a word, then fell over dead.

"You got him straight through the heart, Zed," Jake announced in approval. "Good job."

Emily could scarcely draw a breath. She leaned against the wall for support. Caeden came to her and pulled her into his arms. She tried to say something but found the words stuck in her throat. She couldn't take her eyes off the dead man lying in the middle of the cabin.

Caeden pulled back and put his hand to her face. "Emily. Emily, look at me."

She did so and began to shake so hard her teeth chattered. Caeden led her to a chair and forced her to sit. Only then did he see the pistol in her hand. He reached down and gently took it from her and put it on the table. He left her side for a moment, then returned with a glass of water.

"Drink."

Emily's gaze was fixed on Zed, who was dragging Taber's body from the cabin. Caeden pulled a chair close to hers.

"Have a drink and tell me what happened."

She felt a bit of reasoning return. Tears formed in her eyes, but she took the glass and drank. Lowering the glass, her hand began to tremble, sloshing water over the rim. Caeden took it from her and put it on the table beside her gun.

Emily buried her face in her hands. The realization of how close all of them had come to death settled on her, and she began to cry in earnest. The next thing she knew, Caeden pulled her into his arms and held her while she sobbed.

"Seems like you're always given to tears, Miss Carver," he whispered against her ear.

She had no idea how long she cried. Minutes had seemed like hours when Davies had held them captive, and at the moment, time seemed to be completely displaced. Emily finally slumped against Caeden, her tears spent and her body exhausted from the ordeal. She said nothing, and Caeden didn't force her to speak. He just held her in his warm, safe arms. It was more than enough.

Little by little her breathing eased and the tension in her body settled. It was finally finished. The Davies brothers and their determination for revenge were at an end. Maybe now she and her father would be safe.

"Emmy?"

She felt someone touch her. Raising her face, Emily saw that her father had walked to the table. "Are you hurt, Emmy?"

She shook her head, and her father smiled. "You did real good, Emmy. Made me proud."

Her senses returned, and she realized all at once what her father was doing. "You shouldn't be on your feet. Not without help. You need to get back to your chair."

He broke into laughter and slapped Caeden on the back. "She's naggin' me already. She's gonna be just fine."

Emily looked at Caeden's smiling face. She would be just fine, because she had the love of two good men and her Father in heaven. She drew a breath and let it go, along with the trauma and anguish of the last hour. They were finally all together and safe. Nothing else mattered.

"Before we get any other hornets' nests stirred up," Caeden said, sinking to one knee beside Emily's chair, "I want to ask you to marry me." He held up a ring, a diamond surrounded by sapphires.

"Those little blue rocks," she murmured, touching the ring almost reverently.

"Those little blue rocks turned out to be very valuable sapphires," he said with a grin. He looked over at her father. "It would seem, Mr. Carver, you have struck it rich."

# 25

*E*mily stood in a beautiful gown of pale pink silk and tulle, surrounded by her dearest friends and father. Reverend Morgan had come at Caeden's request to join the couple in holy matrimony, much to Emily's delight.

Millie insisted the wedding be at her place, and Emily thought it a good compromise, since it was much too cold to hold the wedding outdoors, where she would have really preferred. The beauty of Montana's great outdoors was greater than any church cathedral built by man. God's touch on the landscape throughout the state was evidence of His divine artistry, and Emily found herself quite in love with Montana.

They had delayed the wedding long enough that Emmy's father could stand beside her and give her away to Caeden. He looked quite fine in the new suit Caeden had bought him. He had laughingly told them that it would do to marry her off and bury him in when the time came. Emily prayed it wouldn't be anytime soon.

While Millie stood up with Emily, Caeden had the surprise

of his life beside him. His uncle had showed up just the day before, telling them both that he couldn't miss such an important occasion. The moment was quite emotional for both men.

"Who gives this bride to be wed?" Reverend Morgan asked.

"I do," said Emily's father with tears in his eyes. He leaned over to kiss her cheek. "I love you, Emmy."

She nodded and fought back her own tears. "I love you, Pa."

"Then if there are no objections," the reverend continued, "we shall get on with the ceremony."

Emily felt Caeden clasp her hand in his. She glanced up to find him looking at her with that same serious expression he'd had when they'd first met. As if reading her mind, his lips twitched slightly and his eyes seemed to sparkle in delight. She couldn't help smiling.

"Yes," she said, turning back to the minister, "let's get on with it."

The ceremony, though traditional, was quite short. What followed was a party to beat all, and despite there being fewer than a dozen people present, the atmosphere was one of celebration and great joy. Caeden's uncle had thoughtfully brought a great many delicacies from back east, and the old miners were digging in with absolute fascination over the likes of caviar, canned oysters, pickled quail eggs, and a bevy of sugary treats.

By now everyone knew about the sapphires. Jake's own evaluation had come back with a hefty check of over three thousand dollars. It would seem that Yogo City was to have a rebirth, and Emily's father was most enthusiastic.

"I told you, Em, God had a plan for me to strike it rich." He had returned to the wheelchair, but Emily could see he was anxious to be rid of it. "Won't be long till I no longer need this. Then I'm gonna see that Caeden is paid back, get on my feet, and go pan out some more of those pesky pebbles."

"You aren't paying me back for anything," Caeden declared. "Everything I gave was a gift, and you don't repay gifts." He put his arm around Emily. "Besides, I've already received the finest thing I could want. A beautiful wife, a treasure once concealed but now revealed." He stole a quick kiss, causing the miners to cheer.

"Did you tell her your secret yet?" Uncle Jasper asked.

Emily looked at Caeden and narrowed her eyes. "Secret? I thought we weren't going to have secrets."

"I kind of like secrets," he replied with a mischievous expression. "And no, Uncle, I haven't shown it to her yet, but I was just about to."

Uncle Jasper laughed and winked. "I think you're going to like this secret, Emily Thibault."

"Mrs. Thibault . . ." She tried the name on for size. "Emily Thibault. It has a nice ring to it, don't you think?"

"I think it's perfect." Caeden gazed down at her with such desire in his eyes that it made Emily blush and look away.

He took Emily's arm and led her to the door. "I hope you won't think us unsociable for leaving our own party, but I believe it is time for us to depart. As my uncle mentioned, I want to show Emily her surprise." Protests filled the room, but Caeden didn't let it detain them. He continued pulling Emily along and out into the snowy day.

Their friends followed behind, still protesting but in a good-natured way. Within seconds, the sky rained down rice on them and cheers went up from their friends. Emily felt tears come to her eyes, but after months of sorrowful tears, these were from joy. Even her father smiled and waved from the doorway, where he'd managed to maneuver his chair. He looked so happy Emily thought she might break into tears once again. Caeden had assured them just the night before that he was more than happy for them to make their home nearby so that Emily could continue to help in her father's recovery. Her father, however, had assured them that he was doing just fine.

"Come along, Mrs. Thibault. I truly do have something I want to show you."

Caeden led her to a carriage and a black Morgan horse. He helped her up, then joined her in the single seat and lifted the reins. "I think you're going to be quite surprised."

"I'm starting to think that with you surprises are quite normal." Without her coat, she shivered and snuggled closer in the cold air.

Caeden shifted the reins in order to put his arm around her. "I'll have you all warmed up in just a minute."

He directed the horse down the road and away from the heart of Yogo City. They wound their way through the trees and across the river before Caeden turned the horse down a narrow path that was barely wide enough for the carriage. At the end of this path sat the biggest log house Emily had ever seen. She was particularly in love with the beautiful porch that spanned the length of the front. Smoke puffed out of a stone chimney, evidence that someone had gone to great lengths and expense to prepare this cabin.

"I didn't even know this was here," Emily admitted in awe.

"It wasn't until a month or so back. I arranged to have it built—for us."

She looked at him and shook her head. "Again, it would seem that surprises are to be our normal way of life. You amaze me, Caeden."

He laughed and jumped down. After tying off the horse, he came and helped Emily to the ground. "I hope that I might always do so, madame." He swung her into his arms. "Now to carry you across the threshold."

She giggled and snuggled her face against his neck. She had never known such happiness. In a flash he had her inside the cabin, where the warmth welcomed her like a mother's arms. Emily didn't even notice the room as Caeden put her back on her feet. She gazed up into his eyes and sighed.

"I do love you," she said softly. "I prayed for most of my life that I might one day have a home of my own and a husband to love, and now you have made those dreams come true."

Caeden's dark eyes revealed his amusement and joy. "And I love you, Emily. I think I've loved you since I saw you fresh out of the bath, wet hair hanging over your shoulder, clothes clutched to your neck in absolute terror."

"It was a most embarrassing moment. After having spent a lifetime of concealing my feminine form, you walked in and exposed me for who I was. At that moment I regretted it, but now I'm quite happy that you did. I think you've been exposing me for who I am ever since."

"And I love what I've found." He pulled her into his arms and gave her a long and thorough kiss. He lifted his head just a hairsbreadth from her lips. "Now I want to show you our little home." He kissed her again, this time in a quick, almost chaste manner. Then without further ado, he turned her in his arms.

Emily gasped at the beautiful interior. The log walls were completely chinked, and several paintings had been arranged on the walls to add a homey feel. Blue damask drapes hung at the three front windows. Beneath her feet was a polished wood floor. This was no backwoods cabin.

She looked up at Caeden in disbelief. "This is a mansion. I don't . . . don't know what to say."

"You haven't begun to see it all," he said, laughing.

Emily shook her head and gazed around the room. Some lovely pieces of furniture graced the main room. She moved away from Caeden and touched a wingback chair in dark blue upholstery. To the right sat a wooden rocker, and to the left was an amazing sofa of flowered chintz. All three sat in front of the massive stone fireplace that had been trimmed out with a large wooden mantel. Atop the mantel were an arrangement of knickknacks and a lovely clock.

Caeden drew her along with him to the opposite side of the large room, where a magnificent wood dining table with six chairs stood in welcome. Beyond that was a kitchen with real cabinets and counters, an icebox, and the largest stove Emily had ever seen. She reached out to touch the enamel handle on the oven door.

"I understand it was quite the ordeal to get that up here," Caeden told her.

"I can well imagine." She couldn't believe the things she was seeing. "I'm sure to wake up from this soon, but I'm going to enjoy it all while I can."

"It's no dream, Emily. It's a fitting home for a beautiful woman. If there's anything you don't like, we'll change it."

"It's perfect. All of it." She turned to look at him, marveling that he had cared so much about her pleasure that he'd arranged such a home. "You have truly blessed me. There simply aren't words to express how I feel."

He grinned and again reached for her arm. "You haven't seen the best."

"But surely there can't be more."

"Oh, but there is. There are two bedrooms and a room for bathing so that no one will ever walk in on you again. You can even do the laundry there." He drew her to a door and opened it. "However, this is our room."

Emily gasped and stepped inside the large bedroom. There were several pieces of furniture and a large oval rug on the floor.

But in the center of the room sat an elegant four-poster bed, done up in the finest bedding and pillows.

Tears came to Emily's eyes as she ran her fingers down the smooth footboard. "It's . . . it's . . . amazing."

He turned her in his arms and reached out to catch a tear on his finger. "I don't want you to ever have to sleep on the ground or on a cot again. Not unless you want to. When you marveled at that simple hotel bed, I was determined then and there to get you the most luxurious bed money could buy."

Emily wrapped her arms around him. "Although that hotel bed was quite comfortable, it was very lonely, and you were ever on my mind."

"Why, Mrs. Thibault, that's positively scandalous." He winked. "But rest assured, if I have anything to say about it, you'll never again sleep alone."

She sighed. "I wish my mother could have lived to see this. I thought about her during our ceremony and prayed that God would somehow tell her that she was right about you—all along."

Caeden laughed. "Right about me? So your mother told you about our conversation, huh?"

Emily laughed. "Oh yes, and I was horrified that she should tell you such a thing! I never had any intention of proving her right, you know."

"Your mother had no doubts about being right. It turns out we were the only ones who doubted that we belonged together."

Emily reached up and touched his cheek. "I don't know about you, but I don't have doubts anymore."

He pressed his hand against hers. "It's a good thing you don't, because it's too late now." He kissed her tenderly, then whispered, "You're stuck with me."

**Tracie Peterson** is the award-winning author of over one hundred novels, both historical and contemporary. Her avid research resonates in her stories, as seen in her bestselling HEIRS OF MONTANA and ALASKAN QUEST series. Tracie and her family make their home in Montana. Visit Tracie's website at www .traciepeterson.com.

# More From Tracie Peterson

To learn more about Tracie and her books, visit traciepeterson.com.

Nanny Lillian Porter doesn't believe the dark rumors about her new employer. She feels called to help the Coltons, especially young Jimmy, who hasn't spoken since his mother's death. But when dangerous incidents begin to plague the farm, will they find the truth in time to prevent another tragedy?

*Beyond the Silence* with Kimberley Woodhouse
kimberleywoodhouse.com

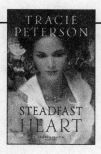

Brought together by the Madison Bridal School in 1888, three young women form a close bond. In time, they learn more about each other—and themselves—as they help one another grow in faith and, eventually, find love.

BRIDES OF SEATTLE: *Steadfast Heart, Refining Fire, Love Everlasting*

# You May Also Enjoy ...

Three LONE STAR BRIDES seek out marriage for very different reasons. They each face difficult choices and obstacles on the road ahead. But they'll also find friendship and adventure, as well as romance and a place to call home.

LONE STAR BRIDES: *A Sensible Arrangement, A Moment in Time, A Matter of Heart*
by Tracie Peterson
traciepeterson.com

Rose McKay has plenty of ideas on how to make her family's newly acquired pottery business a success—too many ideas, in longtime employee Rylan Campbell's opinion. But can these two put aside their differences and work together to win an important design contest?

*The Potter's Lady* by Judith Miller
REFINED BY LOVE
judithmccoymiller.com

◈BETHANYHOUSE